To ~

I thank you
so Much for
Your Support!

Truly
Marie

The Haunting of Dr. Andre C. Brass

Maxine Wilson-Perry

iUniverse, Inc.
New York   Bloomington

iUniverse books may be ordered through booksellers or by contacting:

iUniverse
1663 Liberty Drive
Bloomington, IN 47403
www.iuniverse.com
1-800-Authors (1-800-288-4677)

ISBN: 978-1-4401-6819-2 (sc)
ISBN: 978-1-4401-6821-5 (dj)
ISBN: 978-1-4401-6820-8 (ebook)

Printed in the United States of America

iUniverse rev. date: 10/05/09

Dedicated to my husband and mother,
along with my beloved dog, Blue

Chapter 1

On a summer day in the Bay State of Cambridge, Massachusetts, Dr. Andre C. Brass sat in his luxurious living room quarters, relaxing and reflecting on his life. Andre had one of the most prestigious positions at Harvard University as a professor of historical music. But it wasn't enough to satisfy his status in American society. He often felt something was missing. Andre wanted more in life; he thought love wouldn't be a bad thing. It would be just what was needed and what he been missing.

He would love to share his success with a woman, and he knew the woman in question—she'd been plaguing his mind and heart ever since he first met her. So when summer break began, he knew he would take a journey—a journey to the same place as always but this time without his closest friend, Craig, whom he loved like a brother. While sipping one of his finest merlots, his phone rang. Andre's eyebrow raised as he wondered who could be calling at such a late hour.

It was her—Lanassa, one of the most beautiful women Andre ever had the pleasure of meeting. They met during one of his many trips to New Orleans and he still loved her to this very day; he couldn't forget her, no matter how hard he tried. Her smile was the most brilliant, and her hair always flowed with the silkiest of curls. Lanassa had the most beautiful smooth brown skin that he'd ever seen. She was the answer to why he'd planned his upcoming journey to New Orleans: his beloved Lanassa.

What a lovely surprise to hear her voice. But how did she get his unlisted number after so many years had passed? This is what he'd been dreaming about for years—to speak with her again—and it was better than he could ever have hoped or wished.

"Lanassa, what brings this call from you after all these years? How did you get my unlisted number?" Andre could almost hear her smile and it made him feel instantly fulfilled.

Lanassa replied in that same saucy voice with her Louisiana accent that he remembered. "You must be kidding me, Dr. Brass. I have my sources and getting your number was easy."

Andre felt the heat of her voice as he swirled the dark red liquid in his wine glass, while waiting for her to continue. Her answer didn't surprise him. Andre knew Lanassa always got what she wanted. "It's your summer break, isn't it? It's time to stop being the boring professor of historical music. I want you to join me and my friends, listening to jazz and dancing in the streets of New Orleans. I hope you haven't forgotten the fun we shared together."

He wondered how Lanassa knew he was a historical music professor. Last time they spoken to each other he still was a student at Harvard. He also noticed the difference in Lanassa's tone. She sounded nothing like the young girl from the past. She sounded womanly with a sexy voice. Andre took a sip of his wine and pondered the memories but for only a second or two. "Oh, yes, how can a man forget?" He replied.

He hadn't; Andre remembered those times as if they were embedded into his rich brown skin. He also remembered the way those times ended. "Lanassa, are you inviting me to New Orleans to be with you, along with your circle of friends?"

Andre could hear her smooth laughter while she spoke. "Of course I am. I have missed you dearly. We had so much fun; it seems like yesterday, the joy we shared together."

Her words took Andre by surprise. It seemed like yesterday to her, but it had been many years since they been together—eight, to be exact. He felt those years weighing heavily upon his shoulders, but he refused to mention that fact to Lanassa. He also wondered if this was truly the journey he wished to take again after hearing her smooth voice. To New Orleans, yes, but Lanassa was where all his concerns lay open and deep. Lanassa had been unable to return the love he tried so very hard to share with her. What should a man do when the one woman he most loved in the entire world wanted to spend time with him in her world, even though it was a woman who could reopen the wounds he tried every day to keep closed?

Then again, how could he resist Lanassa? She gave him life those many years ago, and he forgave her for the pain. He'd never found another woman to take her place. Andre's answer to her request was simple after all. He needed her warmth to stop the cold that had been invading his body for far too long.

Still, Andre knew she wasn't good for him. During their relationship, Lanassa was egotistical and distanced herself from him. Nevertheless, Andre needed the life she'd shared with him, regardless of the way in which they parted—it had been painful, but the memories of the joyful times still plagued him.

Each day that went by without her seemed to be sucking the life right out of him. Lanassa brought out things in Andre that he should never cross paths with. Loving a woman like her could cause Andre his sanity, leading him to a road of pain. But maybe this time it would be different. Maybe this time she'll be able to accept his love and return that love back to him. And not push him away by flirting with other men. Her flirtatious ways always drove him to a point of pain and insanity.

Joining her in New Orleans this time might give him the opportunity to be loved by her in return. Or should he think twice and skip the trip to New Orleans altogether, avoiding the possibility of the pain he knew she was capable of causing? But New Orleans gave him air to breathe again—and it was Lanassa who moved that air and began his blood pumping throughout his body.

At age thirty, Andre felt like an old man, as if something spectacular was missing in his world. Life was a constant routine. No excitement, no love, and most times, very lonely. Yes, he had a Porsche, a small mansion on the hill, and more money in the bank than he needed. But material things could never satisfy his soul. Only a woman to share his life could make him feel like the richest man in the world. He wondered now if Lanassa was that partner after hearing her sexy voice. He would soon know the answer; he would walk right back into her life with eyes wide open, with hope in his heart that she would return his love this time. He needed her in his life, no matter what the consequences might be. Still, he didn't want to seem too easy. Lanassa had once wrapped him around her finger—and sometimes her whole hand.

So he relaxed into his plush leather chair and tried to keep his cool, while feeling the blood pumping to his heart. Although Andre wasn't a man for games, he knew games were the only way to excite Lanassa's interest. He couldn't make this easy for her—at least, not yet. "I have to say, Lanassa that your offer is very enticing, but I already made other plans." Andre could feel the smile dropping from her gorgeous face— and the smile widen on his. He knew she was sulking.

"Well, Andre, I must have overstepped my confidence when it relates to you and what we shared." Lanassa knew Andre was madly in love with her during the times they shared together. It was Craig who had to convince him to leave her. She knew he would have stayed regardless of her flirtatious behavior toward other men. Andre accepted her phone call without many questions had proven that fact to her.

Andre was getting a little nervous—he didn't want to miss this opportunity of being with her again. He decided to back off from the games, just a little. She had a way of making him feel just a little insecure at times; this was one of those times.

At six foot two, with wonderful bright brown eyes and rich brown skin, which included a dimple in his chin, Andre was a very handsome man. Still, he wore his insecurities on his sleeve when it came to Lanassa.

She was the only person on earth who could make him doubt himself. But he loved her anyway. Maybe he could spend time with her and persuade her that he was all the man she would ever need—as a lover, a friend, and ... who knows? ... a husband. Andre contemplated his next move. "Plans at times are meant to be broken, Lanassa. I'm sure I could push back my plans and come join you in New Orleans."

He could hear her smile again. "So when may I expect your company? Andre, tell me the date you'll fly out and be with me." Lanassa replied with excitement in her voice. The joy was back in his heart. His only reply was, "Soon, very soon. Let's say next week." Andre looked around the living room at all that he had worked so hard for, yet all he could see was her face, staring at him with a seductive smile.

Chapter 2

The flight to New Orleans seemed to take forever. Andre couldn't wait for the airplane to land. He'd been anticipating this day for years. Finally, he was here in New Orleans, with the airplane touching the soil where his life with Lanassa would begin again—and without Craig watching over him.

He hadn't mentioned this trip to Craig, his closest friend, or Bryan, Craig's brother, both of whom had been like brothers to him. Craig and Bryan had been his partners through the ups and downs, the good and bad. Andre knew his trip to see Lanassa would be a topic that could get heated in a matter of seconds. Craig remembered all too well the condition that Andre was in after he fell in love with Lanassa, only to have that love stomped on as if it were a bug. Craig felt that Andre was too good for a woman who played games with men for her own selfish gains.

Andre remembered his last conversation with Craig concerning Lanassa.

"Lanassa is a user, Dre," Craig had said. *"Can't you see through her? How blind can you be when it comes to this woman? She left you almost insane."*

Craig always had been the pessimist and Bryan the optimist, but when it came to Lanassa, both brothers could never forgive her for the pain she had caused Andre. No, this visit must be his secret … for now.

As Andre walked off the airplane and crossed the field to the terminal, his heart started to pound. He was feeling like a junkie who was about to get his fix. Yes, he had it bad for this woman. She would be waiting for him at gate four; Andre couldn't wait to feast his eyes on her.

But when he entered the gate, he didn't see her. He entered the building and walked toward the claims area and waited to claim his luggage, but still didn't see her anywhere. Then, as he turned around, his panic was replaced by a warm sensation spreading throughout his body—there Lanassa stood, staring at him with a smile that could make a man drop to his knees.

She was wearing a sexy blue dress that exuded sophistication, which hugged her body perfectly. Was it all a mirage set up by Lanassa to convince him how much she had changed? If so, it worked; Andre began to relax. Then another part of his body came to life—he couldn't wait to get his luggage.

He needed something to hide the part of his body that was involuntary responding to her beauty. How he'd missed this woman. Lanassa just stood there, staring right back at him, but she didn't move to greet him. Was she starting with her games already? The memories came back as if it was happening to him at that precise moment. Or was Lanassa just being proper and waiting for him to approach her?

Andre picked up his designer luggage then walked toward Lanassa—she still hadn't moved. Andre was starting to wonder if he'd changed that much in these last eight years. Of course he had, but was it for the better? She really knew how to give a man doubts.

Lanassa finally approached Andre. She walked right up to him and hugged him, then proceeded to give him a kiss that left him in a dream-like state—it was better than he could ever have imagined after so many years. Andre dropped his luggage and placed his masculine arms around her tiny waist, then started kissing her back, like a man thirsty for water after being in the desert for far too long. She felt all so right in his arms. And the taste of her lips, tongue, and mouth were all too sweet. Andre wanted to stay like this forever. Who cared about leaving this building when he was wrapped up into this most pleasurable state of mind? Not him. Andre loved this woman—God in heaven knew how much he missed her. Although he wasn't a religious man, Andre did believe in the Creator. He hoped that this time, the Creator could help him convince Lanassa that they belonged together, as true soul mates.

It seemed neither one of them wanted to break the hold of the kiss or the warmth it provided, but a security guard passed by then whistled at them. Andre didn't know whether it was a suggestion to stop the display of physical affection in public or a flirtatious remark toward Lanassa. Whatever it was, Andre wanted to get this woman someplace where he could be alone with her.

He thought *his woman*, while breaking the kiss. Andre and Lanassa held hands as they walked out of the airport. Andre wore a wide smile, while Lanassa had an expression on her face that he couldn't read. Would the outcome of this trip turn in his favor or crush him like a ton of bricks? He tried to push the thought from his mind. He'd take what happened moment by moment, minute by minute, hour by hour, and day by day.

Outside, waiting for them, was a sleek white 1967 Cadillac convertible. Andre turned toward Lanassa and asked, "Is this yours?" She looked up at him and winked. "Darling of course, I've always driven in style."

Andre observed how proper Lanassa was now. Time had made a big difference in her; there wasn't any trace of her wild ways. She no longer wore her hair wild with curls blowing across her beautiful face or a tight short dress that left nothing for the imagination. She was more refined. Lanassa wore a sophisticated dress that hugged her body and went just a little above her knees. She also wore her hair pulled back into a French-twist professional hair-style. Andre helped her into the driver's side of the sleek automobile. He placed his luggage in the trunk then got in the passenger's seat. Andre wondered what Lanassa did for a living, but he held his question—he had so many questions for her. Instead, Andre looked at her and asked, "So where is our next stop?"

Lanassa winked at him again. "It's a surprise. Don't you like surprises, Andre?"

At that moment, Andre wasn't so sure. He wanted everything to be in the open when it came to Lanassa this time. He didn't want to guess at anything, and he really didn't want to play games with her. His feelings ran too deep, and his soul was too vulnerable. After being away from her for so long, however, Andre decided to relax in the comfort of the smooth leather seat and take in the sights on this journey with her; he gave up his control in the matter—not that he had any other option. Andre was on her playing field and at her mercy ... by his choice.

Lanassa turned to Andre. "Why are you being so quiet? Is there something on your mind that you would like to share with me?"

Andre shook his head while returning her gaze and smiling a sexy smile letting her know that he preferred quiet at this particular time.

Lanassa, being the woman she was, wouldn't accept this for an answer. She placed her right hand on his thigh and gave him a gentle rub.

This woman could drive a man crazy. Andre thought. Then he replied. "Lanassa, it was a long night for me before the flight. I'm just riding along with you, enjoying the scenery and inhaling your sweet scent. Can a man enjoy this time for a little while, in silence? Believe me. It won't be long until I'm talking so much you'll wish I've never started."

"Impossible. Andre. You're the most reserved man I know when it comes to expressing yourself. I guess I'll just have to pick your brain to get your mouth working."

Oh, lord, Andre thought. He knew what kind of picking she would prefer, and it all centered on pillow talk. It was fine with him. But for now, he would stay that man of reserve.

Everything felt so new to him, even Lanassa. He just wanted to observe as much as he could, while trying to hold in his heart. He was really speaking the truth when he spoke about her scent. She smelled so sweet that he couldn't wait to lick each and every part of her body, especially the sweet core of her heat. But he would treat her like a lady. Wine and dine her to the point that she would enjoy his visit as much as he would.

Chapter 3

They finally reached a long, narrow, red-brick road lined with colorful bungalows. Lanassa pulled in front of a yellow and purple house with hanging flower vines. Andre thought it was charming. He turned and faced Lanassa. "Is this our stop?"

"Yes, it is. I can't wait until you see inside, so hurry up and open my door for me" Lanassa was never one for mincing her words.

Andre did as he was told and opened the door for Lanassa. As he did so, he noticed that Lanassa was studying him—he hoped she thought he looked good in his tailor-made suit—or maybe even absolutely gorgeous. He reached out and took her hand in his, and she gave him another wink.

Funny, Andre couldn't recall that Lanassa winked so often during his last trip to New Orleans when he spent time with her. He didn't know what to think about all of the winking. Lanassa held on to Andre's hand while he closed the car door behind him. She finally released his hand and dug the house key from her purse, then gave it to him as they walked toward the house.

Andre opened the door and stepped aside to allow her to enter first. He followed her inside and looked around the narrow, long hallway with the very high ceiling, which was painted white. The walls were covered with burgundy wallpaper. Yes, he was in New Orleans, without a doubt—the colorful scenery of the home was one of New Orleans trademarks, and the bungalow fitted the scene perfectly with an old-style of hospitality that gave him a warm welcome feeling like the city. And he would be spending time in New Orleans with the most beautiful woman who had ever captured his heart.

Lanassa took Andre's hand again and led him to the end of the hallway, where there was a dining room with rich pieces of furniture. The china cabinet was filled with floral porcelain plates and cups and crystal glasses. The dining room table was long and made from mahogany. The fabric on the eight cushioned chairs was the same pattern of burgundy that was on the hallway wallpaper.

To Andre, it was surreal to be in Lanassa's home. Last time he was in New Orleans with her, Lanassa was too young to have her own place. She was only eighteen and lived with her mother and three siblings.

"Do you live here alone, Lanassa?" Andre asked.

"Yes, this is my place, no roommate. Do you like what you see?"

Andre more than liked what he saw, and it had nothing to do with her home. Lanassa crooked her finger at Andre, indicating he should follow her into another room. She had such a wicked smile on her face.

She gave him a tour of her home—the comfortable living room had a long sofa with beige fabric and lots of burgundy and beige pillows thrown on it. The hardwood floors were made of mahogany that seemed to gleam. There was a burgundy rug with a glass-top mahogany coffee table placed on it in the middle of the room. And two beige armchairs were between a rust-colored brick fireplace. Then Andre followed Lanassa into her kitchen, which was small but included everything one would need to prepare a hearty meal. The appliances looked new; it seemed as if she didn't cook much. Everything was in perfect position, as if they were used for display only.

Lanassa saved the best for last. She led him up the narrow stairway to a white door. *This must be her bedroom*, Andre thought. Lanassa opened the door and led Andre inside. All he could see was the huge king-size bed with a sheer red canopy covering it. It was like a big "welcome home" sign. He looked at Lanassa, and she licked her lips and gave him another one of those wicked smiles and winks.

She walked toward him. "I want you; I've wanted you for some time now. How about you take off those clothes and I do the same, and you join me in the shower." Before Andre had the chance to respond, Lanassa was taking off her clothes, without shyness, just boldness and readiness. Andre wasn't too surprised; after all, this is the woman who turned him out those many years ago with her take control desires to please him sexually. It had made him fall so easily in love with her. Andre always loved Lanassa's boldness and the lack of shyness when it came to sex. But Lanassa was also the woman that took his heart and refused to return his love. *Can I do this again?* Andre wondered. *Can I set myself up for the pain that might come, if she is the same person from years gone by?*

What was he doing? Maybe he should have called Craig or Bryan instead of avoiding all calls by throwing the cell phone inside his luggage. He should excuse himself, ask for the key to her car, and get his cell phone from his luggage, which he left in the trunk. But his dick was speaking far louder than his mind at the time. Things were getting pretty heated. Andre knew he couldn't turn away and slow things down with her. He never had that kind of strength when it came to Lanassa. He watched her strip for him as his eyes covered every inch of her smooth brown skin.

Lanassa had the kind of body that was built to please any man's eyes, even if he never got the opportunity to touch her. But Andre did touch her at one point in time and even had the opportunity to bury himself deeply inside her heated core. He didn't want to start the trip this way. But whatever Lanassa wanted, he'd give it to her. In time, she'd want more than just the physical from him. After all, she was a woman now and there must be more to her needs than making love and partying. Surely, she was at the stage in her life when she needed more from him. She missed him, he knew, and needed this first, before anything else could begin. Andre was really counting on that.

Still, it had to go deeper than the physical; he needed more from her than just her body. He needed her soul to love as well. So he watched that beautiful brown body being revealed to him and the sight made him tremble all over, except one place. That part was very hard and ready to enter her welcoming core. When Lanassa was fully out of her clothes, she looked at Andre. "What are you waiting for? Is this enough invitation for you, or should I come over there and help you remove your clothes myself?"

Andre swallowed hard, with so many thoughts running in his head. Was this still a game to her? *Just give her what she is asking for,* he thought. *It will play out in your favor and hers as your wife at the end.* Andre was mesmerized by her beauty; he wanted her in that king-size bed with his arms wrapped around her.

He smiled, and it surprised Lanassa. She felt warmth coming from the smile, and it touched her. Lanassa had secrets, however, that could jeopardize this welcome-home reunion with Andre. She had to be careful. She walked over to him and wrapped her hands around Andre's neck, then started kissing him while standing on her tiptoes. The kiss was amazingly warm, deep, and desperate. She was feeling confused—was it coming from her or him or them both? Lanassa released her hold on Andre's neck, then started unbuttoning his shirt, first the buttons, then the golden cufflinks. She tossed the cufflinks on the bedside table and allowed his shirt to fall to the floor.

Most men Lanassa was into didn't wear white T-shirts under their shirts, but Andre did. Dr. Andre C. Brass wasn't like the men she typically spent her time with. They were the partying, jazzy type, with opened-up shirts that showed their chests. That was one of the many secrets Lanassa felt she must keep from Andre—and the man she lived with.

Andre was different he didn't try to control her and always made her feel special. The man she lived with did try to control her. Lanassa laughed in her mind at the thought of him, trying and failing every time. She shook the thought from her mind and started concentrating on this heavenly looking, tall specimen of man in front of her. Lanassa unzipped Andre's pants and witnessed one huge-sized bulge. Her heart started pumping. Instead of the blood going to her brain, it pumped straight down to her heated core. She was ready—no, more than ready—to take Andre. His pants dropped to the floor—thank God, he wasn't wearing boxers; Andre was wearing briefs. Lanassa liked that.

She started rubbing her hand across his bulge, feeling it getting tighter, ready to escape. Andre took off his shoes, then his black silk socks, and kicked them to the side, then Lanassa assisted him with removing the T-shirt. He was hard as a mountain. Lanassa started rubbing her body up against Andre's body while purring like a cat. He embraced her closer to his rock-hard body and rubbed his hands over her smooth body, from her waist to her spine. *How much more of this can I endure?* He wondered. Lanassa pulled down his briefs, and the smooth-veined muscle came to life, pointing straight at her. Andre pulled his feet from his briefs and kicked it aside with no regard. He picked Lanassa up in his arms and whispered in her ear in a low sexy voice, "Where is the shower? It's time we both got wet." He wasn't just referring to the shower. She giggled in a wicked way then pointed him in the direction of her bathroom, which was across the hall.

Andre reached the bathroom and before he placed Lanassa on her feet, he bent down and gave her another deep, tongue kiss, which took the breath from them both. The adrenaline started running through their bodies; it was hard for them to catch their breath. Andre pulled away from the kiss, then reached behind the shower curtain and turned on the water, checking the temperature to make sure it was just right.

Once Andre was satisfied with the temperature of the flowing water, he picked Lanassa back up into his arms and placed her inside the shower, then he followed her. The water felt inviting. Lanassa reached for the lavender soap and started rubbing it between her hands. Then she rubbed her soapy hands over his wide chest, around his broad shoulders and down his arms. Andre removed the clip from her hair allowing the curls to flow over her shoulders, then he grabbed her hair gently. He started kissing her again, while allowing his thick bulge to press into her stomach. Lanassa pushed herself against him, accepting all he had to offer. And what he offered was amazing.

Andre pulled her away from him then reached his hand out from the shower curtain to grab a washcloth that was on a vanity nearby. He soaped up the washcloth, then washed her body from head to toe and between her precious jewels. She loved it, every part of it. No man had every made her feel this way; after all, Andre had been her first sexual partner. She missed him dearly.

Lanassa knew what kind of woman she was; it was like she was born a certain way. She was born to give herself physically, but never mentally. She pushed him to the edge and away from her so many years ago. She could only blame it on her youth and inexperience in a relationship. But over the years her behavior with men had only worsened. Maybe Andre deserved better, but then again, Lanassa was a very selfish woman. Her behavior hadn't changed; it had strengthened with time. That little fact, however, she would keep to herself; she wanted him to stay around until the end of the summer. Then she knew he would have to go back to Cambridge. But for now, he was hers, on her playing field. She hoped Andre knew that fact.

Her body was all she was willing to share with him, along with the fun of jazz music and dance to come. Lanassa knew she must be careful. She didn't want this to end the way it did those many years ago. If Andre really took a good look, he would see it was more than a possibility he would be going back to Cambridge without what he had been seeking. Lanassa would keep that to herself—no need to ruin the time they had together.

So she relaxed and enjoyed his hands, with the washcloth rubbing smoothly over her body. Then she took it from him and returned the favor. Oh, she really loved running her hands and fingers across his body, so she disregarded the washcloth and started washing him with her bare hands. When Lanassa got to his testicles, she gave them just a little squeeze and heard Andre moan. She wanted to hear more and louder, so she started to rub her hands up and down his shaft, while licking his throat. Andre was going crazy in her gentle hands. He stopped her play and turned her around toward the bath tiles and started playing with her small but sweet breasts, while pressing his bulge against her soft bottom. He pinched her nipples with his fingers until he heard her moan. Then he rubbed his hands between her sweet butt cheeks and spread her legs apart and started rotating his index finger around her clitoris.

Lanassa was feeling good, but she wanted to be the one in control. So she turned around and faced him then placed her right foot on the edge of the bathtub. She was ready for him. "Enter me, Andre, now, or I'll leave this shower and leave you hanging." The aggression in her voice took him by surprise. But Andre wanted the same thing so he entered her with one smooth push inside. This was the first scream Andre had heard from her throughout the play. It reached a point of seriousness. Andre pushed in and out of her body while sucking her breast. Lanassa's head started to move from side to side while she screamed out all of the pleasures Andre was providing her. The loving was affecting him as well, and they both got pretty vocal. She grabbed his short curly hair hard, while pressing her tongue inside of his mouth. She sucked his tongue to a point in which Andre knew without a doubt he needed more from this woman. He needed her in mind, body, and soul.

After the loving, Lanassa was exhausted. Andre held Lanassa around her waist with one arm after they both had climaxed together; then he reached behind her and turned off the water. He grabbed a large white towel and started drying her body and hair. He dropped the wet towel and wrapped a dry towel around Lanassa's body. After attending to her needs, he dried himself off with another towel. Then

Andre picked up Lanassa and carried her to the bed, placing her under the sheets, where he joined her. They both fell asleep in each other's arms in a matter of minutes, each one having different dreams about their future together.

Chapter 4

Lanassa woke up, blinking her eyes, as the morning sun shone brightly through the bedroom window. She felt strong arms around her tiny waist—was she dreaming? She turned toward the warmth against her back, and memories of the day before came into view. *Oh no!* She thought. *I must get dressed; this is going to be hard to explain.* But the strong arms tightened their hold around her waist. Lanassa looked at Andre, and he was smiling at her. He gave her the most pleasure she had received in a long time. Come to think of it, he was the only man who ever completely gave her fulfillment when it came to experiencing the ecstasy of sex.

No wonder she had overslept in his arms. Now, it was in a state of urgency that she excused herself from him to go home—to her real home with the other man, the man who couldn't possibly compete with Andre; the other man who was controlling, who was so different from Andre. The only similarities they shared were that they were both professional men who earned lots of money. Yes, Lanassa knew all about Andre's success. She kept a private investigator on him for years, knowing one day she'd seek him out. She laughed—no man could control her. And if a man could, it wouldn't be the man she lived with. It would have been Andre. If only she were the kind of woman who could give in a little for the man in her life who needed her.

If that were the case, she would be with Andre. She wouldn't have sent him away from New Orleans, with Craig's help. She would have been a better woman to him. And Lanassa certainly wouldn't have spent the past eight years without him and with other men so she wouldn't be reminded of him. And then she met the man she now lived with, who brought memories of Andre back to her.

She wondered on many occasions how it would have been to be married to Andre. Lanassa knew the answer; she would have made him miserable.

"What are you thinking, Lanassa? You seem to be in deep thought."

Lanassa looked into Andre's eyes and smiled. "I'm thinking of you, of course."

"Oh, I like that, me on your mind. I hope the thoughts are pleasant ones."

"Of course they are, you silly man."

"I wouldn't use the word 'silly,' Lanassa. You should replace the word with 'serious.'"

Lanassa became nervous; she hoped that Andre couldn't pick up the turn in her mood. She didn't want the time they shared to become serious. She wanted nothing more other than sex with him and to keep her secrets hidden. Lanassa knew she had to relax and not give anything away, so she settled back into his arms.

"What are our plans for today?" Andre asked. "You did invite me down for enjoyment, and so far, I must say, you are a woman of your word." Andre felt a small tremble in Lanassa's body.

"Oh, I have many plans for us, but first I must go someplace."

"Good, I'll go with you."

It wasn't a question, and Lanassa became even more nervous. Could she pull this off? "No, Andre that won't be necessary it's only business. That will take me away from you for only a little while. I'd like for you to stay here and become comfortable in my home. Remember, I invited you here for enjoyment, not business. You'll have enough of that at the end of the summer, waiting for you back in Cambridge."

Andre gazed at her suspiciously, but he was feeling somewhat tired, so he agreed with her request.

Lanassa bent down and kissed his warm lips, then jumped out of the bed. She took a quick shower and got dressed, then told him where everything was that he needed. There was food in the fridge, wine in a cooler, which was built in the kitchen wall, and books on the bookshelves. There also was a large-screen television in the living room and a collection of DVDs in a glass cabinet.

Andre became skeptical that her "business" would only take an hour. She was making it sound like he'd be without her company for some time.

Once Lanassa was out the door and driving down the street, it hit Andre—he'd forgotten to retrieve his luggage from the trunk of her car. *Great, just great,* he thought, *And what the hell is all of the rushing about? It's only six in the morning. What kind of business does she have that she rushes out before I can get my luggage? No, this isn't her fault. I should have gotten my tail out of this bed and slowed her butt down. It would have giving me enough time to adjust my mind so I could have remembered that I left my belongings in the damn trunk.*

Now, however, he had no cell phone, no toothbrush, no toiletries, and no clean clothes.

Andre got out of the bed and walked across the hall to the bathroom to start a hot shower. While taking the shower, Andre wondered again about Lanassa's life. What kind of job did she have? He barely knew her anymore but he loved her dearly. *I'm Blind, without questions. Yes, that's me all right—damn.* Andre chastised his-self with thoughts.

After the shower Andre got dressed in the same clothes he'd worn the day before. He thought about calling Craig but was sure that would only make his mood worse. Instead, he rinsed his mouth out with some of Lanassa's mouthwash then took a look at himself in the mirror. He needed his shaver and his wave hairbrush. *What the hell?* He started brushing his short curls back with Lanassa's hairbrush. Andre went into the bedroom to straighten up the bed, and then he did the same to the bathroom, throwing the damp towels into a hamper.

Now he was ready to find a café somewhere nearby, but then remembered he didn't have the house key to lock the place up. *Damn!* Andre started pacing the living room, back and forth, while rubbing back his black short curls with his large hands. He kept looking at the phone on Lanassa's end table. *What the hell?* He picked up the receiver and punched in Craig's number in the phone. It rang four times before it was picked up.

"Hello?" Craig's deep bass voice was a welcome relief for Andre.

Andre sat in an armchair and started opening up to his best friend. "Hey, Craig, it's me."

"Dre, where have you been? Bryan and I have been trying to get in touch with you for days. It's not like you to become MIA." Craig said with anxiety in his voice.

Andre usually spoke with Craig just about every day. Craig considered himself something of a philosopher, and Andre has always found it enlightening to talk to his friend. The debates they had were the best. The only time things got a little heated was when Craig brought up Lanassa, telling Andre he need to find a good woman of quality.

Andre did date a little, but it never worked out, because he was still in love with Lanassa. Now, Andre appreciated the MIA statement. He needed Craig's support although he felt bad about the anxiety he heard in his friend's voice. "I'm out of town, man. I know. I should have dropped you a line before I left. But I was kind of in a hurry. It was at a moment's notice, and I had to get my flight schedule in order."

Craig cleared his throat. Andre could tell that Craig knew the exact direction the airplane had flown. "Want to talk about it, Dre?"

Craig knew Andre better than Andre knew himself, at times, but Craig could not understand the hold that Lanassa had on Andre. Still, Andre could use his friend's perspective. "I don't know, Craig, something isn't right. I just can't place my finger on it. I mean, last night with her was amazing. She drove me to her home, which I must say is very nice, and before I knew it, we were at it. No dinner, no talking, just straight-up loving; then we crashed."

Craig blew a wild vocal sound of concern through the telephone.

"That's the good part, Craig; the bad part is that this morning, she was looking sort of strange to me. Lanassa told me she had to go out on business. Before I got the opportunity to clear my head from the morning fog, she was getting dressed and running out of the house. To top that off, she drove away with my luggage in the trunk of her car, along with the house key. Man, I feel like a hostage sitting up in this house."

Craig feared the worse was yet to come for his friend. How could he explain that to a man who had no common sense when it came to this woman? His friend wasn't stupid—he had worked hard and received a doctorate degree in music, but he got a fat F—for failure—when it came to Lanassa. Did she have some kind of spell on him? After all, she was born and raised in New Orleans, where some did believe in voodoo. All Craig wanted to do was tell his friend to catch the first airplane back home. And kiss that baby good-bye forever. But all he said was, "You know what I think, Dre. You don't have to be a mind reader to know what's on my mind concerning your being in New Orleans with Lanassa."

Yes, Andre did know what his friend's thoughts were concerning the situation. But he wasn't the one in love with the woman. Andre loved Lanassa to the point that he couldn't explain that fact to himself. Lord knows he tried.

Maybe it was the fact that he'd taken her virginity. He was the first man to feel right down inside of her heated core. He held her tightly afterwards, soothing her with his low voice because he knew she was sore. He was not afraid to see the drops of blood on the sheets after they made love. He then picked her up and placed her in a warm bath, while washing her all over, as if this all made her belong to him.

No, Craig would never understand; no one would ever understand. One thing Andre did know was that he wasn't leaving Lanassa. He was going to stay with her and show her the love she deserved. Was she too blind to see his love for her, or was he too blind to see that she didn't love him? No matter; he was here now and before he left, he would know which one of those statements was true.

"Craig, I'm all right—just a little upset with the abruptness of her actions. I'll speak with her when she returns. Don't worry about me, man. I just needed to get this out. Thank you for being there for me. I'll see you when I return home."

Before Craig was able to say another word, Andre said good-bye and hung up the phone. Craig couldn't call him back; the number was private.

Chapter 5

Lanassa ran through the spacious house like a chicken with her head cut off. She knew he was going to be furious with her. After all, this was the day he would be flying out to Africa. What was she thinking? It was as if Andre had drugged her in the way he handled and took care of her body. It put her into a deep sleep every time. She should have known that nothing about him or what he did to her had changed.

"Douglas, I'm home, sweetheart. Where are you?" Lanassa climbed the stairs to the master bedroom. Suddenly, she felt him behind her and turned around to face him.

Douglas had a razor in his hand … and then she noticed the aftershave on his face. Good thing. Or Lanassa would have thought that razor was meant for her throat.

Douglas was a tall man, though not as tall as Andre. He didn't have the good looks that Andre had. Where Andre was truly handsome, Douglas was average and had lips that rarely displayed a smile. Lanassa needed a man like Douglas, a man who would at least make her think about her actions. However, he needed to give up that controlling crap. Now that she had Andre back in her life she wasn't about to give him up until summer was over. This business trip to Africa that Douglas was about to take would keep him away from New Orleans during the summer season. Lanassa felt she had all the time in the world to spend with Andre.

"Lanassa, dear, you look like a child whose been caught with her hand in the cookie jar. May I ask where have you been, or is it one of your many secrets?"

Lanassa smiled nervously. "Darling, you know how I need my space from time to time."

"Yes, I remember that you love to get away to go play with your young jazz friends. I guess this was an all-nighter."

Lanassa took a few steps back from Douglas—he was making her more nervous as he stood close to her with that razor in his hand.

Douglas looked at her through narrowed eyes. "Were you having so much fun that you didn't remember I have a plane to catch this morning? I thought we could at least spend some time together, making love under the sheets. It would have been nice if my wife could have pried herself away from those young thugs for such a departure."

"I'm sorry, Douglas; I'll make it up to you."

As if a departure would have made a difference, Lanassa thought. *The only difference is how much older you are as compared to me. How much entertainment can I get from you when you're forty-eight and I'm twenty-six? Andre is the right age for me. Douglas, you need to get real. You're just too boring in all departments. I love your intellect, but Andre has that and the appreciation for jazz music and dance.* She smiled to herself. *If Douglas only knew … the man I spent time with last night is intelligent as well as being candy for my eyes.*

Lanassa was so deep in her thoughts that she didn't notice that Douglas was staring at her. *Chill, girl, just chill.* She could blow this if she wasn't careful. She wished he would hurry up and leave so she could get back to Andre.

"I'll surely take you up on the offer, my dear Lanassa, as soon as I get back home. So please be prepared to please me." Douglas bent down and kissed Lanassa hard across her lips, leaving behind a mask of aftershave on her cheeks and lips. Then he turned and went back into the bathroom.

Lanassa could hear the water running in the shower and the sound of the curtain being pulled aside as Douglas stepped inside. Once Lanassa was sure he was taking his shower, she wiped the aftershave from her cheeks and lips then pulled her phone from her purse and called Andre. He picked up the phone on the first ring. "Hello, it's me. I'll be there within an hour, hugs and kisses." Lanassa whispered into the phone. Before Andre got the opportunity to reply, she hung up the phone. Andre noticed the number was private.

Lanassa busied herself around the house, until the car came for Douglas to take him to the airport. Douglas called to her and in seconds, she was before him. He bent down and gave her another hard kiss while caressing her bottom. Douglas moaned into her mouth while taking her tongue hungrily.

"Be good while I'm gone, sweetheart," he told her. "Try not to burn yourself out from partying too late. You know what they say?"

Lanassa looked at him quizzically. "No, Douglas, I don't know. What do they say?"

"When the lion's away … I'll leave it at that, food for thought." He winked at her and was out the door.

Since when did he speak in riddles? Lanassa thought. Right now, she didn't care. She ran upstairs and took another quick shower hoping it would relax her nerves. Lanassa couldn't wait to be back in Andre's arms.

Chapter 6

Andre paced back and forth, until he heard the key in the door—and Lanassa walked in with a smile on her face. It was hard for Andre to keep his composure. She was more than a few hours late. It seemed as if he had been pacing through the living room all day. Lanassa approached him and wrapped her arms around his waist, placing her head against his chest. Andre felt as if he had no other choice but to accept her embrace. He just shook his head and hugged her back. "May I ask where have you been?"

She looked up into his eyes with the innocence of a child. "I told you, Andre, I had a business appointment. Please don't tell me you missed me for such a short period of time. I'm flattered, but please don't become controlling; it isn't in you. And it hasn't been long."

But it had been. Still, Andre didn't want to ruin the time he had with Lanassa during this trip, even though he had a nagging feeling that something wasn't right. *Keep it together, Andre. It might not be anything at all.* "I guess you rushed out of here so fast, you must have been late for your appointment," he suggested.

"No, I made it just in time."

Andre removed her arms from around his waist. "Well, I'm glad you made it on time. At least one of us had a productive day."

Lanassa gazed at him as if she was puzzled. "What do you mean by that statement?"

Andre looked into her eyes, as if she was far from his view. *Something just isn't right with her. Please don't let this be the same woman from years gone by*, Andre thought. "Lanassa, you rushed out of here so fast, it didn't give me time to retrieve my luggage from the trunk of your car. I've been stuck here without fresh clothes, without my shaving and hair products, not to mention my cell phone. I also was left without a spare key to your house. Time seems to go slower when you feel stuck, if you know what I mean."

Lanassa knew Andre was pissed. She could tell he was trying to keep it together. "I guess the only thing I can say is that I'm truly sorry for inconveniencing you." Lanassa looked like a spoiled child with pouting lips.

I love her; all I want is for both of us to be smiling right now. Andre was somewhat upset, but he was more than eager to make it happen. He wanted to see her smile. So he took her hand in his and gave a gentle squeeze. "Let's forget the whole day ever happened. Let's concentrate on the here and now—and yesterday, during the time we enjoyed together in the shower, you in my arms while we slept together. What do you say?"

Lanassa leaned into Andre's chest and inhaled his scent. She looked up at him. "I say it sounds great, so kiss me and make it official."

Andre gave her a gentle kiss; then asked for the key to the trunk of the car. The kiss reminded him that he needed to get his luggage and groom himself. Then they could go someplace for a nice dinner together.

The real reason Lanassa had been gone so long was that she felt as if she was being followed. Lanassa drove to her girlfriend Patricia's home to waste some time, until the feeling of being watched was gone. They exchanged small talk, as Patricia busied herself getting ready for work. She was one of the bartenders at the nightclub called Peeks where Lanassa frequently went partying. She decided she'd introduce Andre to the place after dinner for some music, drinks, and dance.

Lanassa thought about her reasons for the delay in returning to Andre after promising him the appointment wouldn't take long. Once Lanassa felt comfortable that she wasn't being watched she said good-bye to her friend then drove her car as fast as she could back to be with Andre. She turned toward him with another one of her amazing smiles, along with that not-so-familiar wink, and said, "Okay, go and get your luggage, and we can get this party started." Lanassa kissed Andre's sweet lips again, then handed him the key to her car.

As Andre went to the car, he felt as if he was being watched—not by the woman inside the house but from a stranger, outside. *I'm losing it*, Andre thought. He retrieved his luggage and headed back inside.

Andre told Lanassa he wanted to take another shower and get ready. She kissed him and nodded her head.

It didn't take Andre long. After the task was completed he felt like a new man, with his hair the way he preferred, his breath fresh, and wearing a tailor-made suit and clean shirt.

He took Lanassa's hand and out the door they went. Andre was in the driver's seat this time. He turned to her and asked, "Where to, my sweet Lanassa?"

Andre's term of endearment took her by surprise and it relaxed her. Lanassa told him about a fine-dining restaurant she been dying to go to—Torches Restaurant.

When they arrived, Andre helped Lanassa out of the car while handing the key over to the valet.

Inside the restaurant they were greeted by the hostess, who introduced them to their waiter, a tall man with smiling eyes. The restaurant was very dim; lighted by candles on every table, along with a huge crystal chandelier hanging from the ceiling. The decor was pure quality. The aroma of the food smelled delicious, and the atmosphere was one of romance.

Andre was pleased with her choice and felt the romance of it warming his entire body. He placed his hand on Lanassa's hip while the waiter led them to a quiet booth for two in the back of the restaurant. This was what Andre needed—to be with the woman he loved in a place that catered to the romantic at heart.

Lanassa was comforted by the choice of their table. It helped calm that feeling of paranoia, which been lingering inside of her since they left the house. The waiter left them with menus; then returned in a matter of seconds and placed fresh water in crystal glasses on their table. "Are you ready to order?" he asked.

Lanassa looked into Andre's eyes and asked him to order for her. She couldn't decide—everything on the menu seemed delicious. The waiter recommended the summer salmon kabobs, along with the spicy rice, and aged sherry walnut vinaigrette salad. Andre ordered the recommendation dinner for Lanassa and himself, along with the restaurant's finest white wine. The waiter took their order with a nod of approval, smiled, and walked away.

Andre reached across the table and held Lanassa's hand in his. He gazed into her eyes, trying to read her mood. But Lanassa seemed to be guarding her emotions from him, and the atmosphere was taking her over. Andre's eyebrows raised and he smiled at her.

Sitting this close to Andre, she could see how handsome he was but could also feel the kindness within his heart. Still, she couldn't allow her emotions to get the better of her when it came to the pull he had on her.

"Tell me was your business this morning productive Lanassa?" Andre asked. He could feel her hand tremble.

"Yes, it was," she said in a low voice. "We don't have to talk about business," Andre replied. Lanassa looked down at the masculine hand holding hers and couldn't speak. She was hiding so much from him and her selfishness kept a hold on her. She wanted all the time she had to spend with Andre during the summer, but the guilt Lanassa felt inside was trying to over take her selfishness. *I wish I could be the kind of woman a man like Andre deserves. Don't think foolishly*, Lanassa thought. She took her other hand and placed it over Andre's. She concentrated on the warmth of Andre's hand. She brought his hand up to her lips and gave it a soft kiss. It took Andre by surprise, especially since her eyes were telling a different story. He loved Lanassa unconditionally. Andre hoped that whatever was going on with her, he would be able to handle it. He witnessed the emotional battle Lanassa was having inside by looking into her eyes. Andre hoped the fight she was having inside to control her love for him was losing, if she loved him at all, which was still the question. Andre was praying that he would win her love and devotion, before he left her to go back to Cambridge. *Maybe she would come back with me.* He thought. Hope is what he needed and a lot of praying. He couldn't imagine leaving her behind this time. He'd spent too many years without her and couldn't stand losing her again, going back home with an empty soul, without his mate, would be too much to bear.

Lanassa saw the concern on his face. "Smile for me, Andre. I have a surprise for you after dinner."

"I hope it includes more of me inside of you," he replied. That made Lanassa blush—the most beautiful expression he had seen since they both were seated together.

Before Lanassa could respond, the waiter brought them their dinner. Lanassa let go of Andre's hand and inhaled the aroma of the food; it was heavenly.

Lanassa had been saved by the waiter and the food for the time being. The less they talked, the less she had to reveal. However, being the selfish woman she was, they probably could talk all night, and she would still keep her secrets to herself—to get what she wanted. Andre did most of the talking as they ate their dinner. He tried his best to humor her, entertain her, and make her happy while she was with him. But something wasn't right. If he hadn't kept talking, they would have eaten in silence.

Lanassa listened to Andre and found him to be very entertaining— talking about his home, his friends Craig and Bryan (she remembered Craig all too well), he spoke about his students, and the music he composed for the classes he taught. His conversation was interesting, not like Douglas, who didn't share with her what his business trip to Africa was about … or anything else, for that matter. She was just his sleeping partner, a trophy wife. It suited her just fine, but Andre was having a warm effect on her emotions.

Lanassa wouldn't give up her freedom for anyone. She would share her time but not her space. Douglas stayed away for long hours at the office, and this pleased her; plus, he traveled a lot. She knew Andre would be the kind of man who would like to share and enjoy everything with his partner. Lanassa had believed within her heart for years that it wasn't in her to be Andre's kind of woman. Sitting here with him, she wished it weren't true, but she couldn't change the way she was.

Her world was her own, and Lanassa only allowed men to enter it for a little while. If she believed in working for a living, she never would have married Douglas—after all, a woman needed financial support. What better way of getting that support than marrying a millionaire, one who gave her all the space she demanded and the money she needed? There was no other way, and Lanassa knew it by experience. Lanassa also knew that Douglas was becoming very impatient with her lifestyle lately. Things were changing with him, and the trust was underwater, drowning a slow death.

But she had been thinking of Andre for years, ever since he went back to Cambridge those many years ago.

She started dreaming about him but refused to get in touch with him. Lanassa had evolved into a woman with worldly ways and little value for love, romance, kids, marriage, and the little house with the white picket fence, although she knew Andre lived in a small mansion. She still wasn't the kind of woman he needed. She was wild and couldn't be tamed; this she knew for sure. But those vivid dreams of Andre made it impossible for her to stop reaching out and contacting him—against her better judgment. It was as if she had no other choice. So Lanassa followed through with what she wanted, as always. Now, Andre was here, right before her eyes. With that handsome brown face, those bright brown eyes, the sexy dimple in his chin, and the kind of body women would die to get next to.

Lanassa finally spoke, her words sounding low and sexy. "Mmm, this dinner tastes incredible." She slowly licked her full, perfect lips.

The fabric of Andre's pants became instantly tight. The "boy"— which is the nickname he gave his penis—was trying to break free. Andre shifted in his seat, trying to move his bulge without bring his discomfort to Lanassa's attention. All the shifting in the world, however, couldn't make him comfortable. He had to have her again— and soon—in his arms and in her bed.

Lanassa was a woman with experience in this department—she was no innocent bystander when it came to a man with needs for her. But she played it cool. "Are you all right, Andre? I hope the dinner is pleasing to you. This is one of New Orleans' finest restaurants."

Andre had no doubt that Lanassa knew the effect she had on him. He hoped she also knew it wasn't all about sex. He wanted Lanassa to know how much he loved her and would do his best to make her belong only to him. He wanted to be the man to satisfy all of her desires. Andre thought there might be other men in her life; he could only wish it wasn't true.

Andre was hopeful that the reason for her invitation to come to New Orleans was that Lanassa was ready to settle down with him, growing old together in bliss. He wanted her to love him as deeply as he loved her. *Wishful thinking*, he thought. Andre didn't want his visit with her to end up a lie. "I totally agree—the food is great. Your choice was on the money. I'll never bet against you."

Lanassa thought Andre's words might have more meaning than just the dinner. The nervous feeling came over her again. She had to keep her secrets from him. She was also feeling paranoid again like she was being watched. *If I keep this up, I'll be in a mental ward before the night is over. How could I play this man with the gentle heart?* Lanassa, being as she was, brushed the thought out of her head. *Andre is a grown man, not a boy. I'm sure he can read between the lines. I haven't mentioned love to him, ever. It's not what I want. Surely if I never said it, he can't possibly be looking for it, at least not from me.*

She suddenly felt like a cruel bitch. She was ready to go dancing, to end this romantic dinner so they could play, not get serious. Lanassa also wanted more of his body inside of hers before the night was over. Lanassa did everything she could to restrain herself from tapping her polished fingernails on the table, while holding up her other hand and yelling across the room, "Check, please!"

Chapter 7

Craig and his brother, Bryan, were burning the late night oil with work, going over legal depositions for Brown & Brown, Attorneys at Law, their firm, which was located in Boston. It had been a long day for Craig—that phone call from Andre earlier was nagging at him. He couldn't shake the cold feeling that enveloped him and was very disturbed by the call. Something wasn't right—Craig felt it deep inside. He knew Andre had no idea what he was dealing with. Why would Andre go to New Orleans alone, after all these years, to be with a woman he caught cheating on him? Not just one time but many. Yes, she might have been young and wasn't ready to settle down, but to play a brother the way she played Andre was simply wrong. Something wasn't right about Lanassa. Andre was blinded by this fact, and there was nothing he could do to help his friend to see the light.

Maybe something wasn't right with Andre as well. How could a man love a woman like that, unconditionally? If it were Craig, he would see a mental health professional to help him stay away from a woman like that. And he certainly wouldn't have dropped everything to fly out to see her after so much time had passed—and without a word from her. Craig didn't think she ever apologized for her actions back then. She'd played Andre like his favorite trumpet the one Andre blew jazz through whenever he thought of her. The man just couldn't shake the woman.

Andre had been crushed after his relationship eight years ago with Lanassa. Craig thought his friend would never make it through college when he came back from New Orleans. But not only did he make it, Andre went on to receive his doctorate. Craig always wondered if Andre thought he could get the girl back if he had the prestigious position and the money to go with it. But then Andre went years without contacting her, not even on their trips to New Orleans over the years. Craig thought Andre was doing fine, other than his unsuccessful dates on many occasions. The women Andre dated from time to time lacked something—he'd expressed this fact to Craig and Bryan. Lacking something, he insisted, that Lanassa had. It couldn't have been class; Craig thought derisively, Lanassa was classless. Beauty was only skin deep with her—the inside of Lanassa wasn't beautiful at all.

Craig wouldn't get a puppy with the woman, let alone get married to her and have children, which Andre used to speak about a lot. Craig assumed the idea was still in Andre's head, but he stopped mentioning it in order to keep the peace between them and hold down the arguments. Yes, Craig was worried but what could he do. Andre was no longer his young friend from their days in grade school. He was a grown man. How could he save someone from himself? *Eight years, washed down the drain by a phone call from the bitch.* Craig thought. This time, instead of being crushed by a few bricks, Craig could only hope that when it was over, Andre wouldn't be lying beneath the rubble of the whole building. There would be no way to put so many pieces back together again.

Bryan looked over at Craig and said, "Are you working, man?"

"Yes, I'm working. I'm working." Craig went back to the depositions, with prayers in the back of his mind for the friend who had been like a brother to him, ever since they were dirty-face kids.

Bryan looked over at Craig again, who still seemed to be lost in thoughts that had nothing to do with the documents in front of him. "Tell me, Craig, what gives? You're not into this. We have a trial coming up soon. Maybe you should take a break and talk about what's working your brain cells overtime; then we can get back to work."

Craig wasn't about to share Andre's business with Bryan; he probably would trivialize the matter. Bryan was an optimist when it came to the ones he loved. He viewed their problems through rose colored glasses and refused to face his true emotions. When Andre comes back in one piece—Craig could only hope—Andre should be the one to open up with Bryan. After all, Bryan was close to Andre as well.

But Craig was afraid that something treacherous was about to happen to Andre, and he had no way of intervening. He couldn't share what he thought with Bryan. He didn't want his brother to become worried. Apparently, time hadn't stopped the love that Andre felt in his heart for Lanassa—it was always there in his eyes; Bryan knew it, too. Craig also knew it was an unhealthy relationship—the possibility of its becoming dangerous was always just below the surface.

Craig had hoped during those trips to New Orleans that Andre and Lanassa would never cross paths, which was the reason he went with Andre—to look out for his friend. Now, Andre was there with the bitch. It was as if Andre was being drawn to New Orleans by Lanassa. Craig felt it in his gut but prayed his gut feelings were wrong. He hoped that Andre's visit to be with Lanassa wouldn't turn out to be fatal.

Craig said to Bryan, "I'm cool, so can I get back to work without your analyzing my head?" They both shook their heads at each other, then went back to the business at hand.

Lanassa felt as if she was about to jump out of her skin. The romantic atmosphere was getting to her in more ways than one. Andre was also getting under her skin, making her feel things she didn't want to feel which was loved. There was no doubt about it—it was time to skip the romantic restaurant scene and go to an atmosphere with many people and loud music.

The waiter came back with a menu displaying Touches' many desserts, along with that smile Lanassa had liked at first but which had become annoying to her now. Andre wasn't the type for sweets, so he passed. *Thank God*, Lanassa thought. She said to the waiter, "No, thanks, I can't eat another bite."

Andre smiled at her, then requested the bill. He turned to Lanassa once the waiter was out of sight. "So what's next? Remember, I'm on your playing field."

"I would like to take you to Peaks so we can party our asses off."

Andre chuckled at her childish excitement, but he also observed the wildness in her. It was as if she was still in her teens, not ready to let those years go.

He guessed it was because she really didn't have much time to party back then—she'd been too busy helping to raise her brother and two sisters. Andre remembered all too well how he met her in a grocery store with her siblings and mother. She stood out from the rest—so pretty and young. She dropped a can of soup that went rolling on the floor. He bent down and picked it up for her. As he handed the can to her, they locked eyes. It was the beginning of their relationship that summer. When she told him her name, he thought it was such a beautiful name, one that matched her beautiful face.

He had been smitten by her ever since. They started spending time together when she wasn't busy taking care of her siblings. Lanassa told him she was eighteen and had been helping her mother with her siblings, who were all younger than she was, since the age of twelve. Andre was four years older than Lanassa, and he knew she was excited by spending time with an older man. He took her away from the shack where she lived with her family. Lanassa mentioned that she never knew her father.

Andre was in love with her at first sight but he loved her even more after hearing her stories about being poor and the responsibilities she had, which were many. How could she have enjoyed her teen years with so many responsibilities? She hadn't, so Andre spent time showing her all the nice places that New Orleans had to offer.

They went to the bayou in a boat he rented and swam like fish for hours in the lake. They weren't afraid of the creatures that lived under the water. Andre also took Lanassa to the cafés and to jazz sessions with his friends. She loved it all. The night they made love for the first time, he wasn't surprised that Lanassa was a virgin. He took his time with her, and she was totally pleased. She couldn't get enough of the loving or the music, along with him—or so he thought.

As time passed, Lanassa started going out to the jazz clubs without him. She only called Andre when she was in need of his lovemaking. It was later in their relationship, just before he returned to Harvard, that Andre founded out Lanassa was sleeping with other men. She became wild, but he still loved her. He made excuses for her actions, thinking because she had been so tied down for such a long period of time, her behavior was bound to change. He also faulted himself for showing her so much too soon, like taking her to those jazz clubs.

Andre thought at the age of eighteen that Lanassa would be mature enough to handle that part of life. After all, it wasn't as if they were drinking; it was all about the music and dancing. He enjoyed playing the trumpet and watching her in the audience, smiling up at him. Andre had always thought that if he had taken it slower she wouldn't have changed. But since he only had time to spend with her during that summer, he wanted to share everything with her. Andre forgave her for her wild actions and the fact he found out she had started sleeping with other men. Yes, it broke his heart, but the blame, he thought, belonged to him, not Lanassa.

The tables had turned, and his world became hers during his absence—this he knew for sure. Andre would have to deal with what he thought he created. *But she has taken it all to the extreme*, he thought. Now he had to show Lanassa that what she sought could be enjoyed with a partner at her side, one who trusted her and loved her. Andre was willing to wait—now that he was back in her life, he had hope in his heart again.

Andre shook his head, clearing the thoughts from his mind, and brought his focus back to the woman in front of him. She was ready to party, and he was ready to share the moment with her. *I hope it's not too late and that Lanassa is the woman I wish her to be—and not the wild girl I left eight years ago.*

The waiter brought the receipt for the bill. Andre paid the bill and left the waiter a tip, then took Lanassa by her hand and led her out of the restaurant. He stood with his arms around her waist as they waited for the valet to bring them the Cadillac.

Before driving off, Andre leaned over and gave Lanassa a soft kiss to her lips. But Lanassa was still feeling paranoid, so she asked Andre to take her to a small house, miles from the restaurant, which was in a shady part of the city.

Chapter 8

Andre was starting to feel uncomfortable about granting Lanassa's request. He did know about this part of town. Last time he was in New Orleans it was reported on the news about a big cocaine bust and the police had arrested a big time drug dealer in this part of town. The knowledge led Andre to draw all kind of conclusions. Lanassa directed him to stop in front of a shabby bungalow.

"Why are we stopping here, Lanassa?" he asked. "Are you familiar with this part of town?"

"Of course," she insisted. "There is someone I need to see, then we'll be on our way. Don't worry; it's safe."

Andre had his doubts. "I'll come in with you," he told Lanassa, as he rubbed his hand up and down her arm.

She refused the offer. "I'll only be a minute. Don't worry, Andre. I'll be fine. I know the person who lives here. Just because someone is down on his or her luck doesn't mean it's right to avoid that person. A friend is a friend."

"What kind of friend do you associate with who lives in this part of town?"

The question went unanswered. Lanassa let herself out of the car. Andre wanted to yell at her to get her ass back into the car, but he was trying to trust her, so he let Lanassa go without an argument. He got out of the car and leaned against the car door. He watched everything around him, especially Lanassa. She ran up four steps, then entered a small hallway that was illuminated only by a red light bulb hanging from the ceiling by electrical wire. Andre wasn't comfortable with Lanassa's actions, not at all. *What in the hell is she doing, and who in the hell is she visiting?* Andre was about to go after her, but he decided to give Lanassa the benefit of the doubt.

It took Lanassa about ten minutes to return back to the car. For Andre, it felt like hours had passed. She skipped down the steps into his waiting arms.

"See? That wasn't long, now was it?"

He looked down at her as if she wasn't the Lanassa he knew. There was more to her than meets the eye. "I guess not," He answered, "but do prepare me in the future if we need to stop on dark streets in questionable neighborhoods. Can you do that for me?"

She stood on her tiptoes and kissed his soft lips. "I promise I will, so give me a smile and stop being a spoilsport."

Tomorrow, Andre decided, he would speak with Lanassa and get answers to the questions that were causing havoc inside his head. Andre opened the car door and stepped back, carefully watching the area around him while allowing Lanassa to get inside the car. They drove in silence for about four blocks, until Andre observed that Lanassa's mood had changed. She was singing to herself.

"I see you are in a good mood," he said.

"Yes, I am!" she said with loud enthusiasm. The top was down on the convertible and Lanassa started swinging her arms in the air while singing a song.

What the hell is going on with her? Andre wondered. Something was going on but he still couldn't face the fact that the woman he loved could be into something way over her head. At the present time, he didn't want to think about it; he didn't want to discuss his suspicions. He had to make sure what he suspected was indeed true.

Andre reached over and grabbed Lanassa's swinging arm gently, then placed her hand on his lap. "Would you like to go to your place and relax? It seems as if you are wired up. You did get up early. We can party another night."

Lanassa looked at him as if he was crazy—Andre didn't see her look—he was focused on the road. "No, I don't want to go home," she responded. "This is the right time to have fun. I have too much energy inside of me to go and relax."

Andre decided to give in, but he would watch her closely—and protect her from herself, if the need arose. One thing he did know was that tonight would not be a party for him. Something wasn't right.

Lanassa's mood had changed drastically, and he wasn't going to let his guard down.

Craig's advice popped into Andre's mind. *Lanassa isn't good for you and it could be your downfall, Dre, if you keep up this pursuit of winning her over.* But Craig's advice faded into the wind that blew around his body. She was here with him and the past was just that—the past. He would keep his optimism alive for being with the woman he loved. Craig had no idea how he'd tried to forget her; it just wasn't possible. Lanassa was embedded in his soul—the good and the bad.

Chapter 9

Andre headed for Peaks as Lanassa continued to sing. She had a lovely voice that he remembered all too well from the time she joined him and the band for those jazz sessions. She sang like an angel back then, and he could clearly hear the talent was still there. He tried to convince her to record a demo back then. Lanassa's only reply was that it would feel like work, and she didn't want something she loved doing to become work. The freelancing on her time felt right to her. She didn't want to take orders from a group or a producer. It wasn't in her to accept suggestions on how she should sing a song. After a short while, Andre stopped asking her—he wanted nothing in the world other than her happiness.

They finally reached the nightclub Peaks, where he could hear the music from outside. The place was jumping. There was no need for long lines at the door; everyone who frequented the nightclub knew the bouncers. Andre parked the car and turned to Lanassa. Her eyes looked glassy to him. Was she on drugs? Did she get it from that shabby bungalow in the rundown part of the city? Everything was becoming clearer to Andre. Lanassa was high. Before he could get out of the car and walk around to the passenger side, Lanassa was dancing toward the door of the nightclub. Andre ran to catch up with her, grabbed her by the arm, and turned her to face him. She gave him a sexy look, then brought his lips down to hers and took his tongue into her mouth, kissing him thoroughly. He could taste the chemical substance on her tongue. She tasted like sweet berries from her lipstick and a chemical substance he wasn't familiar with. *What the fuck? She was on drugs.* Andre thought. He started to pull her away from him, but Lanassa only deepened the kiss while grinding her body into his. He felt like picking her up and throwing her ass over his shoulder and taking her home. This wasn't what he expected from the woman he was truly in love with.

Craig had always mentioned that Lanassa wasn't the innocent girl Andre made her out to be. *Dre, Lanassa isn't innocent, you're creating an illusion of this woman in your mind." Damn, was he right.* The revelation of those words from Craig entered Andre's thoughts. Andre was completely caught off guard, as if he was still driving down that dark lonely road they'd just left behind. All he wanted to do was plead with her that they should go to her place. But after the kiss ended, she started pulling him by the hand toward the door of the club. He didn't want to cause a scene, so he followed her. Andre felt as if she would party with or without him. And there was no way he was leaving her here by herself, unprotected. Did she love him? The doubt was crushing him. Why did he accept her invitation? Love. L-O-V-E. He knew the answer as if it was written in stone.

They went inside, passing the bouncers as they stepped through the door, each one greeting Lanassa with a hug and a kiss to her cheek. This got Andre's blood boiling. There shouldn't be other men touching her, period. The four burly bouncers in tight black T-shirts and jeans greeted him with a smile after Lanassa did the introductions. Andre, however, didn't return the smile. He was about to freak out, but he kept his cool while placing his arms around Lanassa's waist, protectively.

The music was pumping through the speakers in the club—it sounded explosive and was a mixture of reggae and jazz. It was music that Andre was very familiar with, but without the explosive, loud sounds. The lights overhead were of multiple colors. People were gyrating all over the place. The whole scene was uncomfortable for Andre. It hadn't been this wild back when he had met Lanassa and introduced her to the sound of mellow jazz and reggae music. Andre felt like he was stepping into a different world, one that Lanassa obviously embraced.

She led him across the dance floor and straight to the bar. Lanassa introduced him to the bartender, whose name was Patricia. She hugged Lanassa from across the bar and shook Andre's hand. "It's my pleasure to meet you. I have heard from Lanassa so much about you, it's like I know you." Her statement surprised Andre but didn't lighten his mood. She was friendly, but Andre just wasn't feeling it at the time—he was too concerned. He knew without a doubt that Lanassa was high, and it put a strong damper on his mood. Andre was very protective of Lanassa, knowing her state of mind. He kept his arm around her and didn't move more than two inches from her side. It didn't matter that Lanassa had spoken about him to her friend or anyone else; the scene wasn't what Andre expected.

Patricia asked, "What do you want to drink? It's on me."

Lanassa grinned. "Shot of tequila."

"And Andre?" Patricia said.

"Soda water with a twist of lemon."

Patricia looked at him as if they didn't carry the stuff in stock, but she made the drink for him with a raised eyebrow. Patricia turned to Lanassa. "Your friend is conservative with his drink selection."

Lanassa giggled, but Andre wasn't about to order anything stronger; he felt that he had to stay alert. After receiving her drink, Lanassa swallowed it in a matter of seconds. She licked her lips as if she was licking candy from them. Andre's heart dropped. He knew this wasn't the first time Lanassa had behaved in such a manner. Lanassa then ordered a second drink. She swallowed that one just as fast as the first one. Andre dragged her to the dance floor, trying his best to stop her from ordering a third drink.

Once they were on the dance floor, Lanassa was in her glory. She gyrated all over Andre, and he noticed she was very steady on her feet. He was trying his best to keep her dancing and away from the bar. It didn't work. After the music stopped and the band was taking a well-earned break, Lanassa went back to the bar, dragging Andre along with her. She did order the third drink, and it went down her throat like water. Then she faced Andre. "I have a surprise for you," she said. The only surprise he wished for at that moment was that she would tell him she was ready to go home.

The band was back on stage and introduced Lanassa for a solo. She kissed Andre on the cheek and whispered in his ear, "This one is for you." One of the band members crossed the dance floor to escort Lanassa onto the stage. As Lanassa stood in front of the mike, she cleared her voice and dedicated the song to Andre.

The band started playing a smooth, low-tempo tune. Lanassa started singing in a voice that matched to perfection the music that the band was playing. Lanassa sang of love lost never found; she sang of appreciation for the man who loved her deeply; she sang of her lost soul and the love she didn't have in her to share. She sang until a tear dropped from her eye. Lanassa didn't wipe it away. She allowed the tear to roll down her cheek. The club became quiet with emotion. Andre's mood was one of heartbreak and understanding. His eyes closed slowly.

It was killing him inside; the song was telling him all the answers to his many questions. The woman he loved with all his heart, he now realized, would never be his. Andre wanted that sweet soulful voice to stop singing. Then again, he wanted to hear her sing forever. He was in pain, and he could hear the pain coming from inside of Lanassa, through the song she was singing to him. Andre opened his eyes and moved away from the bar and walked through the thong of people as he listened to the woman he loved more than life itself. He stopped right in front of the stage.

Lanassa saw Andre approaching and walked to the edge of the stage. Once he was in front of her, she bent down and sang the song close to his lips. Their pain ran so deep. Andre would never understand the reasons why Lanassa was unable to share love with him. But one thing he did understood for sure—the woman he loved would never belong to him. It hurt her as well—Andre could feel it coming from her body.

All he could do was stand there and tremble as he listened to her sing, "Forgive me, please," in the song she was singing so sweetly to him.

After the song was over, Lanassa handed the mike to one of the band members and went back to the edge of the stage. Andre helped her off the stage, then embraced her in his strong arms. He was running his fingers through her hair that she now wore in a wild curly hairstyle. He was trying to let her know it was all right. But one thing he could never do for her was to stop loving her, even if the love would never be returned. He gave his love to her and refused to take it back. Andre didn't know how to hold back his love, even if he wanted to. He picked up Lanassa in his arms and carried her out of the club and into the fresh air.

She was crying in his arms all the while. He placed her tiny body in the car and then got in the driver's seat. He turned to Lanassa and told her to stop shedding tears over him. He understood. It only made her cry more. She relaxed her head on his shoulder as he drove them to her place.

Chapter 10

Douglas Armstrong sat in the dark spare bedroom in Lanassa's house, barely breathing in air. Everything was going all wrong for him and he knew it. Life in prison wasn't going to be a piece of cake. His men had let him down. They had traded him for things much smaller than the things Douglas had provided for them while under his command. The men who were under investigation couldn't help him. And the men, who still were clear, according to the Federal Bureau of Investigation, wouldn't come within his radius or return any of his calls. The trip to Africa came to a sudden halt—his shipment of diamonds had been confiscated.

Douglas held the title of financial investor, as a front for the people who thought he was legitimate. He was far from legitimacy. Douglas Armstrong was a diamond smuggler, one of the best in the world, with connections ranging from country to country. He knew how to get the diamonds in and the money out of the countries where he did his business. Douglas was indeed a circulator—he had been in the business since the age of twenty-eight. Climbing up the ranks was a slow process, but Douglas made it. Now, it was all crumbling down, right before his eyes. Yes, he knew without a doubt that he would be indicted and spend many years—if not life—in a prison cell.

He accepted these facts, but his wife—she was a different dilemma for him. Douglas had been pulled in Lanassa's direction after taking one look at her. In her eyes he had seen the same empty soul that possessed him. They were the same, incapable of giving love but wanting to receive it. To top that off, he loved the sex. She was one of the best, and her uncaring attitude after it was over always turned him on. She didn't know what he did for a living, so she claimed. All Lanassa cared about was the money and that it kept coming into her greedy little hands. Douglas appreciated that as well—two people bonded together by their soulless hearts.

Her purchasing the bungalow, however, had him suspicious, to say the least. Was little Lanassa planning on leaving him? *When hell freezes over,* was Douglas' first thought. She belonged to him, like every other thing in his possession. She might as well be compared to his 2009 Mercedes Benz, because that was just the way Douglas thought of her—as an object, not a person. What the hell—she thought of him in the same way. No guilty feelings—it was their unspoken reality.

Now, Douglas wondered if Lanassa would visit him in prison when the judge sentenced him to do time. He doubted that. She wasn't the "bake cookies; bring them to the husband in prison" type of woman. So Douglas sat in the dark bedroom without much to care about—lights out; eternity was welcoming to him.

Andre drove up to the bungalow, got out of the car, and opened Lanassa's door. He reached inside and brought her into his arms, then carried her up to the house. Andre handled her with ease, while he took the house key and opened the door for them. He didn't turn on any of the lights; he just carried Lanassa upstairs to her bedroom and kissed her hair as he laid her on the bed.

Andre took off Lanassa's designer high heels. She was still crying quietly. He began to massage her feet; the only light in the room was coming through the bedroom window from the streetlights. He didn't want to say a word; he was trying his best to focus on something other than the woman next to him. Andre couldn't bear hearing her weep and knowing she would never love him. He also couldn't bear that Lanassa was a drug user. The pain for him ran so deep with the revelations he discovered.

Lanassa finally sat up and motioned for Andre to join her on the bed. They lay together in silence; it seemed like forever, each not knowing what to say. Andre thought all of his questions had been answered with the song she sang to him that night, along with her chemical kiss. He held her tightly in his arms, resting his chin on the top of her head, feeling her silky curls. They both were in emotional pain, and he knew it. There would be no life with Lanassa. She would be the woman he could never have, and that conclusion started to come down on him like bricks. He still held her tightly because the knowledge of the outcome didn't erase his love for the woman lying in his arms.

Lanassa finally turned to gaze into his handsome face. She could see the shadow of his features in the dim light, and she thought how many decisions in her life had caused him pain, along with her brother and sisters. She blamed her father and mother for what she had become.

But the man holding her in his arms—the blame could never be his burden. Andre would have been good for her in so many ways, but Lanassa knew she had been broken many years ago—or shattered, to be accurate—and Andre couldn't put those many pieces together, no matter how hard he tried. Lanassa knew she should have walked away when she met him years ago but instead, she was selfish and needed what he offered. She took and never gave back, but she had no regrets. Being here with him like this, she still was that selfish bitch. Now that Andre knew the facts for himself, she felt he needed her to explain—not that it would make a difference.

Maybe it was the selfish part within her; maybe it was because she needed to free herself from the guilt. Whatever the reason, she now said to him, "Andre, please listen to what I have to say. After you do, you may leave or stay; it's up to you." Andre started to speak but she silenced him by placing her finger to his lips. "Please, just allow me to explain to you."

Andre gazed at her and nodded his head in agreement.

Lanassa began her story.

"My life wasn't one that I would have wished on any young child. My father abused my sisters and me when we were very young. He never entered our bodies but touched us inappropriately; my mother turned her head from the acts, as if nothing was happening. I received the worse of his actions. I guess it was because I was the oldest. A slap on the ass or a squeeze or those despicable kisses—it didn't matter to him or my mother. She was a very weak woman. I told myself at a very young age that I would never fall in love the way my mother loved my father. It reached a point in my life where I became incapable of loving at all. It went on for years. Finally, my father left my mother to pursue a singing career. That was a joke; the man's voice sounded so bad from all of his drinking and smoking. He was nothing but an alcoholic. And I refused to acknowledge him after his departure. That was the reason

I told you I never met my father, and I never forgave my mother for what she allowed."

Andre was seeing red, becoming very upset by Lanassa's words of how her father abused her, and his hold around her waist became a little tighter without his noticing it. She didn't mind. Lanassa believed she deserved the pressure. In a way, it felt good. Yes, Lanassa knew she wasn't the woman for Andre. Everything bad felt so good to her, even the pain she was experiencing now; the pain she had caused Andre. Every man was going to suffer because the one man, her father, who should have protected her years ago, failed to do so. And the result of that treatment from her father had made her cold. She accepted pain because that's all she knew from such a young age. After time had passed, she learned to embrace pain with welcome arms. Lanassa become narcissistic.

The only regret Lanassa had was for the man lying next to her. Andre didn't deserve what she had put him through. He had a good soul, and she only wished it would remain that way after he left her to go back to Cambridge. Lanassa continued telling her story.

"For so many reasons other than the downfall of my father's singing career, I refused to make singing a career of mine. I love the freedom of doing what I want and when I wanted to do it." She giggled, although her heart was filled with sadness. "But you were making it hard for me to fight the curiosity. All the possibilities you were putting in my head. You were too good for me. So I tried to stop you by sending you away, by sleeping around with other men. The more I saw your pain, the more men I sought out to fuck. I finally succeeded. You left, with Craig being the reasonable one, convincing you to go. Andre, you need to know, out of sight, you were never out of my mind. I thought of you each and every day. Until this summer I couldn't resist contacting you—not for anything serious. I just missed you. I had to have you back in my bed."

Lanassa looked into Andre's bright brown eyes—they seemed to go dull with her confessions. "I love you; I'm just not in love with you. I'm sure you know the difference. I'm not capable of loving anyone. I don't even believe I love myself. But I do love the act of sex and with you it had always brought me so much pleasure. I couldn't get it out of my mind."

Andre didn't need to hear this; the song had been enough. Was she trying to draw out more pain from him? He would leave her tomorrow. But in leaving her, he knew his heart would be left behind. Andre had given it to her many years ago, unconditionally.

Lanassa requested one more thing from Andre. She looked straight into Andre's eyes and said, "Please, Andre, I beg of you … please make love to me."

Andre sat up quickly. "Why would you ask such a thing," he gasped, "especially after what you've just said to me?"

Lanassa raised herself to her knees and placed her arms around his neck, drawing Andre to her lips. She took him like everything else in her life—with disregard of his feelings and more for her own selfish needs.

Her kiss was desperate. She held on to him, refusing to let him go. Lanassa sucked his tongue into her mouth like she was dying from hunger. Andre couldn't resistance the assault. He loved her madly. He also needed her this one last time. Then they would go their separate ways—staying in New Orleans with this woman would surely cause him to lose his sanity.

Andre embraced Lanassa in his strong arms, taking in all of her hungry kisses and returning them ten times more. Andre stripped Lanassa from her dress, then her panties and bra, hearing rips along the way. Then he ripped his clothes from his body. Now they were both nude, and gently rubbed each other's bodies with their hands. The adrenaline started kicking in for Andre, and he pushed her back against the mattress and pillows, spread her legs wide apart, and took her clitoris into his hungry mouth, sucking, licking, and gently biting her at times. He took in all of her sweet juices, trying to get her inside of his system. Andre wanted her to be a part of his bloodstream. All he heard from her were loud screams. They made him take more of her juices, with madness. Then he climbed up her body and touched her breasts, rubbing them feverishly. *Yes, I'm insane, I love you, I love you, and I love you,* he thought wildly.

He sucked her breasts, licked her breasts while biting her nipples. Andre could only hear Lanassa's screams of pleasure. Then he entered her with his enormous penis, not gently but hard. He pushed up inside of her like a man gone mad, taking her legs and placing them over his broad shoulders. Andre kept making love to her pussy, knowing he could never have her heart. He was making love to her very well, leaving her out of control for once in their unusual relationship. Andre heard Lanassa's cries, but he kept making love to her. He knew she was in her glory—they both became exhausted and climaxed together, and Lanassa started crying in Andre's arms. She wished she could be the woman he needed, wished she wasn't the damage goods that didn't deserve a man like Andre, one who loved her with all her flaws in her life.

Impossible—a life with Andre. Lanassa knew she could never completely make him happy. She refused to let go of her past. Lanassa didn't want Andre to leave her. She wanted him to stay as long as it was convenient for her. It was thoughts like this in Lanassa's head that made her realize he must leave her—and soon, before she got on her knees and begged him to stay, until the end of summer. Lanassa knew he would, and she was the kind of selfish bitch that would ask such a thing from him.

Lanassa knew she wasn't the only child who had been abused by a parent. Some of them came out fine, but she was determining to inflict as much punishment as she could on others for her suffering. She really should have taken some of her money and sought mental help. Now it was too late. Lanassa was comfortable with the life she lived.

Andre and Lanassa stayed physically bonded without speaking. Finally, Andre said, "I never told you that I was a foster child."

Lanassa gasped at his words. "No, you never mentioned that to me."

"In so many ways, Lanassa, I felt your pain. I was shipped off to so many different foster parents throughout my young years, never becoming adopted. I felt unwanted. I tried to do everything right to please each foster parent I lived with, but no one was really interested in adopting a black kid back in those days. It's hasn't changed that much to this day. I thank Craig and Bryan, who followed me from house to house and gave me the feeling of worth; I don't know how I would have turned out without them. They both gave me the courage to keep up my grades, which allowed me to enter Harvard on a scholarship." He paused briefly, swallowing hard before he went on. "I could no more hate you than I could hate them or any of the foster parents that put a roof over my head. They all allowed me in, if only for a little while. And Craig and Bryan took me in completely."

Lanassa was more surprised by his confession than he knew. He'd had a hard life but was so kind and loving.

"I guess in my way of loving you so much, Lanassa, I wanted you to know how special you are. I was hoping the abuse wouldn't ruin you. It didn't have to. I knew something was wrong, much deeper than you let on. I met you too late. The self-destruction had already taken a hold of you and affected your life.

I was too blind to see it, and I hate the fact I wasn't able to heal you. I want you to know I will always love you and be in love with you. You have my heart and if that makes me a foolish man, so be it. And now, confessing your full story to me concerning your father, I know I wouldn't have left you if I'd had that kind of knowledge. I would have stayed, no matter what."

Lanassa refused to shed another tear. It would only make her weak. She had to be strong—because after tonight, Andre would be out of her life forever. She held on to him for the little time they both had left to share. Lanassa closed her eyes and went to sleep in Andre's arms.

Chapter 11

Douglas was still in the spare bedroom next to Lanassa's bedroom. He heard just about every word shared between her and this man named Andre. He'd heard the name before—Lanassa's savior who couldn't save her. But by the screams from her bedroom, Douglas knew the man could fuck her well. She never responded to him in such a way. During the lovemaking they shared, she made him feel as if it was nothing other than a fuck. No sounds escaped her lips, no groans or screams. Maybe she loved the fool and didn't realize it.

Her betrayal infuriated him. He'd given the bitch everything a woman could ever want in life. She'd even purchased the bungalow behind his back—no doubt for the man sleeping with her in the next room. Of course the bungalow was purchased as a love nest for Lanassa and her lover. It was right around the time he came across a bill from a private investigator who kept tabs on Dr. Andre C. Brass' whereabouts for his wife. She'd thought he would be gone for the summer on the trip to Africa. The feds had spoiled that plan—and hers as well. Now he found his wife with her ass flopping around in this cozy little nest, parading herself around like a single woman. He'll bet millions the fool didn't know she was married.

Lanassa played him the same as she had played the fool she just slept with. The only difference was that the fool loved her, and Douglas found her to be nothing more than a convenience. *I'll let them sleep for a while—what's the hurry? I have the time, but seeing the surprise on that beautiful fucking face of hers, once I enter that room, is going to be priceless.* Douglas' sick mind was enjoying this far too much.

The morning light came through the window in the room where Douglas had been waiting since two o'clock in the morning—the time his sweet wife and Dr. Andre C. Brass arrived. It was now 8:17 in the morning. He couldn't wait to wake them from the bliss of their early morning fucking into the reality of the day ahead of them. Douglas walked slowly down the hall with the excitement of anticipation. He couldn't wait to see the shock of his presence on Lanassa's face, along with the .45 caliber gun in his hand. Douglas crept into the room— good thing the door wasn't closed. He wanted to be the one to surprise them, not the squeaking noise coming from the hinges of the door.

They both were still asleep in each others arms. He sat down quietly in the chair at the end of the bed and smiled eerily. Douglas knew his fate, and now they would know theirs. He sat there watching them as they moved gently in each other's arms.

Douglas was furious, thinking Lanassa to be nothing more than a whore. And the man with her was dumber than bark from a tree. How convenient—this little setup Lanassa arranged for her lover. *What a bitch.*

Finally, Lanassa started to stir. She sat up slowly, so as not to disturb her lover. Lanassa's eyes squinted, then they seemed to bulge out of her pretty little face. She didn't say a word—the look on her face was all Douglas needed; it was priceless, as he knew it would be.

Next to her, Andre raised himself up on his elbows. "What the hell!" Andre shouted as he saw Douglas with the gun in his hand.

"What the hell indeed," Douglas mocked him. "Do you make it a habit of sleeping around with other men's wives?"

Douglas question took Andre by surprise. His mouth opened in shock. *Lanassa—married? Can this be true?* Andre didn't take his eyes from the man with the handgun, but did ask Lanassa, "Is this man your husband? are you married, Lanassa? Please tell me it isn't true."

Lanassa didn't speak—she seemed to be in shock. Douglas revealed her secret to Andre caused her blood to boil.

Douglas started laughing. "Of course she is married—and married to me. I guess you also aren't aware that my wife is a whore."

Lanassa finally sat up quickly and started shouting at Douglas. "Shut up, you bastard!" Andre grabbed her arm, quickly pulling her back next to him. Andre knew they were dealing with a mad man, but learning that Lanassa was married sent sharp pains through out his entire body. *Might as well pull the trigger*, Andre thought. *It couldn't be as painful as this.*

Douglas laughed out loud—the fool hadn't known Lanassa was married; he had no pity for the fool.

Still, Andre kept a strong, protective hold on Lanassa, trying his best to shield her from the gun, which was pointing right at her face. She was struggling, trying to break free and get at Douglas.

"Don't worry," Douglas said calmly. "She didn't marry me for the love; it was for the money. She's always been a greedy bitch—has been since the first day I met her and then married her greedy ass. She wanted her freedom, and I gave her as much rope as possible. Looks like she hanged her ass with it this time."

Andre looked at Douglas and saw the craziness in his eyes. He would die before he allowed this man to shoot Lanassa.

Douglas saw the protective stands in Andre's eyes. *The dumb fool should be pushing her away and grabbing the gun from me and shooting the bitch himself,* Douglas thought. Douglas knew Lanassa had played the doctor. He didn't understand the protectiveness that Andre was showing for his deceitful wife. "Tell me Dr. Brass," Douglas went on, "how does it feel to know the woman you loved played your ass?"

Andre shivered involuntarily. *How did Douglas know about him?*

Douglas read Andre's thoughts as clearly as if he shouted them at him. "You want to know how I found out about you? It's very simple—a private investigator. I wouldn't have married the bitch without a background check. Dr. Brass, you should have been smart enough to have done the same before you agreed to allow such a tramp to enter into your life. I, on the other hand, love living with danger and on the edge. She fit my world perfectly."

Lanassa gasped. She'd had Andre investigated, and Douglas had investigated her.

Andre's blood was boiling but he saw no way out of this predicament. What kind of world had Lanassa been living in during all those years since he'd last seen her? Andre pushed the thought to the back of his mind and concentrated on how to save their lives. He knew for a fact Douglas was going to kill them both if he didn't take action. But Lanassa was making it hard for him, fighting in his arms as if she could fight the bullets back into the gun if the man decided to pull the trigger. She was making it harder for him to think. Andre had fear in his heart for her, the woman he still loved. He tried to remain calm, tried to hold her back, but she kept lunging toward Douglas. Andre wanted to be rational and talk the gun out of Douglas' hand—he wanted to fight without weapons in this combat. But there didn't seem to be much chance of that.

The end results were that someone was going to die, but he refused to allow that someone to be Lanassa. Andre continued to hold Lanassa while trying to reason with Douglas. "Why don't you put the gun down? It doesn't have to end this way, with anyone getting hurt."

Douglas' smile was crazed at that point—and a crazed look was showing all across his face, in his eyes as well as his smile. Andre could tell that this man could not be rational. He wanted blood, with that .45 caliber gun in his hand. The man was completely out of his mind, even though he seemed calm.

He's going to kill us both, Andre thought.

"Don't worry, Dr. Brass," Douglas said, "I'm not going to kill you. I just want you to watch Lanassa die and have you live with that image in your head for the rest of your life."

Before Andre knew what was happening, Lanassa leaped from his arms too fast for him to grab her back. As if in slow motion, Andre heard the trigger being pulled and the bullet released from its chamber. The bullet hit Lanassa straight between her lovely eyes, and she fell back against Andre's chest. Blood and flesh were everywhere. As she lay in Andre's arms, he could hear a gurgling sound coming from her opened mouth. Then he felt her take in her last breath.

Lanassa was dead in a matter of seconds—the woman he loved was dead in his arms, with her blood covering him. In shock, Andre held Lanassa, brushing her bloody hair from her face. Without saying a word, he held her, stroked her hair, and started rocking back and forth with her in his arms, both of them covered with her blood.

Chapter 12

Douglas left the room and walked down the hall and down the stairs with the gun still in his hand. He pulled out his cell phone from his shirt pocket and called the New Orleans Police Department. He sat in the chair by the fireplace and waited for them to arrive. He was fully aware of what he had just done. He wasn't in shock, like the fool upstairs. Douglas was feeling pretty good about the whole situation. No way in hell was he going to prison with that bitch still able to live her life in glory and take his stash of cash with her. He had to kill her.

Andre hadn't moved—he was holding Lanassa in his arms. Clearly in shock, he was staring straight ahead. Andre couldn't speak; he could only rock back and forth like he was in a trance.

This would be the end of him. The death of the woman in his arms—it was all too much. He felt as if he had died along with her—his beloved Lanassa.

The homicide unit and law enforcement officers from the New Orleans Police Department entered the bungalow to find Douglas in the chair, still holding the .45 caliber handgun. One of the policemen shouted, "Drop the gun slowly to the floor or I'll be force to shoot!"

At the time Douglas was thinking it wouldn't be a bad idea, but he wasn't about to lose his life over a whore. He could accept a sentence of life in prison, if it came to that, for smuggling diamonds across the countries where he did his smuggling business.

But dying over a bitch wasn't in the cards for him. She was gone, and Douglas felt justified by his actions, no matter if man-made law ruled otherwise. He lowered the gun to the floor, and four policemen rushed Douglas, then pushed him to the floor, knocking over the chair where he'd been sitting just moments before. Douglas still had that crazed smile on his face as his body was pressed hard against the floor. Two of the policemen cuffed Douglas' hands behind his back, pulled him off the floor, and dragged him out of the house while reading him his legal rights. He was still wearing that insane smile as a third detectives said, "What a crazy son of a bitch. I know his reputation. He is being investigated for smuggling diamonds. Now add homicide to that crime. What a sick son of a bitch."

As the two policemen were dragging Douglas from the house, other units ran upstairs to the scene of the crime. Police detective Morgan quickly assessed the situation—a jealous rage that ended in a murder. The answers to specific questions would no doubt be revealed eventually—he was the best at what he did for a living. And Detective Morgan wouldn't rest until he had all the answers. One thing he knew for a fact—Douglas Armstrong was going to be indicted, not only for the crime before him but also for operating the largest diamond smuggling ring in the country and across borders.

Morgan knew Douglas was a dangerous man who usually kept his hands clean, letting others taking the fall or doing the deed for him. But the scene before his eyes was proof that Douglas had slipped. That suited detective Morgan just fine. Morgan had wanted to lock up the murderous asshole for some time now. Douglas had killed before—he was sure of it; he just couldn't prove it. Now Douglas had presented him with a clear case of murder in the first degree. Morgan would work with the FBI and make sure the man was sentenced to life in prison.

The police and detectives were in the process of trying to get answers from Andre, but he wouldn't speak—or couldn't. He just stared straight ahead, just as he had when they entered the bedroom. They also were trying to take Lanassa from Andre's arms but his grip on her was strong. It took three men to pry Lanassa's lifeless body from his tight hold.

Once she was free from his arms, Andre kept his arms in place, as if he was still holding her.

One of the paramedics nodded to another and pointed at Andre. "The guy looks like he's a statute—made of stone."

"Maybe we should take his vital signs," said the other.

They found his blood pressure was very low and his heart was beating irregularly. The paramedics gave Andre oxygen and wrapped his nude body in the sheets they brought with them. Then they placed him on a gurney and wheeled him out to the ambulance to transport him to the hospital.

Chapter 13

It took Craig two days to get ready to fly out to New Orleans. He hadn't heard from Andre in days and couldn't reach him by his cell phone. And Craig was growing very concerned. He hired a private investigator named James, who worked from time to time for his law firm and also was a good friend, to accompany him to New Orleans. He didn't have any information regarding where Lanassa lived or any information regarding the friends she hung out with. Calling New Orleans didn't help either.

At the airport in New Orleans, Craig was introduced to Nick, one of James' investigation partners. Nick looked grim—a cause for alarm.

Craig started trembling—he knew whatever it was it wasn't good for his childhood friend. Nick refused to answer any of Craig's questions until they went to his office, which wasn't far from the airport.

Craig wanted to shout, "What the fuck is going on?" but he kept himself composed, even though the short ride to Nick's office seemed interminable. When they reached Nick's building, he rushed Craig and James inside—it was immediately calming. The walls were all beige and there were bright marble floors and doors made of walnut colored wood. They finally stopped at a door with the number fifteen written on a glass panel above the door, which also displayed the words, "Nick Williamson, Private Investigator."

Nick pulled out his keys, opened the door, and stepped aside, allowing Craig and James to enter. His office was neat, except for the many files stack high on each file cabinet. It was obvious he had a heavy case load.

Nick sat in the large black leather chair at his desk; Craig and James sat in two smaller leather chairs in front of him.

Craig was the first to speak, in a calm but deliberate voice that only slightly masked his impatience. "Mr. Williamson ... Nick ... tell me what you found out concerning Dr. Brass."

Nick began, "Dr. Brass got involved with the wrong woman down here. Her full name was Lanassa Kilmore."

Craig leaned forward in his chair. "Was?" he repeated. "Was her name?"

Nick nodded. "She was killed by her husband, Douglas Armstrong, who had been one of the biggest diamond smugglers in the country. Mr. Armstrong confessed to the New Orleans Police Department that he killed her—and he did so when Dr. Brass was present."

"What the fuck ...?" Craig said. "My friend Dre ... is he alive? Did the bastard shoot him too?"

"Your friend wasn't harmed," Nick assured him, "but he is in a mental ward at one of the local hospitals in a state of shock."

Craig couldn't believe what he was hearing. "Why hasn't there been a report about this on the news?"

Nick looked Craig straight in his eyes, then replied, "Before the day is over, it will be on every news network across the country and in the national newspapers. You can bet on it. The story has already hit the local press."

Craig's light-brown complexion turned a shade of gray and his body became rigid. After hearing the whole sordid story about Andre's visit to New Orleans from Investigator Nick Williamson and what was waiting for Andre here, Craig realized he should have gotten on an airplane days ago and dragged Andre's ass back to Cambridge. After Andre phoned him from New Orleans, Craig knew his friend visit wasn't going to end pleasantly. Investigator Williamson had just confirmed Craig's gut feelings. The feelings he been plagued with after speaking with his friend over the phone. Now it was too late, and guilt caused his guts to feel as if they were twisted in a knot. All Craig wanted to do was visit his friend in the hospital. He needed to see for himself that Andre was still alive.

How could one man be so much in love with a woman, then witness that woman being killed in his arms, shot by a husband that,

Craig knew without a doubt, Andre knew nothing about. This was bad, really bad—what a fucked-up tragedy.

Craig was hurting for Andre and himself, then realized he would have to tell Bryan before he heard about it on the national news. Then the tears started to run down his face. He tried to brush them away with his large hands, but they kept coming. His pain was burning him, inside out.

James wondered how in the hell a great guy like Dr. Brass had gotten himself involved with a woman like Lanassa.

James had met Dr. Brass on more than one occasion and found him to be honest, an outstanding citizen. Dr. Andre C. Brass was a hard-working man with a serious gift for composing music. He also admired the connection that the doctor had with his students, with Craig and Bryan, and with the charities in which he was involved. But as far as James knew, when Dr. Brass attended social functions or fund-raising events, he never had a woman accompany him. James found that to be strange at the time; now he knew the reason why the doctor never had a date—he was in love with a woman he couldn't have. Now that the truth had surfaced, it had turned into a bad situation.

Love is a powerful thing, James thought. *It can make or break a good man, pulling him back into the woman's clutches.* In this case, the man was broken, and putting him back together might be impossible.

James glanced over at his employer, his friend, who was being swept up into something that was out of his control—a damaging spiral. Something like this could take many victims, James knew from experience. He also knew that Bryan would be a victim as well. Craig had told many stories to James about his and Bryan's exploits with Andre by their side. Growing up together, they did what three boys did—caused mischief. The stories had James laughing so hard that tears streamed down his cheeks, every time Craig spoke about growing up together with Dr. Brass.

Now the story had changed, and the laughter would be a long time coming for the three of them—if they ever laughed together again. James placed his hand on Craig's shoulder, unsure of any other way to show his support and understanding.

"Craig, would you like me to call Bryan down from Boston?" James asked. He didn't think Craig should face this alone; he needed his brother by his side. "There really isn't anything you can do for Dr.

Brass. Waiting a few more hours before going to the hospital won't make much difference to Andre's condition. Why don't you wait for Bryan?"

Craig seemed to ponder the request while trying to control his internal pain. Yes, Craig needed the support from his brother, but Craig had little patience. It'd been days since he had spoken to Andre. No, Craig wouldn't wait; he wanted to see Andre right away. "No, James," he finally said. "I refuse to wait for Bryan. I must see Andre now. Andre needs to know that he has family who loves him and will see him through this ordeal. I do agree I must contact Bryan as soon as possible, before he hears about it on the news, but that can wait until after the visit."

Nick cleared his throat. He already knew that only family was allowed a visit with Dr. Brass; his condition was grave. "Craig, no one is allowed to visit the doctor, other than blood relatives," Nick explained. "The District Attorney's Office has him on their witness list, but to my knowledge, Dr. Brass hasn't spoken a word since the crime. I know Dr. Brass placed you as his executor and custodian of his estate. I recommend at this time that you try to be a lawyer for him as well as his friend. You would need that proof if you wish to enter the hospital and visit with the doctor. You should call your brother and request that he bring those legal documents before you attempt to see Dr. Brass. Also, you need to provide proof that you and Bryan are licensed to practice law in the state of Louisiana. Keep in mind, there is still an ongoing investigation." James had explained to Nick over the phone that both Craig and Bryon were Dr. Brass' Power of Attorney. Nick had to bring these legal issues to Craig's attention in hopes that he would try and focus on the legal battles he was about to face. He also hoped Craig emotional state of mind concerning his friend's condition wouldn't hinder him from what needed to be done to help Dr. Brass.

Craig faced Nick with so much anger in his eyes. "Why didn't you explain all of this to James before we came down here without the documents? What is going on here? Bryan and I heard nothing about this in the news. And I've never heard of such a request from hospital administrators. I need to know the truth, and I need to know it now. Don't dance around me and continue to waste my time. This is serious, and it's not all about business. He is my family. I don't want legal games being played out here. Tell me how bad Andre's condition is and the legal situation I'm facing that warrants such a request from you. Why must I go through all of this, just to be able to enter the hospital for a visit with him? Andre isn't a criminal."

"Of course he isn't a criminal," Nick said quickly, "but he is involved in a case, as a witness to a murder." Nick and James didn't explain the situation to Craig before his arrival to New Orleans. They knew it would be best to speak with him in person and in the privacy of Nick's office. And by Craig's reaction regarding the information Nick knew he was right by withholding the information until now.

Craig's rage was about to boil over; he'd lost the little patience he might have had. All he could think about was that Andre was dying. The legal shit could wait. He stood up so abruptly that he knocked over his chair. "You're both trying to keep something from me!" he ranted. "And time is running out! What the hell is really going on with Dre? No, I'm not waiting for Bryan. I'll lie to the hospital staff if I have to. There is no way in hell I'm going to wait another minute to see Andre. Do I make myself clear?"

James stood and put his arm around Craig's shoulder and said soothingly, "Of course you're clear. Don't worry. We'll take you to the hospital and try to get you into the room to visit Andre." He knew that weight of waiting was taking its total on Craig. *No one should have to go through this*, James thought.

Nick got out of his chair. "I'll accompany you to the hospital."

The three men started for the door with only one mission in mind—to get Craig in to visit Dr. Brass.

Chapter 14

Craig sat in the backseat on the way to the hospital—he wanted to be alone with his thoughts. *Something isn't right—even the details of Andre's ending up on a mental ward.* He was beginning to think was Andre dying, and that James and Nick knew about it but failed to tell him the other side of the story. *Could things possibly get any worse?*

Craig hated Lanassa now more than ever—not that he ever liked her to begin with. *What a treacherous bitch*, he thought. He knew Andre loved the woman, and he also knew that Andre had enough knowledge to know she wasn't any good for him. But Craig doubted that his friend knew the dangers of that kind of love. *The deceitful bitch, how selfish could she be? Did she think she could have a diamond-smuggling husband and Andre as well? Apparently she had her cards spread out so she could have them both. And at the end she had lost them both, along with her life. The bitch never loved either one of them; life was nothing but a game to her. But why contact Andre after so many years? Why didn't she just leave him the hell alone? Oh, God, Dre, what have you allowed the bitch to do to you?*

The car finally arrived at the hospital. As Craig got out of the car, his heart was pounding so hard that he could hear it. He was suddenly covered in perspiration, but he rubbed his sweaty hands on his tailor-made pants. His knees were weak and he felt his legs buckle. *Death of a family member could be a traumatic experience. But Andre wasn't dead ... or was he?*

Craig cleared the thought from his mind and tried his best to keep his composure. Craig knew what he had to do—he had to be the attorney with rational and logical actions, not emotional ones ...

but Andre wasn't a court case; he was family. How could he not be emotional? Craig's eyes burned as he fought back tears.

Taking a deep breath, he walked quickly and with determination across the parking lot, toward the revolving doors of the hospital entrance. James and Nick were fast on his heels. As they stepped inside, they were hit with a blast of cool air from the air conditioner. It was a welcome relief for Nick and James, but Craig felt as if he had just entered a morgue. This wasn't the place he wished to visit his friend.

Pull yourself together; you can do this; you have to do this, he thought as he approached the front desk. He told Nick and James to stay behind, so they both took seats in the waiting room. Craig planned to tell the nurse at the front desk that he was Dr. Brass' brother.

"Do you think he'll be able to pull it off?" James whispered to Nick.

Nick just shrugged. The ongoing investigation concerning the murder case might mean guards were posted at Dr. Brass' room; the situation was serious—a diamond smuggler who murdered his wife, whom he caught in the arms of a prestigious professor from Harvard University, while they were in bed together. The people of New Orleans couldn't get enough of the news.

The stories placed Dr. Andre C. Brass as a victim, but the stories concerning Mr. Douglas Armstrong and his wife, Lanassa Kilmore, were different altogether. New information was revealed about them every day. Douglas Armstrong's attorney spoke to reporters and gave interviews every chance he got. Douglas' attorney knew his client wasn't about to be set free, but both he and Douglas seemed to want as much publicity as they could muster up.

Nick believed the motive was to try to discredit Dr. Brass' flawless reputation—it was one way Armstrong could exact more revenge, as he was out to destroy Dr. Brass. *The son of a bitch doesn't realize he already accomplished that feat,* Nick thought.

Nick looked around the waiting room as they waited for Craig to return, and something caught his eye—it was a national newspaper with a headline that read: *The Saga of Dr. Andre C. Brass and His Part in the Murder of Lanassa Kilmore.*

"Oh, shit," Nick muttered. He jabbed his elbow at James and pointed to the paper. James' mouth dropped open, and they both rushed out of their seats and to the front desk before Craig was able to carry out his plans to visit with Dr. Brass. Now, it was no longer an option for him to say he was Dr. Brass' brother. To start off with such a lie could postpone the visit all together. The hospital administrators couldn't allow just anyone to visit with Dr. Brass under the circumstances of the ongoing investigation. They would most definitely request proof from Craig to prove he was indeed Dr. Brass' brother, proof that Craig didn't have because it was untrue. —Craig heard the heavy footsteps pounding down the hall and saw Nick and James running toward him. Craig turned from the reception desk, where he'd been about to request to see someone in charge of Andre's care, and looked in surprise at the two men. James was the first to speak. "Craig, things aren't good; I'm asking you with urgency to get those legal documents down here as soon as possible."

Craig was confused by the sudden request and just stood staring at Nick and James.

James convinced Craig to follow him and Nick back to the waiting room. Then he showed Craig the national newspaper. The story finally had gone beyond the local press.

Craig dropped into a chair, his mouth hanging open, his eyes wide. He knew Andre had played no part in Lanassa's murder. Why were the reporters trying to drag Andre's good name through the mud? *What a bunch of vultures.*Craig thought with anger. He knew now that the plans had to change. He must bring out the lawyer within him in order to see Andre and get him the hell back to Cambridge.

Chapter 15

Craig stood in a corner and pulled out his cell phone. He called his brother at the office. Bryan's receptionist, Brenda, answered the call and, upon hearing the urgency in Craig's voice, put him straight through to his brother.

"Craig, what's going on? Has Dre's condition turned for the worse? I told you we should have taken the flight together. I'm here but can't concentrate on anything but what's going on down there."

Craig replied, "You haven't watched CNN?"

"No, I haven't. Why?"

Craig took a deep breath; he was furious and his pain over Andre's condition was making his emotions erratic. "I don't know exactly what is going on with the local or national newspapers or news networks, but they have Dre's name spread across the front page, no doubt trying to get paid big time, but who is feeding them this garbage is beyond me."

"Craig, I … I … don't know what to say."

"Listen, Bryan, I need you to get the documents concerning the executor of estate and the custodial rights down here as so as possible. And bring along our bar license, giving us the right to practice law in Louisiana. Don't fax anything. I don't trust the situation. I need for James to do some investigating. Someone is trying to destroy Dre, and I have a pretty good feeling who that person is. We need to bring out our attorney skills and be Dre's family at the same time. Something just isn't right."

"How is he, Craig? Is Dre doing that bad?" Bryan asked, his voice breaking..

"I don't know," Craig answered. "I didn't get the chance to visit with him. And lying about being his brother at this time will not do. The situation warrants us to do this the legal way, if we are to protect Dre. I hoped we could have prevented all of this from happening."

Bryan always knew Andre would meet up with Lanassa again; Craig was the one always in denial. Having that knowledge didn't diminish Bryan's pain—the same pain that was taking over Craig. "I'll get the documents together and be on the first flight out. Are you at the hospital now?"

"Yes, I'm here and will stay here until you get here. Then I'll explain the whole story."

Craig placed his cell phone back inside his suit jacket and went back into the waiting room to give Nick and James the update. He could see the relief on Nick's face and the understanding of what both brothers would be facing running across James' face. Not only would the brothers be faced with a legal battle regarding a visit with Dr. Brass. They both have to represent him against the news press with their garbage of allegations trying to tie Dr. Brass into the murder case. Nick gave Craig his business card. "Call me when Bryan arrives," he said.

James told Craig, "I'll stay by your side no matter how long we have to wait."

While in the waiting room, Craig started reading the newspaper. The story was unbelievable to him—accusations that Dr. Andre C. Brass had come between a ruffian diamond smuggler and his wife, who was known for sleeping around and taking illegal drugs, and speculations of what part the prestigious professor from Harvard University played in the treacherous lives of the two known criminals.

Craig became so enraged that he threw the newspaper into a trash basket with force, causing other people in the room to look at him as if he'd lost his mind.

James had never seen Craig so angry. "Maybe we should go and get something to eat. There must be a cafeteria around here." James said.

Craig nodded, aware of James' attempt to calm him. "If we stay in this waiting room any longer, I will explode. I'm about ready to start throwing things." Craig replied. James placed his hand on Craig's shoulder, and Craig gave James a half-hearted smile—a smile that didn't reach his eyes. "Okay, James, let's find the cafeteria. I need to get some control over my emotions. Thanks for your support, James. It's just so hard; that article is way off. They don't know how it affects the victims and right now, I feel just as much a victim as Andre. He doesn't deserve this, just for loving the wrong woman. I just want to see him. Everything has gone so wrong, but I'll make it right, not for my pain but for my brother Dre."

James nodded his head and they both walked out of the waiting room in search of a place to eat in the hospital.

James knew Craig all too well, so he said as they walked together, "Don't try to find the room where they placed Dr. Brass. I'm sure they have security watching."

My exact thoughts, Craig thought. *Am I that transparent?* He gave James another half-hearted smile that still didn't reach his eyes and replied, "Wouldn't do it for the world and mess things up. I was just thinking it, but believe me, I'm running on all cylinders, which are pointing me in the right direction—getting Dre back home legally and stopping these vicious lies."

James smiled at Craig, glad that he could comfort Craig, if only by his company. *A man shouldn't be alone during a time like this.* James thought. And right now, everything was unknown, except for the punishment that was awaiting Douglas Armstrong and the death of Lanassa Kilmore. Dr. Andre C. Brass' future, on the other hand, was still unknown, along with the condition he'd be in once they got the opportunity to see him.

Craig and James finally found the cafeteria. It wasn't crowded, only a few people sat at the tables, some in their street attire, others in business attire, the rest in hospital uniforms.

James stopped at the food stations, getting a salad, sandwich, and soup, along with a cup of fresh coffee with sugar and cream. Craig went straight to the beverage station, getting black coffee. They sat at a small table by a window overlooking the hospital parking lot.

"Craig, is that all you're having? You need to eat. Running on empty isn't going to help."

Craig avoided answering James' question by placing the cup to his lips and taking a sip of the strong beverage. He didn't have the stomach for anything more.

It was easy for James to understand Craig's lack of appetite. Given the pressure he was under, no amount of food was going to comfort him. They sat in silence—James because he was busy eating; Craig because he was lost in thought.

A couple seated behind them was talking loudly; James could clearly hear their conversation. No doubt they'd read the daily paper, as they were busy expressing their opinion on the matter. If Craig heard them, he didn't show it. His facial expression remained the same, as if he was in his own world. James could only thank God for that, because what the man was saying would cause Craig to go ballistic.

"If I ever caught my wife cheating on me with another man," the man said brashly, "not only would I kill her but I would take out the man as well."

Ignorant son of a bitch, James thought, *stating something like that when he had no idea of the circumstances. Read and believe.* James started eating faster, so they could leave before Craig became aware of the conversation. *Yes, this must be the talk of the town by now, everyone with an opinion, regardless of the facts.*

James didn't finish his soup and Craig didn't finish his coffee. He couldn't wait until Bryan got there; he wanted to leave New Orleans as soon as possible, but first they had to take care of business.

James pushed back his chair. "I'm ready to go back to the waiting room, if you are," he said. He really wished they could go someplace other than that damn waiting room, but Bryan was expecting them to be at the hospital upon his arrival.

When they reached the waiting room, Craig turned toward the front desk.

"Don't even think about it," James warned. "We only have a couple of hours, then Bryan will be here. Do you want to go outside and walk around, view the sights? I'll come with you.". *What a dumb thing to say,* James chastised himself. *If the man isn't eating, what makes me think he would like to view the sights of New Orleans?* James wondered if he was losing a few of his own marbles. He really didn't know how to deal with Craig's silence. Being a mind-reader would have been a great asset during a time like this. *Please, Craig, just keep it together a little while longer.*

Craig finally spoke and it took James by surprise. "James, thanks for staying with me. If you weren't here, no telling what I'd do. The police probably would be taking my ass down to the station. I heard that crap upstairs. I wanted to take the bastard's head off."

James felt relieved to finally hear his friend speak. "You got me there. I wanted to do the same thing, but we need to keep it together. No doubt it's going to get ugly before we leave—it's just a feeling I have but one I hope doesn't become reality."

"You might be right. We just have to be prepared."

They took seats in the waiting room. James kept looking at his watch, while Craig closed his eyes and tried to remain calm. It was like a clock ticking in his head. *Tick tock, tick tock* was all he could hear. Time was moving like a turtle's crawl. Craig felt as if he'd been in New Orleans for weeks.

Chapter 16

In a cab headed to the hospital, Bryan wished the cab driver would break all of the speeding laws and place the pedal to the metal, hard. He was stiff from the flight and exhausted with worry for Andre. Bryan had turned his eyes away from every newsstand in the airport he passed by. He didn't want to read one word that was being printed. Being a lawyer, he didn't take everything he read as fact—the attorney in him always left room for speculation. Those were the reasons why he did a thorough investigation with James, to get the facts straight. But it disturbed him that things were being printed about Andre—it was personal and hurtful.

He was proud that he and Craig were honest attorneys. They had passed on many cases because they refused to tell lies to win a case, even when those cases would have brought the firm lots of money. He was proud of that. A person never knew when he or she might become a victim, on the other side of the fence, and right now, they were on the other side.

The traffic was very slow due to the number of tourists in the area. Bryan reached for his cell and called his brother, advising Craig that he was in New Orleans, on his way to the hospital. Bryan heard relief in Craig's voice.

Bryan held his briefcase like it was a life jacket. He was sweating profusely and his nerves seemed raw—he was so close to the end of his rope. The summer of 2009 would be a bad memory for Andre, Craig, and him forever.

Bryan thought about Lanassa. He'd always refused to call any woman a bitch, but he knew his brother was throwing that term around to describe the woman, regardless of the fact she was dead. It was after her death, however, that the term seemed most fitting—she just might be Andre's downfall. *We could be at the place of no return, especially under the circumstances,* Bryan thought. *She left him with a bang—how ironic.* Now, however, his main concern was for Andre's mental health and the task ahead.

This ride is way too long. Please let everything work out for the best, he thought. He tried to concentrate on the positive during the remainder of the ride to the hospital. But it was hard. He remembered the first time Andre introduced him to Lanassa; she was such a flirt. What a turn-off; she was not a lady. Why hadn't Andre noticed how she came on to every man who crossed her path? And the sad part to the whole story was that Andre was the only man who treated her like a queen. Bryan had seen the deceit in her eyes; Craig had, too. But Andre was blind.

Bryan knew the reason that Andre always wanted to go to New Orleans was to find her again. And after Hurricane Katrina, Andre became even more desperate to find her—at one point, he'd wanted to hire a private investigator. He didn't want to hire James because he didn't want Craig to find out. But Andre had approached Bryan and asked for referrals. Bryan had always managed to talk him out of it. So Bryan assumed those vacations to New Orleans were hopeful ones, in which Andre hoped he'd run into her.

Craig always convinced Andre to allow him to come along—Craig wanted to protect Andre, just in case Lanassa crossed his path. The support from Craig, years ago, had saved Andre's career—and possible his sanity. When Lanassa started sleeping around, Craig had to speak up and point out what kind of woman Lanassa was to Andre. He told Andre if he wished to finish college, it was best to leave the woman and get his ass back to Cambridge to his studies. It worked—and Andre went on to earn his doctorate. But sadly, he never was a complete man, regardless of his riches. And Bryan knew that Lanassa had destroyed Andre long before the call she made to him this summer. *Why did she have to call him after so many years?* Bryan thought.

Finally, the cab pulled up in front of the hospital. Bryan couldn't wait to see Craig and relieve him from some of the stress. He had the necessary documents; now using their skills as two great attorneys—who planned to get their brother back home and restore his good name—would be their priority.

Chapter 17

Dr. Andre C Brass looked straight ahead at the woman across the white room. The image was all in his mind because his eyes were covered with cotton patches. Her eyes weren't the angry eyes he had last witnessed, nor did she have blood pouring from her head. Now, her eyes were kind and gentle. And her face was beautiful. She kept calling his name in a low whisper; she wanted him to follow her. And he wanted to go and be with her, but every time he got close to her, he felt a chill and something pulled him away from her.

She was so beautiful, just like he remembered. Why was someone or something keeping him from reaching her? He was held down and couldn't move and when he was able to move, that pulling came back and held him back in place. Where was she? Why couldn't he get to her? Her voice was so very clear, as if the whisper was close to his ear. *Come, Andre, don't leave me hear. I'm alone; please come, Andre. Don't leave me here; I'm alone. Be with me. Please come and be with me, then I'll never be alone again.* Andre wanted to be with her, but he couldn't reach her. All he could do was gaze at her sad eyes and beautiful face.

He heard her whispering in his ear again. *Try harder, Andre, for me, please. Try harder. Come to me. I'm so alone with out you.* Andre tried again and again to reach her. He'd keep on trying, until they were together again. His life belonged to her and her alone. He felt love for the woman who whispered in his ear. Her words reached very close to his mind. If only her words could reach inside of his mind, then he'd know they were finally together.

Nick received the call from James that he'd been waiting for, informing him that Bryan was in New Orleans and en route to the hospital. He had been doing some investigation work, concerning the leaks to the press, as he'd waited for the call. What Nick found out was trouble with a capital T, and it had Mr. Douglas Armstrong's name written all over it.

Douglas Armstrong was in the county jail, held there for the murder of his wife. The judge denied him bail. The feds were also pulling together their information concerning Armstrong's involvement in the diamond-smuggling business. Douglas knew that once their investigation was over, he'd be spending a long time in federal prison. The city and state would argue over who should have jurisdiction over his punishment first.

Regardless of the ongoing investigation, however, Douglas had sent out his attorney to give interviews with the press. He was obsessed with spreading his lies, and the reporters were eating it up. He was feeding them a big paycheck that could turn out becoming a lawsuit. Nick had no doubt that Craig and Bryan would file a law suit against the news networks for their allegations trying to link Andre to the whereabouts of the diamond smuggling cash in order to sales their stories to the public. But first their priorities were on Dr. Brass' condition. The proper care of their friend took precedence over everything else for now. They knew of Dr. Brass' connection with Lanassa and after the completion of the police investigation, along with the FBI, they would have all the facts they needed and the truth would be discovered and revealed for all that Dr. Brass had no knowledge where the cash was hidden. There had been no contact between Dr. Brass and Lanassa over the past eight years, not even a phone call. The only connection was that the man who now rested in a hospital bed on a mental ward was madly in love with the woman.

That didn't stop Douglas, however, from creating a story that Lanassa had shared with Dr. Brass were he'd stashed the cash from his diamond-smuggling business. If he was going to sink, he was going to bring Dr. Andre C. Brass along with him for the drowning.

Nick had spoken to his old friend Detective Morgan, who informed Nick that the District Attorney's Office was trying to get a court order that would prevent Dr. Brass from leaving New Orleans until after he was questioned.

Yes, Nick knew all of this wasn't going to sit well with Craig or Bryan. They'd have a fight on their hands. Nick only hoped their emotional connection to Dr. Brass wouldn't cause them to lose perspective.

Nick grabbed his suit jacket and headed straight to the hospital to share the information he'd discovered with the Brown brothers, attorneys at law.

Craig was still on pins and needles. He decided to wait for Bryan at the entrance of the hospital. James stayed behind, pacing the floor in the hall near the front desk. Neither one of them could stand to be in the waiting room another minute. Waiting, in Craig's mind, was time wasted. It was time for action, and those documents would bring the fight straight to their opponent. Those documents would give them the rights to practice their law skills and protect their friend who they loved like a brother.

Bryan entered the hospital through the revolving doors and was greeted by a look of tension on his brother's face. The closer Bryan got to Craig the more he could feel Craig's fury. Craig pulled Bryan into a hug that was strong but showed his relief.

"How are you feeling Bryan, circumstances notwithstanding?"

Bryan stepped back from his brother's embrace. "I'm holding up. I just can't wait any longer to visit Dre." "I agree." Craig replied.

Both men approached James, who then followed them to the front desk. Before they could proceed, Craig's cell phone rang.

He opened up the cell phone and said, "Not now, Sharon, I'll get back with you a little later." Then he flipped the cell phone closed and turned it off. Sharon was Craig's female friend who wanted a more serious relationship with him. She hoped he felt the same way about her.

Bryan's left eyebrow raised. Sharon knew what was going on with Dr. Brass. He explained to her as much as he could before leaving Boston. Sharon was really beginning to get into Craig. She showed so many feelings for his brother. Bryan knew Sharon was falling in love with Craig. But this wasn't the right time for Craig to take time away from what needed to be done, to help Andre.

Craig wasn't feeling it. Bryan could tell by the expression on his face after he flipped the phone closed. Then all three men walked to the front desk to take care of the business at hand.

Sharon's feelings shouldn't have been hurt, but they were. She knew what was taking place in New Orleans. It'd been on all of the news networks and in her evening newspaper. Like Craig and Bryan, she, too, was concerned for Dr. Brass. She just couldn't resist trying to contact Craig. Before this all happened, she was trying to win him over. *Great timing; why did I place that call?* Sharon thought. She should have gone out shopping with her friends, but how could she shop at a time like this?

Sharon knew about Lanassa and how the woman's treatment of Dr. Andre C. Brass almost caused him the career he was seeking and working so hard for during his college years. Sharon often wondered how a woman could be so cruel. It wasn't like her to judge others, but when it came to Lanassa, Sharon couldn't help herself. She tried on so many occasions to introduce the doctor to her eligible friends.

After trying so many times without success, she gave it up, only to have Craig ask her to keep trying. He was desperate to find a good woman for his friend. And after Sharon heard the sad story concerning Dr. Brass' love for Lanassa, she became just as desperate as Craig, after meeting Dr. Brass. Sharon tried her best to find an ideal woman for the doctor but failed every time.

She visited Dr. Brass at his small mansion with Craig on many occasions. Sharon found him to be very handsome, just as handsome as Craig and Bryan. She also found Dr. Brass to be very talented at playing the piano and the trumpet. Sharon marveled at his intelligence, along with his talent for composing music. Craig and Dr. Brass would get into conversations that enlightened her mind every time she visited the doctor with Craig.

Now she sat out on the patio of her home, praying for Dr. Brass, Craig, and Bryan. Bryan looked very worried and tired when he'd explained the doctor's situation to her. She knew Craig must be in the same shape as his brother.

How one woman could cause such a mess in other people lives? Sharon thought sadly.

Chapter 18

Craig approached the nurse at the front desk and requested to see the person in charge of Dr. Brass' care. The nurse smiled and turned toward a phone on the wall, then placed a call. Craig heard the name Dr. Marvick. Then the nurse told Craig the doctor would be down within an hour. *Damn, I don't know if I can take "within an hour."* One thing was certain—Craig wasn't about to wait in the waiting room. He requested a place they could use to go over the documents that were still in Bryan's hand.

After all three men shown her their identifications the nurse directed them to the doctors' lounge. They entered a small room, with power-blue wallpaper and colorful pictures displaying the care of patients on the walls. The room had a comfortable feel to it. It was designed to relax the mind and body. But it wasn't working for the three men who now were seated in light gray chairs at a table in the room, going over the documents that would be valuable, if need be.

Within twenty minutes, a medium-height man with white hair and a tan complexion entered the room and introduced himself as Dr. Marvick. He sat down at the table, and all three men introduced themselves to Dr. Marvick.

Bryan showed Dr. Marvick the legal documents and explained that they had legal rights to visit Dr. Brass, along with the right to receive any medical information concerning Dr. Brass' condition.

Dr. Marvick didn't blink. He knew about the investigation, surrounding Dr. Brass situation. But he was a doctor, and the man was under his care. Dr. Marvick felt no need to keep the truth from these men; he even allowed James to stay while he discussed the medical condition of Dr. Andre C. Brass. "Your friend's medical case is like no other. It's hard to explain. There is really no treatment program we have for him, other than to keep him warm and feed him with an intravenous tube."

"I don't understand your meaning, Dr. Marvick," Craig said. "Dr. Brass is under your care. He has been diagnosed, hasn't he? Or are you telling us his condition isn't written in any medical books?"

The doctor looked at all three men, then replied, "That's exactly what I'm saying. When Dr. Brass arrived, he had all the medical symptoms of a person who was suffering from shock. Now, all of his vital signs are normal, but his eyes stay open at all times. So we have to place drops in them around the clock and place cotton patches over them with medical tape to keep them closed. If not, his eyes will stay open, staring straight ahead."

Craig and Bryan gazed at each other in confusion. James looked blank.

Then Dr. Marvick went on, "The nurses have observed that no matter how high the temperature is in the room, they can feel a chill in Dr. Brass' room. We keep the thermostat on eighty at all times, but the chill remains. I have no explanation regarding the chill in his room."

Bryan had one thought entered his mind, but he wouldn't dare repeat out loud: Lanassa. Her spirit came back for Andre. He knew all about the undead from his research during his spare time. It was something that he was interested in. Now it seemed to be his reality. What he learned from his research had made him a believer regarding dead souls that refused to rest.

After everything was explained, Dr. Marvick took them to the sixth floor. Craig and Bryan both were on pins and needles and nervous as hell. James didn't display any particular expression at all; he thought the doctor was a quack with his talk about Andre's room having a chill that couldn't be explained. He believed Craig and Bryan should hire a specialist and get Dr. Brass out of that hospital.

While walking with the men, Dr. Marvick began to explain that the room might feel hot to them, as it did for him. However, the female nurses were the ones who experienced the difference in the temperature of the room. James shook his head with that bit of shared information; he thought the doctor should be placed in a bed next to Dr. Brass'.

James looked at Bryan and noticed he seemed to accept the information as fact. Craig just looked concerned. The doctor stopped at room number 4D and opened the door, allowing all three men to enter before him. Once they all were inside, they felt the sultry heat— all of the men except Craig.

Dr. Marvick, Bryan, and James started sweating immediately, but Craig's teeth started to chatter. To him, the room felt extremely cold. *What the fuck? I'm freezing my tail off.* Craig thought. He rushed over to his friend lying in the bed, and it took him by surprise. Craig was the first to see the condition Andre was in. Craig noticed that Andre looked so frail and aged beyond his years. Bryan and James walked over to Andre's bed. They both gasped at the same time.

Dr. Marvick explained, "We are doing everything we can for him. Dr. Brass isn't in any kind of pain."

With that being said, Craig touched Andre's arm and found that his arm wasn't cold; he was warm. He then turned toward Dr. Marvick. "You're telling us that medical science doesn't have answers regarding his condition?"

"Yes, that is what I've been explaining to all of you. There are no medical answers to what is taking place with Dr. Brass."

Craig just stood there, still touching Andre's arm and considering the doctor's words with great concern.

Then one of the window blinds fell to the floor with a thump. It seemed to have fallen because of a lose screw, but Bryan had doubts about that. Still, too much was going on; he couldn't tell Craig what he really was thinking—not yet.

Bryan knew for sure he would have to talk with Craig. The simple fact Craig was freezing confirmed some of his suspicions. Lanassa hated Craig—that came to Bryan's mind loud and clear. Bryan turned to Dr. Marvick and asked, "All the nurses providing care for Dr. Brass—are they females?"

"Yes, they are. None of our male nurses are caring for Dr. Brass. They're assigned to mental patients who could pose harm to themselves."

Craig turned to face Bryan, wondering why he would ask that kind of question. It had nothing to do with Andre's care.

James didn't understand anything that was going on and wanted to keep it that way. All he wanted was for Dr. Brass to be able to fly back to Cambridge and get the medical care he needed. This medical stuff wasn't something he could figure out. It also was freaking him out for reasons unknown to him. James glanced at Bryan and noticed he was acting as if he understood everything that was happening to his friend, who was lying in the bed with Craig's hand still on his arm.

Andre felt the cold hand on his arm; it felt good but not like the softness of the other touches. He was wondering if this person could help him get to her, his beloved. *No Andre, this is not the person to help bring you to me. Please don't feel good with the touch of that hand. Please come to me. The touch of that hand will try and pull you away, far away from being with me.*

At that moment the chill left Craig's body so fast, he was hardly able to ready himself from the abruptness of the temperature change. He placed his hand to his temple, as if he was experiencing a headache.

"Are you okay, Craig? You look as if you're about to become sick," Bryan said, even though he knew the answer. Lanassa had just attacked his brother. Bryan went to Craig, steadying him with the support of his hand. *No way in hell*, he thought, *will Craig believe me about this.* One thing Bryan was very sure of—they had to get Andre back home as soon as possible. It was urgent.

He turned to the doctor. "We'll be setting up care for Dr. Brass back at home. How fast can those discharge papers be signed?"

Craig was in perfect agreement with his brother. They needed to hire a doctor and nurse for Andre around the clock and do it fast. Craig believed that when Andre returned home and received proper care, he'd be able to heal and fight whatever was going on with his current health.

Dr. Marvick responded, "Once I go over his case with the doctor you hire and the nurse concerning his care, then I'll allow him to be discharged, with the courts approval. Remember, Dr. Brass isn't a healthy man; he is going to need the best care you can provide."

Craig and Bryan had no problem with his answer. They both placed a kiss on their friend and brother's forehead, then left the room with Dr. Marvick and James.

Chapter 19

Outside the hospital, Bryan turned his cell phone on and dialed the law firm. He explained to Brenda what they needed and whom to call. They would hire their physician, Dr. Baines. He'd be able to recommend the best live-in nurse possible for this kind of case. Although Bryan knew it wasn't a medical condition afflicting Andre, he also knew he needed medical care, which included those daily eye drops, along with a feeding tube and daily bed baths. While Bryan was thinking they'd hire the best help money could buy, a man approached them.

Craig turned and gave Nick a handshake, then introduced him to Bryan. Nick shook Bryan's hand firmly, then turned and said hello to his friend James. James knew there would be two parts to the process concerning Dr. Brass. Now they had the facts concerning Dr. Brass medical condition; it was time for the legal part to begin. Nick came to the hospital to give them the information that James and he had talked about earlier.

James turned toward the brothers. "Now the legal fight begins."

They look more than ready.

Nick drove all three men back to his office. When they arrived and all were seated in the chairs in Nick's office, he began to explain the legal battle ahead of them. "I was doing some investigation work while you two were at the hospital, waiting for Bryan. What I've found out is that Mr. Douglas Armstrong, along with his crooked attorney, is trying their best to drag Dr. Brass' name through the mud. They're saying that Lanassa told Dr. Brass where Douglas stashed his diamond-smuggling money. The FBI wants answers concerning the whereabouts of that cash. However, Mr. Armstrong refused to comply with their request. Mr. Armstrong is more than aware he is facing life in prison. So all of this means nothing to him; it's like a game. And so far, he is winning. Mr. Armstrong and his attorney are feeding this shit to the press every chance they get."

With that information Craig was losing it inside of his head and hit his fist on the arm of the chair where he sat. He wanted to request a visit to see this Mr. Armstrong and cut off the man's head—he felt like doing just that. Logically, he would never actually perform the deed, but at that moment, he felt furious enough to do so.

Bryan explained to Nick that he would file a petition with the court for a gag order. That would put a plug in the live-wire socket of Mr. Douglas Armstrong and his attorney. Craig thanked God that Bryan was there—he had on his attorney's hat, while Craig felt emotional and furious. *Get it to together Mr. C. Brown. attorney at law*, Craig thought. He placed the anger in the back of his mind and started thinking like the great attorney who had won 98 percent of the cases he took on.

Bryan smiled at his brother. He knew what was going on inside of Craig's head. The same thoughts were trying to invade Bryan's thinking as well. But he was an attorney on a serious mission. He knew Craig would come to the same conclusion: fight them hard in the court of law.

"Okay, try and keep it together," Nick cautioned. "I have another bomb to drop. The District Attorney's Office placed a request with the courts, trying to prevent Dr. Brass from leaving New Orleans. They don't want their star witness out of their sight until they speak with him.

"The FBI and the District Attorney's Office have the evidence they need to disprove the accusations of Mr. Armstrong and his attorney, concerning the knowledge of the whereabouts of the money. They have the records proving there hasn't been any contact between Lanassa and Dr. Brass for years. So the timeline that Mr. Armstrong is speaking of concerning Dr. Brass' knowledge about the money wouldn't hold up in a court of law. It would only weaken their case to bring such a fabrication into the trial.

"But the public, as well as Dr. Brass' employers at Harvard, don't have the facts. This is the reason why they are spreading these allegations, trying to place doubts in people's minds and bring down Dr. Brass' reputation."

"This is a smear campaign! It's time Bryan placed a gag order with the courts and shut their asses down with the lies!" Craig shouted. "And as far as that little petition the district attorney just placed with the courts, no problem. Dr. Baines could provide medical records from Dr. Marvick to prove the state of mind Andre is in. He isn't a flight risk, nor has he committed a crime. You don't treat a victim like this, and I refuse to allow it."

Everyone in the office could see the determination on Craig's face.

What great attorneys Craig and Bryan are in a time of need, Nick thought. *Dr. Andre C. Brass is lucky and blessed to have them on his side.*

Bryan was the next to ask questions. "Do you have the names of the persons handling the case in the FBI and District Attorney's offices?"

Nick smiled. "Wouldn't leave home with out it. The person in charge concerning the investigation for the FBI is investigator Michael Verrico. The district attorney's name is Scott Cobb."

James looked at Craig and Bryan. He noticed they looked tired and needed a good night rest before they tackled the obstacle ahead of them. He cleared his throat, then stated, "I know you two want to get the show on the road, but the courthouse is closed, and it's late. I suggest we get a nice hotel and get some sleep so the both of you can be fresh for the work you must perform tomorrow. You don't have to act on this tonight. Besides, the two of you look as if you haven't eaten or slept in days."

There wasn't any arguing about that; they were beat. Craig turned to Nick. "How much do we owe you for the important information you've given us?".

"James covered my fee," Nick replied.

Craig should have known James put Nick on the payroll during the time he was waiting at the hospital with him. Both brothers thanked James at the same time. Then they turned and shook hands with Nick and thanked him for the great investigation work.

"If you should need further assistance, let James know. I'm out in the field a lot, but he is my source of contact. Or call me on my cell; you have my card."

Craig and Bryan both nodded their heads. Then Craig, Bryan,

and James left Nick's office building, catching a taxi to one of New Orleans' finest hotels.

All three men were beat from the long day. Bryan wanted to take a nice long shower then eat something and rest. Craig wanted to work out but was going to follow Bryan's lead concerning a shower, eat, and rest. James was just going to shower and crash. He was still freaking out a little concerning Dr. Brass' medical case. Something was wrong, and his experience as an investigator didn't help him concerning the medical aspects of the case. One thing he was sure of—something was going on with Dr. Brass, and it had nothing to do with his medical health.

Being an experienced investigator, however, James knew Bryan was holding something back. Yes, Bryan knew something and wasn't ready to share the information. *Something weird, without a doubt, is going on with the doctor, and Bryan knows a little—or all—about it. But, what is making him hold in his tongue during a time like this?* After James noticed Bryan's reaction to the window blind falling to the floor, as well as Craig's condition during the visit with Dr. Brass, these thoughts kept swimming in his head. *Freaky* was one word that kept playing in James' mind during the taxi drive to the hotel.

Chapter 20

Andre, you are not fighting hard enough for me. You are leaving me her alone, by myself. That hand belonged to the enemy. He'll try and keep you away from me; you and I must fight him every inch of the way, until we are together again.

Andre heard the voice in his ear again, then she started crying. He hated hearing her cry; he loved her and he wanted to be with her, but how? Still, the other hand was strong and comforting. It was familiar to him. He didn't want to fight against that person. All he wanted was to go to his beloved.

Craig, Bryan, and James finally made it to the hotel. Craig booked a large suite that could accommodate a family of four. All the other hotels were booked full, due to the tourist season. Therefore, they found themselves booked in the most expensive hotel in New Orleans. It didn't matter to Craig because he knew money wasn't being wasted. They weren't about to be flying out of town any time soon. They also needed a suite that could accommodate their laptops and that had a fax machine.

They were all in the suite when Craig's cell phone started to ring. He took it out of his suit jacket and flipped it open. It was Sharon. Craig answered the phone, feeling pretty bad about the last phone call he'd had with her. Although he'd just gotten to the suite, Craig knew this time he must be more pleasant with her.

"Hello, Sharon."

"Hello, Craig. I know I shouldn't be calling you this late. I just couldn't help myself. I've been so worried."

That really made Craig feel even worse. "No need to apologize. It's good to hear your voice." Craig could hear the relief coming through the phone with the deep breath Sharon exhaled. Then he went on to say, "Sharon, I don't want you to be worrying. This trip might take longer then we expected. There is so much that has to be handled down here concerning Dre."

"Of course, I understand. Please tell me that Dr. Brass is fairing well."

That was one thing he couldn't tell her, but Craig didn't want her to be worried. Sharon was a good woman, beautiful inside and out. She had long legs with a slim body. Sharon also had deep dimples in her smooth, dark brown cheeks. Her hair was short and tightly curled, which she wore with class. Oh, how he loved running his large hand through her short silky curls. Sharon was so beautiful to him.

To tell the truth, Sharon could have been a model, hands down, but had decided to become a physical therapist with a master's degree in her chosen field. Those hands of hers were like magic to him. They had released a lot of tension from his body after those late nights and hard days working on legal cases. She was good for him. However, Craig didn't know if he was ready to settle down. It had nothing to do with Sharon and everything to do with him.

Craig pictured her face while he continued with their conversation; it gave him comfort. "Dre isn't doing that great. But it isn't as bad as I thought it would be. Bryan and I are working on the legalities and setting up medical care for him. It's going to be a while before you and I have the opportunity to see each other again. I hope you understand."

"Craig, I do understand. I just want you all to come back home safely. That is the priority in front of you right now. And for me, please make it happen."

Craig wasn't surprised by Sharon's understanding; she always had that quality about her. He guessed that was the reason she went into the physical therapist field. She cared about the well-being of others. Sharon was truly gentle. A man could fall in love with a woman like her. He just wasn't close to falling in love at this point. It didn't matter who the woman was. Right now, when it came to a relationship, Craig wanted to hold on to his freedom a little while longer. For now, they were friends that shared more with each other. Sharon accepted their relationship as it was. If Craig ever felt that Sharon wanted more from him, he didn't know if he would risk losing her or give her more of what she wanted from him. Right now, he still had time; she wasn't pressing anything on him.

"Trust me, Sharon, we will all be home soon. We'll fight tooth and nail to get Dre back home where he belongs. As for Bryan and me, we both have the fight in us to make it happen. So please don't worry, okay?"

Sharon responded with her low, sweet voice. "Okay"

Craig could hear her relief. "I'll call you tomorrow. Please try and get some rest."

"I will."

With that, they both said their good-byes.

Dr. Andre C. Brass felt those soft hands touching him again. He was happy that she came back. Why did she leave in the first place? *I left you because you won't take heed to what I'm telling you. Don't trust any other touch other than mine. They'll try and take you back with them. You're so close. Please come to me. You belong to me. I'm the only one you ever loved. Please remember that.* Then the velvet voice that visited him and whispered into his ear was gone. Dr. Brass didn't know where he was or how he got to the place that kept him on his back.

That pretty face, with blood pouring down her soft skin, along with a hole between her perfect eyes was all he remembered. Now, she came back to him looking so beautiful, without the pouring blood. He wanted her to be happy. Why was it so hard for him to go to her? He'd keep trying; he wouldn't give her up for the world.

Bryan knew he would have to tell Craig and James what he thought. He knew Lanassa's soul was not at rest. She was all around Andre. Bryan believed Lanassa was trying to kill Andre, taking him with her. But they would take him as a nut, so he decided to keep the knowledge to himself, until the legal and medical cases were wrapped up in their favor. Would Lanassa's spirit follow Andre back to Cambridge? Bryan shook that thought from his mind. No, it would be impossible; her spirit should remain in New Orleans. But it was the thought that Bryan feared the most. He knew Craig would think he'd gone mad. But after a few more of Lanassa's attacks on Craig, Bryan knew his brother would become a believer.

All three men had freshened up. Now they were eating a needed meal that James had ordered from room service. James decided to join the brothers, instead of skipping the meal and going to bed as earlier planned. James wanted to ask Bryan what he knew concerning Dr. Brass' medical condition; he knew Bryan had the answers. James also thought was he ready to hear them. *Nope, not ready—not ready at all.* James gave in and finally went to bed after his meal. Why freak himself out any more than he already had? Because for sure, whatever Bryan was hiding, it was bound to freak out Craig and him to no end. The chill in Dr. Brass' room that Craig experienced didn't make sense to James. But Bryan had acted as if he knew something and the questions Bryan asked Dr. Marvick didn't make sense to James either. Those questions along with the events in the room left him with an eerie feeling. He didn't understand how Bryan could be holding up as well as he was. He saw the look in Bryan's eyes—something wasn't right. James hoped he'd be able to get some sleep without the nagging thoughts causing havoc in his mind.

After Sharon hung up the phone with Craig, she felt a little relief but not much. She could tell by the sound of Craig's voice that he hadn't slept, and he was very worried. He probably wouldn't be able to get a good night's sleep until the whole ordeal was over. *When will that be?* Sharon wondered. Craig did state it would be a while before they returned home. Sharon's only prayer was they all came back the way they left. She knew in her heart that might be impossible. Lanassa's actions during her life were still affecting people now that she was dead.

What a mess. Will there be an end to Lanassa's effect on the people I love? Sharon went inside her home and walked slowly up the stairs to her bedroom. She then got down on her knees by the edge of her bed and prayed, something she been doing all day. For reasons unknown to her, she knew it would take more than man-made laws and man-made medicines to make the current situation right. She got up from her knees and walked to a comfortable, cushioned armchair in her bedroom and sat there for over an hour, with tears pouring down her face.

The next morning, the sunshine filled the entire suite. Bryan entered the room with the enormous sofa and met James' eyes on him. James was having a cup of coffee, while sitting on the sofa, trying to relax. It wasn't hard for Bryan to tell that James had been some what jumpy lately. He had never witnessed James seeming so unglued.

"Where's Craig?" Bryan asked.

"He's still in the bedroom, making calls to get us appointments to meet with Mr. Verrico and Mr. Cobb."

"Did he have breakfast?" Bryan asked.

"He nibbled on a bagel and had a cup of coffee," James stated with concern on his face. Craig wasn't eating that much and would find himself working on empty if he kept going the way he was.

Bryan took a seat on the sofa, then poured himself a cup of coffee from a tray that was on the table. He grabbed a bagel and spread cream cheese over it, then took a bite. While doing so, he noticed James was staring at him. "What?"

James shook his head. "It's nothing."

Craig entered just as they finished breakfast. He had his cell phone placed at his ear and was looking more than impatient. He also was looking rather pissed.

What the hell was going on now? Bryan wondered.

Craig wasn't speaking into the phone, just listening.

During this one-sided conversation, Craig's eyebrows were drawn together in a serious expression. Craig finally spoke. "Yes, I understand that. It won't be a problem if anyone doesn't turn it into one. We're here for one purpose and one purpose only, which is to get Dr. Brass back home. I hope I'm making myself very clear regarding this matter. We'll be downtown within an hour." Then Craig flipped his cell phone closed.

"What was that all about?" Bryan asked.

The look on Craig's face didn't change. "Nothing we can't handle, I assure you. Agent Michael Verrico from the FBI doesn't have a problem with Andre's leaving, but it's District Attorney Scott Cobb, who's trying to make a big name for himself, that's trying to pose a problem."

"Okay, if he wants to look like an overzealous, out-to-get-the-good-guy type of lawyer, so be it," Bryan responded. "We'll eat him up alive in court, if we have too."

With that, Craig, Bryan, and James readied themselves for the day ahead, going over some key points they must present to the court.

This was the only big case that ever went national for District

Attorney Scott Cobb. He refused to allow his star witness to leave New Orleans, especially a witness like Dr. Andre C. Brass. He knew he had the case locked down and won without the good doctor, but the witness' name alone could carry his name across the country. His ambition was high, and winning the case with Dr. Brass' name attached to it could bring him national coverage. District Attorney Cobb's mind was made up. He wanted Dr. Brass to stay put, until he could see his own name in bright lights across the country. The diamond-smuggling aspects of the case would be awarded to the Federal Bureau of Investigation. The state brought charges against Armstrong for the murder of his wife. Yes, the man confessed. But Cobb wanted to carry this one as far as he could so he could get what he wanted—higher and widely exposed recognition. District Attorney Scott Cobb picked up his phone, hit his assistant's speed-dial number, then requested him to put the wheels into motion for a press conference at once. With that request Cobb knew he lost his morals regarding his duties as an attorney. *A man has to do what a man has to do,* he thought with a smile spreading across his ambitious face.

Dr. Andre C. Brass felt the hands running up and down his unmoving body. She'd come back to visit him again. This time, she came without encouraging whispers in his ear. She only came to let him know that she still was waiting for him to join her. He wasn't fighting against her but still tried to get closer to her in the world of the unknown—in the place she was calling him from. He knew their worlds still hadn't connected. And he didn't know what her world would be like. The only thing he knew was that she was there on the other side, waiting, and that was more than he needed to know. She still wanted him in her life.

Dr. Brass tried his best to reach her and be with her, but something was interfering. What was it that prevented him from reaching the destiny she planned for them both? The answer to that question went unanswered. He didn't care. He knew where he wanted to be—back in her loving arms and embraced with her warmth. But every time she came, she brought with her a chill. He couldn't figure out why, but he did know that all the answers would be revealed, once he was on the other side, in the world in which she awaited his return to her.

Then a pretty female nurse entered into his room and the touches were gone, replaced by a swirl of cold air surrounding his body. The nurse sat down beside Dr. Brass' bed and began to read a book to him. She brought with her warmth from the cold air that surrounded his body and the abruptness of his love's hands leaving him.

The nurse's voice was unlike the woman he wanted to hear, but it was soothing and rich with care. Dr. Brass wanted to turn his head toward that heavenly voice, but he couldn't move. Was he in a straight jacket? It felt like he was, because he wanted to move closer to that voice but he just couldn't move any part of his body. Her voice wasn't in his ear; it was inside of his head. He remembered her visiting him on many occasions. She sat down next to him, reading to him, then speaking to him about her life. And what was taking place outside of this room he was unable to leave? Her voice didn't make him forget the person he loved—or did it?

Anna was wrapped in two blankets and wore a thick sweater over her small body. Every time she entered Dr. Brass' room, she was very cold. The whole room was cold, although the temperature read seventy-five degrees. She had no explanation for the temperature. All Anna knew was that she had to be by his side and protect him from something she couldn't explain. Every time she visited the doctor, she would take his vital signs and knew everything was normal. That was something Anna couldn't understand, along with the hospital staff. They had no answer for the events that took place inside of Dr. Brass' room. The other nurses refused to stay long with the doctor. They just came to make sure he was all right and replaced his intravenous bag that nourished him. Then they would put the drops in his eyes and cover them with cotton patches.

But Anna refused to do only the basic duties. She was drawn to the doctor lying in the bed. She would look down and see his frail, handsome face, and her heart was touched. Although Anna knew the whole story behind Dr. Andre C. Brass being admitted to the hospital, she felt he was a victim. Anna didn't believe he knew that the woman named Lanassa was married or even that her husband was a diamond smuggler.

Anna didn't know how she knew these things about Dr. Brass, but she felt that her feelings were true. He didn't have to speak his innocence of a crime for loving the wrong woman. Anna just knew it was the case—his falling in love and getting hurt by being blindsided. She did went on the Internet and read all about him—the charities he headed and the students he mentored. Anna thought of him as an honest person of good morals and character who had fallen in love with a woman who wasn't in his same league.

Whatever it was that was trying to take him away, Anna knew she must hold on to him; keep him among the living. The young doctor still had so much more to live for, even though something or someone was trying his or her best to take him from life. How odd it was for her to think this way. But it was a part of her protectiveness for the young doctor. Anna continued to read to Dr. Brass, while feeling the draft all around her. She pulled the blankets closer to her neck and continued to read, unfazed by the temperature that brought chills to her body.

Chapter 21

Craig and Bryan both were livid by the time they made it down to the courthouse. They both heard about the press conference that Mr. Scott Cobb had given to the public. He was just as bogus as the people who were eating up the lies and ready to get the lies printed as fast as they could. *Is the asshole working for Armstrong?* Craig thought. He wanted to punch the district attorney straight in his face. Bryan, on the other hand, wanted to speak to the court judge immediately and stop the spread of lies, although he did acknowledge that a good punch to Mr. Cobb's face was appealing to him.

The man's statements were all full of garbage. He stated that Dr. Brass was a key witness who knew more about the circumstances regarding the crime of murder and would be staying in New Orleans as a witness. He also stated that Dr. Brass had information that would help prosecute Mr. Armstrong for more than just the murder of Lanassa Kilmore. The whole case was becoming a circus. And the main clowns were Mr. Douglas Armstrong, his attorney Ted Pearson, and District Attorney Scott Cobb.

Now all of the men, except for Armstrong, who was in jail, and James, who was with Nick, furthering the investigation, were sitting in the Honorable Judge Fred Goldstein's chambers. The District Attorney and Ted Pearson were arguing their cases fearlessly with the judge. Bryan couldn't believe the behavior of D.A. Cobb and Attorney Pearson. They went at Craig and Bryan as if they were children, arguing in front of their father. Craig and Bryan were too cool for this kind of arguing. It played no productive role. They both could hardly wait until the judge slammed down his gavel on the two men in order to shut them the hell up, which didn't take long.

Then Judge Goldstein started viewing the documents that were presented to him by Brown and Brown, petitioning a gag order on the case, along with information from Dr. Marvick and Dr. Baines, providing a medical-condition report on Dr. Andre C. Brass. It stated Dr. Brass would need medical care for some time, but they couldn't predict the time frame for his recovery. And it would be in their patient's best interest to provide him the medical care he needed in Cambridge, at his home, where he could feel more comfortable. FBI Investigator Michael Verrico also provided an investigation report to the judge that proved Dr. Brass had no knowledge concerning the whereabouts of the money Mr. Armstrong had hidden. The information Douglas provided the FBI regarding that matter was bogus to say the least, filled with lies.

Also, the medical report stated that Dr. Brass hadn't spoken since his arrival at the hospital, and there was no way of knowing when he might speak again. Craig and Bryan both told the judge that it would be unconstitutional to victimize the victim, especially in his current condition.

The judge cleared his throat before speaking. "Well, gentlemen, with the documents and petitions in front of me, Along with the FBI investigation report I can't find cause for not granting the ruling in the Browns' favor. Mr. Cobb, you don't have to drag this witness through a case in which the prisoner already has confessed to the murder of his wife with a signed statement. Furthermore, there is clear evidence to prove Dr. Brass had no knowledge regarding the whereabouts of the money Mr. Armstrong hidden."

"And as far as freedom of speech is concerned, this case is hereby under a gag order to be placed as soon as possible. If I should read or hear about another interview from either one of you, I'll find that act to be in contempt of this court ruling. Do I make myself clear? No more games. This is serious court business, and I want you to treat this case accordingly. There will be no personal gains. You both will follow the rules of law. I want you to understand what I'm ordering—no more stepping out of line."

Cobb and Pearson both turned shades of dark red, and it looked as if they were about to blow their tops, but they weren't fools. They didn't want to damage their reputations, at least not the district attorney. Mr. Cobb knew any actions against the court would damage his reputation; he wasn't a stupid man. But Craig and Bryan both knew that Mr. Pearson could give them a hard time. They didn't doubt he would land in jail, alongside his client. The man had "crooked" written all over his red face.

The Honorable Judge Fred Goldstein signed the necessary documents putting the gag order in place. Then he signed the documents giving the hospital the legal right to release Dr. Brass. The judge stood and gave Craig and Bryan a firm handshake across his large mahogany desk. He was too furious with District Attorney Cobb and Attorney Pearson to give them any more time; he dismissed them both without a handshake. With that, they all were dismissed from his chambers.

All four men walked out of the chambers into the hall. Mr. Cobb and Mr. Pearson walked in separated directions away from Craig and Bryan. And the two brothers were on their way to visit their friend and beloved brother, Dr. Brass.

Once the brothers were outside the courthouse, the press surrounded them, taking pictures and yelling out questions. The attorney for Mr. Douglas Armstrong and the district attorney were nowhere near to be seen. The brothers walked through the throngs of reporters with coolness and confidence. They were pleased with the outcome, and the press didn't faze them, not in the least. Bryan was the first to notice Nick's car parked at the bottom of the courthouse steps, and James was with him. James got out of the car and allowed Craig to take the front passenger seat. Then he opened the door and allowed Bryan to step into the backseat, with him following.

"I can tell by the look on your faces that it went well with the judge." James stated.

Bryan's smile was one of relief. "Yes, you can say that, and now it's time we get Dre home." His cell phone rang and he flipped it open to see Dr. Baines' number. He answered the call immediately. The doctor informed Bryan that he was still at the hospital waiting for them. Dr. Baines arrived earlier in town to assist Dr. Marvick with the medical report that was given to the Judge to prove the brothers' case. That Dr. Brass should be released from the hospital. *Thank God.* Bryan Thought. He started to feel better by the minute knowing that Dr. Baines was still at the hospital. He shared the information with all the gentlemen in the car. Then he advised Dr. Baines that they would be there within half an hour.

Things were finally looking up. Bryan still needed to find a way to share what he knew to be true facts with his brother and James concerning Andre's condition. He promised himself that once the legalities were over, he would do just that. But he was still very uncomfortable sharing that kind of news. It wouldn't sound right, but it was the truth. Lanassa was haunting Dr. Brass. Bryan was eager to visit Andre and to see Dr. Baines.

Bryan contemplated sharing with Dr. Baines his suspicions of what was causing Andre's current state of heath. But would the doctor view his opinion as off the wall? Bryan's thoughts were a whirlwind inside of his head regarding the restless soul of Lanassa, which was preventing Andre's recovery. He knew he must share the information with someone in order to save his friend.

Who should I turn to who would take the situation seriously? Dr. Baines is a man of logic and science. Could he reach beyond his field and accept there might be another explanation for Dre's condition, something that involved the supernatural? Or would he think I needed a mental evaluation? Bryan knew he must share what he knew with someone, but whom? Maybe he should do some more research of his own, before presenting his thoughts on Andre's condition—but that would only waste valuable time. And Lanassa's soul needed to be released before it took Andre with her to the hereafter. Bryan thought she wouldn't treat Andre any better in the afterlife than she did during life. He had a dilemma on his hands, and no one to turn to.

At the hospital, Nick said his good-byes and said he would keep a watchful eye on the murder and diamond-smuggling case after they returned home. All three men shook his hand and thanked him for his assistance.

"If you should come up with anything that needs our complete attention, please contact us immediately," Craig said.

"I sure will," Nick replied.

Craig, Bryan, and James entered the hospital and walked to the front desk. The nurse remembered them and advised them that Dr. Marvick and Dr. Baines were waiting for them in Dr. Brass' room. James glanced at Bryan and noticed his nervous look had returned. *Bryan is keeping something balled up inside, but what?* James thought.

They took the elevator up to the sixth floor and entered Dr. Brass' room. They were greeted by both doctors with puzzled looks upon their faces. The room was very warm, as expected. Bryan and James could feel the heat, but Craig was shivering, the same as before. Bryan and James observed Craig, along with both doctors.

Dr. Baines asked Craig, "Are you feeling well?"

Craig responded with chattering teeth. "I'm all right; it's just so damn cold in here."

Everyone gave Craig an odd look—except Bryan, who knew exactly what was happening to his brother.

Dr. Marvick responded, "It's the same temperature as always. It's close to eighty degrees in this room."

Craig continued to tremble like a leaf.

Dr. Marvick wondered again why the female staff—and now Craig—felt so cold when they entered Dr. Brass' room. It didn't make sense to him. "Would you like to leave the room?"

Craig just shook his head. Letting the doctor know he was staying.

They all approached Dr. Brass' bed. The man still looked very frail, with his eyes covered with the cotton patches and the intravenous tube attached in his arm.

Dr. Marvick informed them all that Dr. Brass' condition hadn't change, and it should be a sign for concern.

"I agree," said Dr. Baines. "We must get Andre back home as soon as possible for further examination." Right after he made the statement, he felt a chill through his body, and he started to shiver as well. "That's strange; I can feel the chill now in this room. What is going on, Dr. Marvick?"

"We haven't figured this out, the temperature change. So far, the only ones who experienced the cold in this room are the female nurses and Mr. Brown," Dr. Marvick stated. "Now, Dr. Baines, you are telling me you are experiencing the same chill?"

"That's exactly what I'm telling you—but now it's passed. I'm feeling rather hot again."

Then the pole that held the bag of nourishment that flowed into Andre's vein started to shake.

"What the hell is going on?" Craig snapped.

All of the men looked confused—except for Bryan.

James couldn't take it any longer; he saw the look in Bryan's eyes and knew that Bryan had knowledge he was trying to keep hidden. James finally spoke up. "I believe the answers to these questions can be cleared up right now." Then he turned to face Bryan. But before James could say anything more, a pretty brown-complexioned nurse, with her hair pulled back into a curly ponytail, entered the room.

She was wrapped up in four sweaters with a book in her hand. All eyes turned in her direction, and she was startled. "Oh, I apologize! I didn't know Dr. Brass had visitors." She was about to turn around and leave, but her presence caused a reaction in Dr. Brass' body.

"He moved! Yes, he finally moved," Dr. Marvick observed right away.

Then they all felt the cold surrounding them instantly. *Lanassa*, Bryan thought. *She's jealous of the pretty young nurse*. Bryan shouted immediately, "Please stay!"

Anna turned around with a smile, then said, "I already took his vital signs earlier, and everything is normal. I was going to read to him another book."

Craig and Bryan viewed her with much approval. They wondered how old she was—she looked no more than twenty—but her age really didn't matter. She had gotten a reaction from Andre.

Bryan thought, *Not only a reaction from Dre but from Lanassa as well*.

Chapter 22

During Dr. Baines' visit, Dr. Brass hasn't moved—not until the nurse entered the room. He turned and asked Dr. Marvick, "Has this every happened before? Has Dr. Brass moved at any time during your examination of him?"

"No," the doctor replied. "Not one inch, not even when we placed needles in his arms or the cotton patches over his eyes; not even during his daily bed baths."

Bryan was smiling inside. The nurse was the one person keeping Lanassa's spirit at bay and preventing Andre from going to Lanassa in the afterlife. But he had to be sure. He asked Dr. Marvick, "Have any of the other nurses who provide care for Andre experienced a movement in his body?"

"No, not to my knowledge. They would have informed me of such a change in his condition. I must say, this is the first."

Anna didn't want to contradict the doctor, but it wasn't true. Although the other nurses hadn't viewed any movement, she had witnessed it on more than one occasion. Anna decided to speak up. "Dr. Marvick, I've put it in the medical report, but the other nurses refused to believe me. I guess they kept the information from you. I don't think they really believed a word I wrote in the report. After all, he only moved a little and during those times, I was the only one to witnessed it."

"I see." Dr. Marvick looked dumbstruck.

Bryan had to know the name of the nurse that was literally saving his friend's life. Bryan gazed at her with amazement, then asked, "May I ask, what is your name?"

She smiled and said, "Anna. Anna Jordan."

"Nice to meet you, Ms. Anna Jordan—or is it Mrs. Anna Jordan?"

What is Bryan doing? Craig wondered. *Is he trying to get hooked up with Dre's. nurse at a time like this?*

James was the only one who knew there wasn't a hook-up going on here. He hadn't been an investigator for this long without developing some insight—and he suspected that this young woman had some answers that Bryan had been seeking—answers that could shed light on Andre's present state.

Anna walked over to Dr. Brass and said, "My name is Ms. Anna Jordan—there is no Mrs. in front of my name." Then she reached down and touched Andre's arm. He moved again, and the room got colder.

Lanassa's restless spirit was furious with them all; they shouldn't be coming between her and the man lying in the bed. He belonged to her and her only. The room became even colder. The blinds hanging from the windows started to move rapidly. And the curtains started swishing back and forth with the sound of the wind. Everyone in the room started to shiver with cold, their bodies seeming as if they were covered with ice.

Dr. Marvick turned to Anna with questioning eyes. "Has this ever happened before, during your visits with Dr. Brass?"

"No, not to this extent," Anna replied, as her teeth started to chatter.

Dr. Marvick could only shake his head. "This is not logical. The force within this room is not something medical science can explain. I don't understand this at all."

Bryan knew it was time for him to speak up—and speak up fast. He looked across the room at everyone and decided to call a meeting. "Is there some place we all could go? I need to speak to each of you, including you, Nurse Jordan." He said her name with a smile.

It's about time, James thought.

Craig didn't understand. No one seemed to want to leave Dr. Brass while the currents of unnatural events were taking place.

"Trust me," Bryan said, "Andre will be fine. Once we leave, everything will calm down."

Craig and the doctors looked at Bryan as if he'd lost his mind. Bryan knew those reactions were coming; he had to get himself prepared and share his knowledge with them. There was no way in hell he was going to keep the facts to himself one moment longer. If he did, Lanassa would win and possess everything that was alive inside of Andre.

James looked around at the doubtful faces and decided to give Bryan some support. "I think we should listen to what Bryan has to say. Please, is there some place we all can go and discuss this with open minds?"

Craig trusted his brother and could clearly see he needed his support. "I agree with James. Dr. Marvick, where can we all go to talk?"

"To my office," the doctor replied, leading them all out of the room and down the hall.

They all walked just a few doors down the hallway with dreadful looks upon their faces. *What could Bryan possibly know concerning the turn of events and Dr. Brass' condition?* The two doctors and Craig wondered suspiciously.

James was sure all questions would be answered soon. Whether the doctors and Craig would think Bryan should be admitted for evaluations was another question altogether.

But how could anyone dismiss the change in temperature, along with the shaking and moving of objects, and the rattling of the IV pole? How was Bryan going to explain those kinds of occurrences?

They reached Dr. Marwick's office and entered. It was designed for comfort, with huge windows that allowed sunshine to invade the space. The curtains were drawn opened to accept the brightness. On one side of the office, against the wall, was a huge leather sofa in deep red. The desk top was made of glass with four steel leg posts. The leather chair behind the desk was large and made for relaxing and was in the same dark red color as the sofa. The two chairs in front of his desk also matched the sofa. There also was a conference table made of glass and eight chairs that matched the other chairs in the office. Everything was of quality and comfort.

James thanked the stars above that the office was made for comfort, because with the news they all were about to hear, they needed all the brightness and comfort they could get. It was about to become dark, without a doubt, if Bryan shared with them what James had already guessed: Lanassa.

The men all took seats at the conference table, except for Bryan.

Anna removed her four sweaters; she no longer needed the warmth they provided. Bryan pulled out a chair for her, and Anna looked up at him with a nervous smile on her face then took her seat. Bryan smiled in return. Then he took his seat across from Anna and sat next to Craig.

All eyes were now on Bryan.

Anna also looked at Craig. She noticed both brothers were extremely handsome with very similar features. They could have passed for twins, except for the differences in their complexions. Bryan's complexion was a darker brown, while Craig's had a lighter shade to his skin tone. They also wore their hair differently. Whereas Bryan's hair was cut very short with tight curls, Craig wore his hair brushed back in a wavy hair-style the different hair-styles complemented the brothers' looks.

Anna knew that Dr. Brass had the same good looks, which showed through his frail features. She knew that once Dr. Brass was healthy again, he would be as attractive as the brothers. It never crossed her mind that the doctor wouldn't recovery. Anna shook her head, as if to clear it. Why was she sitting there thinking about Dr. Brass in such a way? She had no clue, but she'd never really thought of Dr. Brass as being just a patient. Anna felt more for him. Her protectiveness regarding Dr. Brass was taking over. She always went to visit him when she was off duty and stayed there, reading to him, hoping he could hear her words. Then one night, Dr. Brass moved. Although slightly, he still moved, and from that day forward, she knew he could hear her reading and talking to him. But what was causing his condition? No one knew. She also didn't understand his medical condition—his vital signs were in order. It didn't make any sense whatsoever.

Bryan wondered what Anna was thinking—he almost could see the wheels turning in her mind. He had many questions he wanted to ask her, but for now, his questions must wait. He had some serious news to share with these people. Bryan took a deep breath, looked at the faces around the table, and began telling his theory.

"I know you might think I'm losing it when I share my theory. But I want you all to know my faculties are in proper order."

This is it, James thought. *Bryan is finally going to open up. It's about damn time.*

Bryan saw James' eager expression and wanted to tell the man he was being distracting. Instead, he continued, "I believe Lanassa's soul isn't at rest, and she is trying her best in the afterlife to take Dr. Brass with her."

Dr. Marvick and Dr. Baines shuffled in their seats, trying to compose themselves. Craig stood up and stared at his brother as if he had indeed lost his mind.

Anna, however, looked as if she just might believe Bryan's theory. And James, wanted to tell Craig to chill out, but he knew better than to speak the words. Bryan's theory sounded crazy to him as well. But, they all had been presented with proof while in Dr. Brass' room.

Dr. Marvick cleared his throat. "Finish, please, Mr. Brown."

So Bryan continued, "We all have experienced the temperature change in the room, even though the thermostat reads seventy-five degrees. The temperature definitely dropped during our visit today—I could see my breath."

Craig sat down and considered Bryan's theory. *Is it possible? Is Lanassa's dead spirit after Dre? If it is true, how can we help Dre fight against the supernatural?* Craig wondered. He wanted to hear more. He asked Bryan to continue.

Bryan continued. "Please don't forget the movement of those curtains, along with the rattling of the IV pole. And I'm sure there will be more activities to come. We need to get Dr. Brass out of this hospital and back home as soon as possible. Lanassa's restless spirit wants to possess him. She wants to take him to the other side, to be with her."

Anna became instantly upset. She started biting her lower lip while holding her hands tightly together in her lap.

Bryan felt bad that he'd had to include her in the meeting, but something was telling him she would be the answer to saving his friend's life. He would speak with her immediately after the meeting. There wasn't any way around it.

Dr. Marvick spoke up. "What makes you think that moving him to another location would stop these occurrences?" He made the statement as if he was starting to believe Bryan's theory.

"I can't say that it would. But being here in New Orleans, where she was born and raised—it just might keep her spirit here. New Orleans was Lanassa's life, not Dr. Brass. She had no feelings for him, other than games. I'm hoping she would move on to someone else. Like that husband of hers."

Now it was sounding crazy, even to Bryan, but there were no other explanations. He knew it had to be Lanassa.

Dr. Baines finally gave his opinion. "I do believe in the paranormal, although I'm a doctor of logical science. I have heard from some of my colleagues who have witnessed such occurrences. They explained them to me, and while in that room I have to admit, I became a believer. We all know that Dr. Brass isn't medically sick. The entire test you have provided me, Dr. Marvick, concerning his brain activities, came back normal. It confirmed he is a healthy man. What else could possibly be keeping him in such a state? I'm inclined to agree with Bryan on this. We must start preparing him for the care he needs back home without delay."

All nodded in agreement—except for Anna. Anna's throat felt like it was closing up. Why was she feeling this way about a man she didn't even know? She didn't want him to leave, but how could he stay under such conditions. It might prove to be safer for his recovery if he did go back home. Anna felt a sharp pain in her heart, and she held back the tears that were trying to escape her eyes.

Bryan and James noticed her reaction, and Bryan went to her and placed his large hand on her tiny shoulder. "Are you alright, Ms. Jordan?"

She looked up at him. "I don't know." Anna turned toward Dr. Marvick and asked to be excused.

"Yes, of course," he responded, assuming the talk of dead souls had distressed her. "Please sign out and take the rest of the day off."

Bryan wanted to speak with her before she left, but Nurse Jordan was clearly at the end of her rope. He could see she was trying hard to hold back the tears. He couldn't question her today. But he would need to do so before he went back home with Andre.

Chapter 23

Anna walked quietly out of the room, and she no longer had all of those eyes on her face, she leaned against the closed door and began weeping. Anna wanted to visit Dr. Brass before she left, but took Dr. Marvick's advice and signed herself off duty. She carried Dr. Brass with her in her heart—something Anna couldn't explain, no matter how hard she tried.

After Anna had left the room, all of the men started talking about preparations they needed to take care of for Dr. Brass—the care that must be in place before Dr. Brass could be discharged.

Bryan couldn't let it go. He had to request that Anna come with them, if only for a month. He asked Dr. Baines, "Do you have a nurse assigned for the live-in care for Dr. Brass?"

"Not at the present time. It will not be a problem, I assure you."

James was watching Bryan. He knew what was coming next. The man was too easy to read.

"Dr. Baines, may I make a suggestion?" Bryan asked.

"Of course, you and Craig are his family. The only family he has. I'll welcome anything you have to say."

"I would like you to assign Nurse Jordan to his care, if only for a month."

Craig exploded from his chair. "Are you crazy? We don't know her from Adam, and you want to invite her into Dre's home as a care provider?"

"Yes I do," Bryan said evenly. "You've seen the effect she has on Dre. Nurse Jordan has been the only one to get a response from him. There is a connection between them. I believe she is the one keeping Lanassa's spirit from reaching Dre."

Craig couldn't believe what he was hearing. "Are you so eager to place a woman in Dre's life that you'll do it without any background information on her? Isn't that what got him into this situation in the first place?"

Bryan was trying his best to keep his cool with his brother. "She is a nurse, Craig, not a bar-hopper."

Craig looked at Bryan, dumbfounded. "How in the hell do you know what she does off duty?"

"Let's not get ahead of ourselves" said Dr. Baines. "Dr. Marvick, can you tell us Anna's qualifications and if she could take such a leave, if she agreed?"

Craig's face turned a deeper red as he shouted, "Has anyone in this room been listening to what I'm saying? I can't allow anyone in Dre's home without a thorough background investigation."

Dr. Marvick stated, "Nurse Jordan is more than qualified to accommodate the needs of a patient in Dr. Brass' condition. That was the reason she was assigned to his care. As far as a leave, it's up to her. It's also up to her to agree to the background check that is required in order to get the job."

Craig calmed down with the statement from the doctor. He looked at Bryan and said, "If you want her and if she wants the position as Dre's live-in nurse, she must agree to a background check. Do I make myself clear?"

Bryan smiled at Craig, a smile that reached his eyes. "Yes, I hear you loud and clear, sir." He wanted to salute, but decided he got what he'd wanted.

Craig smiled back at his brother, somewhat sheepishly.

Don't leave me; they're trying to take you away from me. You must fight and fight hard. I'm alone; you left me alone. Don't you love me? You said you loved me once. I feel you still do. So fight them. Fight against them and most important, fight against her—that voice that reads to you. It isn't mine. She isn't the woman you love. I am.

Andre heard her pleading in his ear. He wanted to feel her touches again. He wanted what she wanted. Dr. Andre C. Brass would fight to give her what she wanted, which was him. He felt time was running out. But that voice, the voice of the other woman, was still in his head. How could he fight against that voice in his head? It was smooth, like velvet, and it provided him with so much comfort. What should he do? How should he do it? He couldn't rest that night. Lanassa's voice in his ear kept pleading with him.

Then he saw her face—that beautiful face—and refused to stop fighting to be in her arms again. He was becoming weaker by the day.

Craig, Bryan, and James left the conference room after it was decided that Dr. Brass would be discharged immediately from the hospital. Before they left the hospital, the brothers had to visit Andre again. They had to let him know he would be home soon. They only hoped he would be able to hear their voices. Bryan wished that Anna was with them. She would have been the one to get the message through to Andre. There was some kind of connection between them. Anna was the source for his survival. Bryan had no question about that, but what if she refused to accept the job offer? What then? There wasn't a plan B. Anna was the only plan Bryan had regarding the recovery of his friend and keeping Lanassa from destroying him.

When they reached Andre's room, Craig was not so eager to enter. He was the one that Lanassa hated; Bryan couldn't deny that fact. But once Andre was released from the hospital, Bryan was sure that Lanassa would hate them all. He only prayed her restless soul wouldn't follow them back to Cambridge. They entered the room and instantly, all of them felt the chill.

Bryan had his answer. They were her enemies, but he refused to allow her to win the battle over Andre's life. *I wonder how could Anna endure this kind of cold and stay at Andre's bedside?* Bryan mused. Maybe it's because she cared far more than its being her profession as his nurse that was the reason. *But now she knows what causes the cold and the movement of objects, will she want to follow Andre back home?* He was more fearful of Anna's rejection of the job offer than of Lanassa's spirit.

Now, he turned to James. "I know it's getting pretty late, but could you contact Nick and find out where Anna lives? We have to find out if she'd be willing to be a part of our team."

James was relieved by the request. He wanted nothing more than to leave that cold room with the strange things that happened in it "You know I can't use my cell phone in here. I'll meet you both downstairs, and I'll call up Nick and request that he make it a priority."

James walked quickly out into the normalcy of the hallway. His body temperature returned to normal instantly.

Craig and Bryan pulled up their suit collars to cover their necks from the cold, then approached their dear friend and placed their hands on his arm. It had to be near freezing in the room, but Andre's arm was warm. How could that be?

Bryan looked at Craig and knew they were thinking the same thing. Bryan said. "Dre is still warm because Lanassa hasn't taking over his soul. He is still here with us, but I don't know how much longer that will be. I wish we could take him away tonight."

Craig nodded in agreement. Then the IV pole came crashing down on top of his head, causing a nasty gash. Craig yelled, "You fucking bitch!" while he tried to steady the pole and hold his head at the same time.

Bryan hurried to the bathroom and grabbed a washcloth that was folded neatly on the vanity. Then he rushed back to Craig and placed the cloth over his brother's wound and applied pressure to stop the bleeding. "Thanks, man. I can take it from here." Craig continued to apply the pressure to his head, but his hand was shaking.

This is going way too far and becoming dangerous, Bryan thought. He knew at that point that the restless spirit was also an angry spirit. He wondered if he should involve Nurse Jordan in something that was so unpredictable. The spirit of Lanassa was in a fury. Both brothers placed a kiss on Andre's forehead and quickly left the room.

Craig was the first to speak, while still applying pressure to his wounded head. "Her ass is playing for keeps. How do we stop her?"

Bryan shook his head. How could they stop her? This went far beyond the legal or medical expertise of anyone they knew.

At that time, Dr. Baines, who was supposed to meet them downstairs, was coming out of Dr. Marvick's office. He saw the two brothers and started walking fast toward them; he noticed the blood on the cloth that Craig was holding against his head. "What happened?"

Craig explained, Dr. Baines responded with great concern, "Yes, I have heard about these kinds of incidences that my colleagues had shared with me. Follow me, I need to look at that wound." Dr .Baines went to the front desk and asked the nurse where there was an unoccupied examining room.

"Room C is across the hall. Please feel free and take your time."

She smiled at him, wondering what was going on, but didn't ask. Too many things that couldn't be explained had been happening since the arrival of Dr. Andre C. Brass.

Dr. Baines directed Craig and Bryan into the examining room, where he asked Craig to sit on the bed. He pulled the examining light over Craig's head to get a better view of the wound. "It's not too bad," he said. "The blood is coming from a very small gash. Due to the fact that the heart was beating fast, your blood was pumping faster, causing the blood to rush heavily from the wound, making the wound appear more serious than it is." The doctor put on some plastic gloves, washed the blood from the wound, then applied some antibiotic ointment to it. Dr. Baines then covered it with a large bandage.

After Dr. Baines was done caring for Craig, he advised the brothers that Dr. Brass would be discharged the next day. And if Bryan wanted to have Nurse Jordan as care provider, he'd better act fast or the process would take longer. Dr. Marvick wasn't going to sign any paperwork until he was sure that Dr. Brass had a live-in care provider. The doctor would approve her leave immediately, if she agreed to take the job.

"I think we're placing her in a difficult position, but what other choice do we have?" Bryan said. "I'll just be very open with her about everything—the background check, and what just happened to Craig. I wouldn't want to offer the job unless she's aware of what she is getting herself involved with."

Anna was home, trying her best to stop the tears. She was lying on the sofa with "Blue," her American Staffordshire pit bull terrier. He was her comfort and joy during times like these. Although he was afflicted with cerebellar hypoplasia, a disorder that gave Blue trouble when he walked and prevented him from climbing stairs. Blue had a lot of heart and always was there for Anna during her time of need. And boy, did she need him now. She picked Blue up from downstairs at her mother and stepfather's home when she arrived. They lived on the first floor of the house were Anna lived. Her mother, Florence, and stepfather, John, were great at dog-sitting with Blue during the times Anna had to go to work. Once she returned from the hospital, Blue always wobbled into her arms, licking her face and showing her so much love. At the age of seven, people could clearly see that something was wrong with her dog, and it was obvious he couldn't climb stairs.

But her veterinarian always told Anna she was doing a great job with Blue. For that Anna was happy. Now he was doing a great job for her, keeping her company and showing her support, because it wasn't any doubt in Anna's mind that he knew something was wrong. He always did. "What a precious baby you are," Anna said to Blue, while rubbing him behind his ear. Then that tail started to wag and her emotions started to pick up. "Thanks Blue." Anna was too exhausted to go farther than the sofa when she entered her apartment. So that was Anna and Blue's destination. They both laid on the sofa, curled up together, and fell peacefully asleep.

Chapter 24

After Dr. Baines finished caring for the wound on Craig's head, the three men got on the elevator and went down to the main floor, where James was waiting for them.

"Here's Anna's address," he told Bryan.

"Thanks, James. Time is of the essence—Andre's life depends on it. We have to act quickly because Andre is becoming weaker with every passing second."

Then James looked over and saw the bandage across Craig's forehead. "What happened to your head?"

Bryan spoke for his brother. "Lanassa is what happened."

James was to afraid to ask what that meant. "Are you all right, Craig?"

Craig nodded. "I will be."

James asked, "Are we going to pay Ms. Jordan a visit tonight? It's getting rather late? Do you think we should wait until tomorrow?"

"No, now that we know where she lives, it's best that we get this over with as soon as possible," Bryan insisted. "We can't afford to waste another moment."

While waiting for the brothers to finish their business with Dr. Baines and Dr. Marvick, James had rented a car for them so they wouldn't have to rely on cabs. They said good-bye to Dr. Baines and Dr. Marvick then walked to the parking lot, where the car was waiting. The heat of the evening hit them as they left the building. It was a welcome experience after the cold in Andre's room.

They all got in the rented Chevrolet Impala, with James taking the driver's seat, Craig sitting up front with him, and Bryan in the back. All Bryan wanted to do was close his eyes and try to relax his nerves.

He was worried that Anna wouldn't accept the job offer. He had to concentrate on how to approach her, especially as they were visiting her without her invitation, during the late evening.

The car came to a stop in front of a duplex in an upper middle-class neighborhood. *How will she react?* Bryan wondered. *The last look on her face seemed to indicate she didn't want to see either one of us again. This isn't going to be easy.*

James turned and looked at both brothers. "Well, this is it. I'll stay in the car. Good luck."

The brothers got out of the car, Craig with an expressionless face and Bryan with an expression of great concern. They walked up the steps to the lovely house. Bryan knew from Nick's information that Anna's apartment was on the second floor, over her parents' apartment. He rang the upstairs door bell twice; then they waited.

Blue started to bark. Anna blinked her eyes open and saw that Blue had left her side and was wagging his tail by the door with excitement. She wondered who could be visiting her so late in the evening. She looked out of her front window and saw a black Impala parked in front of her home.

So she told Blue to stay and rubbed him behind his ear. Then she walked down the stairs, turning on the front-porch light—and saw Craig and Bryan standing there. *Oh my God! Did Dr. Brass pass away?* Anna wondered. What other reason could there be for the two brothers to pay her a visit? Anna opened the door and greeted them, with concern plastered across her face.

Bryan smiled, which gave her some relief. If Dr. Brass had passed away, surely he wouldn't be smiling at her. "What a surprise," she said still wondering what was going on and why they'd come to visit her.

"May we come in? It's important that we speak with you." Bryan's request sounded more like a plea. Anna didn't hesitate; she stepped aside, allowing them to enter the hallway. Bryan and Craig followed her up the stairs and entered her apartment.

They were greeted by Blue. And Bryan bent down to rub the dog behind his ear; Craig did the same.

"Let's sit in the dining room," Anna suggested, leading the way. The room was small and comfortable, with thick beige cushions on the four dining room chairs.

They situated themselves at the table, then Bryan said, "You're probably wondering why we're visiting you at such a late hour. But we have a job offer for you, and we both hope you will accept. Time is running out, and you're our only hope, Ms. Jordan."

Bryan realized that Anna was looking at the bandage on Craig's forehead. How would they explain that to her? *I'll just have to explain what truly happened*, Bryan thought. He cleared his throat, bringing Anna's attention away from the bandage.

She looked at him as if she wanted to apologize for staring, but the confusion was clear on her innocent face.

He observed her hair was no longer in the ponytail. It was wild and free with spiraling tight curls, with a rich dark brown color that matched her perfectly pretty face. She was still wearing her nurse's uniform, and her feet were bare from any kind of house shoes or socks.

"Dr. Brass is being released from the hospital tomorrow," Bryan went on to explain, "He will need a live-in nurse. We are prepared to offer any salary you request if you will take the position."

Anna's mouth opened wide with surprise. Bryan wondered if that meant she would take the job or was planning to refuse the offer by telling them there was no way in hell she was going near Andre again.

Craig waited patiently for Bryan to get to the interesting part of the offer. Bryan continued, "I must be very honest with you, Nurse Jordan; it won't be easy. As you know, Lanassa's spirit is haunting Dr. Brass, and we can't be sure that spirit will not follow him home."

"Please, call me Anna," she said. "Is ... is Dr. Brass in any real danger?"

"He could be," Bryan said honestly. "If you're afraid to take us up on our offer, I'll understand. These aren't normal circumstances."

Anna met Bryan's gaze. "I'm not afraid of Lanassa's spirit. I'm more afraid and concerned for Dr. Brass. To tell you the truth, money really isn't an issue. I feel for Dr. Brass, and money can't buy my concern for his recovery. The spirit that is haunting him doesn't diminish my concern for his safety or his health. I just wish I could protect him."

Good answer, Bryan thought, but he still hadn't gotten to the other part of the story at hand.

Craig decided to be the one to lay it all out for her. "The bandage across my head was caused by Lanassa's spirit, Anna. She pushed the IV pole down on me, and it landed on my head, which caused a wound.

Her spirit is wicked. And she will not stop until she takes possession of Andre. In other words, her mission is aimed at taking his life. She is after his soul, Anna. Do you understand what I'm telling you? Things could become dangerous if that spirit decides to follow him home."

"Oh, my," Anna said softly. Then she looked up at the brothers with determination and said, "I accept your offer without hesitation, but I must bring along my dog, Blue. I love him and can't leave him behind."

"Of course," Craig said, "but Anna … do you need to think this through? Do you understand the situation clearly, Anna? We are talking about the paranormal here."

"I don't need to think it through. I've spent time with Dr. Brass. I knew something wasn't normal. Now that I know what is affecting his condition it could only prepare me for what to expect. It was the unknown I feared, but it never kept me away from Dr. Brass, even when I didn't have the answers. Now, the questions are answered. That can only aid me with providing him with the proper care he needs."

Bryan looked over at his brother with victory in his eyes. But Craig wasn't finished. "One more thing, Anna … we must investigate your background, but we need your permission. You must sign papers that I have in my briefcase in order for us to do the investigation."

The victory in Bryan's eyes faded, but Anna said, "Pull them out and let me see them. If everything is in order, I have no problem with signing the papers. I just hope you jump on it right away. You said Dr. Brass will be released tomorrow. We don't have time to waste."

Craig smiled at her and pulled out the papers. He wanted her just as much as Bryan did to be the care provider for Andre. After hearing her responses to their questions, Craig knew they wouldn't find anything that would have them withdraw the job offer. Anna viewed the papers in front of her. The documents were brief and straight to the point. She signed the papers, then handed them over to Craig. He placed the signed documents back in his briefcase. Then Craig mentioned the salary, which was 400 dollars a day, and she wouldn't have any out-of-pocket expenses. If she needed anything, all she had to do was ask either one of them and they'd make sure she was provided with whatever she needed.

Anna looked at him as if he was crazy.

"And there will be no negotiations regarding the pay," Craig said with a smile, realizing it was far more than she made working at the hospital. "Also, Dr. Marvick will release you from your duties at the hospital immediately; it was pending until we knew if you would accept the job offer. I'll call the doctor and advise him after the background check."

With the mission accomplished, both brothers bid her good-bye and advised her they'd see her in the morning. They patted Blue on his head before they left.

Anna called her mother and told her the whole story from beginning to end. Florence already had read about the case that surrounded Dr. Brass, but the part about the restless spirit of Lanassa was information she received from her daughter. Florence wasn't worried for Anna, but she did have some sound advice to give her. "I want you to be aware, Anna, the dead can't hurt you if you have faith in what you believe in. But you must know that if the spirit follows Dr. Brass back to his home, he'll have to be the one to send her away. He must be able to see her spirit and allow that spirit to feel what's inside of his soul.

"You see, it seems as if her restless spirit still believes the doctor wants her and is still in love with her. Lanassa's spirit must be lonely and in need in order to take the doctor's soul. Obviously, she is as selfish after life as she was in life. He must be the one to free her—and free himself from her. Do you understand what I'm telling you?"

"Yes, Mother, I understand, but how can he do that when he is barely conscious?"

"If it isn't too late, he will be able to recover and regain consciousness. At that time, it would be up to him to fight her spirit away. You will not be able to free him. Dr. Brass must allow that spirit to invade his body. If the love isn't there, I'm sure Lanassa's spirit will feel his soul and the lack of love for her. Then it will move on and go to a place of rest, in the afterlife of peace. But if there is any love inside of Dr. Brass for this woman, he will be possessed. And there isn't anything that anyone would be able to do to save him." Florence knew this from experience. She had witnessed the haunting of her husband John years ago by his ex-wife.

Anna started to ponder her mother's wisdom. It scared her to death to think that Dr. Brass might still be in love with the woman who had caused him so much pain. Anna also knew if he was still in love with Lanassa, she herself would lose him forever.

All she could do was take care of Dr. Brass and hope, in the end, he would want to live and send the spirit to its finally resting place. She prayed that he would want Lanassa out of his life for good. But she wasn't a fool. She heard how much Dr. Brass loved the woman. It was causing her so much pain, but she couldn't share this with her mother. Was she just setting herself up for the pain that might be coming her way?

"Mother, I love you and Dad with all my heart and will call you ever chance I get. I'll be taking Blue with me. We'll come down first thing in the morning and say our good-byes."

"We both love you, too, Anna. You be careful." Florence knew her daughter was falling in love with Dr. Brass. She only hoped that it wouldn't damage Anna to a point of no return, especially if Lanassa's and Dr. Brass' souls did join as one at the end.

Anna said good night to her mother then hung up the phone. She gathered Blue up in her arms and carried him to her bed, where they both curled up together and went to sleep.

Craig knew he was wrong to have requested the investigation on Anna before she even signed the papers. He was reading through the papers, and Bryan shook his head at James and his brother. "I can't believe you both investigated her before she agreed to it. James, I'm not surprised at your actions. After all you are an investigator ready to investigate at a drop of a dime. But Craig you should have known not to do such a thing."

Craig glared at Bryan. "How else would we have gotten the background check in time? I knew we wouldn't find anything. And time is running out. The wheels would be rolling tomorrow, and I had to be sure she was as innocent as she appears. Could you find it in your heart to forgive this one transgression?" Then Craig looked up at his brother, who was standing over him, and James, stating with his eyes, *Please, oh mighty, please forgive us.* Then he smiled at Bryan.

Bryan rolled his eyes at Craig, but he wanted to find out what was in the report. He was as guilty as they were. "Let me read what you found out." Then he held out his hand for the background check on Anna. Craig gave him the report.

Anna's family consisted of her mother, Florence, and her stepfather,

John, both of whom were retired. Anna's biological father died of heart failure when she was seven, and her mother remarried years later. Anna helped with her college expenses, working part-time at a local bank. She received a master's degree in nursing. She was twenty-seven years of age, had few friends, and drank an occasional glass of wine. She had been a nurse at the hospital for over six years and often worked overtime. And she had a great love for animals, especially her dog Blue.

Bryan thought she was perfect for the job. Bryan gave the report back to Craig, and they both started smiling. They couldn't wait to pick her up and get Andre home.

Chapter 25

Nick and James found it was very easy to investigate Ms. Jordan, because there wasn't anything hidden in her life. Her life was a constant routine. Bryan thanked James again for a job well done.

"My pleasure. Now these tired bones of mine are off to bed. See you both tomorrow." James O'Rourke always spoke as if he were an old man, although he was only forty-five years of age. Bryan and Craig had hired him during their first case, after they opened up their law office. They all took to each other instantly. It was a great partnership.

Craig was talking on his cell phone with Dr. Baines, advising him that Anna had accepted the position. He bid the doctor a good night and said to Bryan, "Well, brother, everything is a go for tomorrow. I suggest we both pack it in and get some sleep."

"I can't agree with you more. Good night."

Craig had one more call to make and that was to Sharon. She answered on the first ring. "Hello, Sharon, did I wake you?"

"No, not at all, I was just in bed reading."

Craig wished he was in that bed with her, rubbing his hands over her soft brown skin. "I want you to know we will be flying out tomorrow with Andre. I'll call you after work and maybe you can meet me at his mansion. That's if you don't have other plans after work."

"I have no other plans, and I can't wait to see you. Craig, you are truly missed."

Her words touched Craig's heart; he could feel her sincerity. "Good, I'll call you once we have settled in Andre and Anna."

"Anna?"

"Yes, she will be Andre's live-in nurse. She's bringing along her dog, Blue, too."

They said their good nights, and Craig went to get some much-needed sleep.

Craig and James were both ready to pick up Anna. But Bryan was slow as always. Craig called out to him, "Bryan, what's the hold up?"

Bryan answered from the bedroom, "It will only take me another minute, and I'll be ready."

Craig was becoming impatient with his brother. "I've already spoken with Anna. She's packed and ready, along with Blue."

Finally, Bryan came out with his luggage in hand. "I had to make sure I wasn't leaving anything behind," Bryan explained.

Finally, they all were in the Impala and off to pick up Anna. She would have to sign more paperwork at the hospital, requesting the leave of absence officially, although Dr. Marvick already gave his approval that morning.

When they reached Anna's house, Bryan and Craig helped her load her luggage into the trunk of the car. They decided to return and pick Blue up later, after they finished at the hospital.

Craig and Bryan both met Anna's parents, who were with Blue in the living room of their home. Florence advised the brothers that they couldn't have found a better nurse to take care of Dr. Brass. Both men nodded in agreement.

When they arrived at the hospital, James decided to wait in the car, while Anna, Craig, and Bryan went into the hospital. They approached the revolving doors of the hospital, clearly on a serious mission—to get Dr. Brass discharged from the hospital and away from Lanassa's lingering spirit as fast as they could. Everything was going according to plan.

They were greeted by Dr. Baines and Dr. Marvick, who both were going over some medical reports. They looked up and noticed the Brown brothers and Anna approaching them. Dr. Baines stated, "Everything is in order. Dr. Brass will be transported, along with the rest of us, on a private jet."

Anna excused herself to go and sign the necessary paperwork for her leave. Before she left, Dr. Marvick shook her hand firmly as a way of showing his support. "This may be a difficult case, Anna," he told her, "but I have total faith in your abilities. I've always viewed you as someone with a strong will, someone who cares not just with her mind but also with her heart. Dr. Brass will be in good hands, indeed."

Anna smiled warmly. "Thank you, Dr. Marvick. I appreciate your saying that."

After Anna left them, Craig noticed someone coming out of Andre's room. He felt his hair stand straight up, as if he was sensing something like an animal. He saw then that it was Ted Pearson, and Craig became enraged. He left the doctors and Bryan behind in a flash and approached Pearson, grabbed the man hard by the collar of his suit jacket, and pushed him hard against the wall. "What the hell are you doing here, you bug?" Craig demanded. He could see the fear in the man's eyes, but it wasn't coming from Craig's reaction or the fact that he'd just thrown him up against the wall.

Bryan ran to his brother's side and pried his hands off Pearson's collar. The man was white as a ghost. *Lanassa*, Bryan thought. *Her spirit was aimed at the correct person this time.*

Craig was furious and he growled at Pearson, "If your ass leaks this to anyone—and I do mean anyone—I'll sue you for every cheap-ass thing you ever owned in your entire life. You will be left with only the underwear under that suit of yours. Do I make myself clear, you maggot?"

Ted Pearson seemed so incoherent that Craig grabbed him again and repeated his threat. Bryan touched his brother on the arm, and Craig slowly released his hold around Pearson's collar.

Then Pearson told them in a shaky voice, "No one would believe what I just witnessed anyway. What's inside of that room, I don't care to remember." He turned and ran toward the elevators.

Craig and Bryan entered Andre's room and were immediately caught of guard. All of the curtains had been thrown on the floor, along with the window blinds. The IV pole was laying on the floor, and the entire room was in total disarray. They rushed to Andre's bed—he was in the same state as before. They checked him to make sure he hasn't been injured. He seemed okay, but one thing alarmed them—there was blood coming from his arm, where the needle from the IV had come out.

Dr. Baines and Dr. Marvick entered the room after hearing all of the commotion. They were astonished by what they witnessed. Dr. Baines examined Andre and also noticed the needle was removed from his bleeding arm, and the IV pole was on the floor. Dr. Marvick placed a call over the intercom for Nurse Jordan. Anna quickly responded, and Dr. Marvick instructed her to bring an IV pole and the bag of fluids with clean needles to Dr. Brass' room immediately.

Anna entered the room with the supplies. She viewed the way everything was thrown around and hurried to Dr. Brass to set up the IV pole with the fluids. She took out a needle from a sterile package, cleaned the blood from Andre's arm, and placed the needle into his arm. She checked his temperature; it was normal. Then she felt calmer and proceeded to remove the patches from his eyes and wipe them with a warm washcloth. She put eye drops into his eyes; then covered them with clean cotton patches.

Craig and Bryan watched her with amazement. She didn't hesitate not once; she was cool and very calm. When she finished with Andre, she asked, "When do we get him out of here?" The urgency in her voice was clear.

"Now," Dr. Marvick said as he called for the orderlies to remove Dr. Brass from the room and get him ready to be taken from the hospital.

Anna called James on her cell and asked him to pick up Blue and meet them at the airport. Dr. Baines and Anna rode in an ambulance with Dr. Brass, while Craig, Bryan and James, along with Blue were in the Impala. They all were headed to the airport. When they were finally on the jet, Blue was buckled up in Bryan's arms, allowing Anna to be with Dr. Baines and Andre.

Dr. Baines advised them that another ambulance would be waiting for them in Boston to take Dr. Brass home. He already knew a full staff would be awaiting their arrival. That task had been completed days ago. The staff was very familiar with the brothers and with Andre as most of the staff worked for Dr. Brass. This wouldn't be Dr. Baines' first case that required him to make daily visits to examine his patient. Dr. Brass was his client before the whole traumatic situation occurred. Dr. Baines also found it a pleasure working with Nurse Jordan; it was as if she read his mind. He didn't have to instruct her on anything regarding the care of Dr. Brass. She anticipated what was needed to be done and did it. *What an asset*, he thought as he watched her perform her duties.

The jet landed in Boston, and the ambulance was waiting. As they left the jet, Bryan was still holding Blue in his arms. He could swear the dog was smiling up at him. Dr. Baines, Anna, and Dr. Brass rode to the mansion in an ambulance. The rest were headed to a sleek Audi, which belonged to Craig. Brenda, Bryan's receptionist, was behind the wheel.

All three men and Blue settled inside the car. She patted Blue on his head, and Blue seemed to smile at her. Brenda noticed Craig and James looked stressed, but Blue seemed to give Bryan a kind of peace. He kept hugging and rubbing the dog. *It must be true that animals can lift your spirits during times of sorrow*, Brenda thought.

During the ride to Dr. Brass' mansion, Craig made a phone call to Debra, his receptionist who was also a paralegal with the firm. He requested her and Bill Gorgon, one of the attorneys the brothers hired, to meet him at the mansion. Debra and Bill had held down the fort while the brothers were in New Orleans.

The ambulance arrived at Andre's mansion well ahead of the Audi. Now everyone was inside of the mansion, and getting them on the same page regarding Dr. Brass' care was top priority.

Anna and Dr. Baines were in Dr. Brass' bedroom on the second floor, where a hospital bed had been set up. Anna couldn't help herself. She noticed Dr. Brass had expensive tastes. The floors and fireplace in his bedroom were made from rich, polished wood. The room was so spacious that his king-size bed didn't have to be moved in order to accommodate the hospital bed. There were two brown leather armchairs positioned in front of the fireplace. His bookshelf was filled with all types of books. Dr. Brass also had an office area and a music area. She saw two trumpets on stands and a composer stand next to them. The doctor's bedroom invited comfort.

Anna also had noticed the baby grand piano downstairs. It was breathtaking. She hoped the doctor would survive his ordeal and get another chance to enjoy what he had worked so very hard to achieve in life. Anna had to clear her head. She'd never seen a more beautiful home.

The medics had finished placing Dr. Brass on the bed, then lifted the rails on each side. Anna went over and began her work. She replaced the needle in his arm that was connected to the feeding tube and fluid bag, which hung from the IV pole. Then she checked his body temperature; it was normal. She wiped his smooth, full lips with a warm washcloth, then rubbed medicated ointment over them to help prevent chapping. Then Dr. Baines checked over Dr. Brass, and all of his vitals signs were normal. They both knew why he remained in his current state. He was home now; maybe with a lot of praying he would recover. There really wasn't anything medical science could do for him.

After Anna and Dr. Baines made sure Dr. Brass was comfortable, they both went downstairs to greet the others. Everyone had arrived, and Blue was so excited to see Anna. She picked him up and kissed the top of his head.

They introduced Anna to Brenda, and both women shook hands, while Blue lay comfortably in Anna's arms. Brenda stated, "That's some dog you have there." Then she smiled at Anna.

"Yes he is. Blue is the best."

"We set up your living quarters upstairs, next to Andre's bedroom," Craig told Anna. "I'll show you and Blue where the both of you will be staying."

Craig led her to a beautiful wooden door with Victorian carvings around the edges. The room was beautiful and had a queen-size bed that was covered with a huge beige comforter and lots of dark fuchsia pillows thrown across the headboard. The room had a walk-in closet and an attached bathroom, along with a desk with a computer. She also noticed there was a big fluffy dog bed beside hers. She turned and saw Bryan smiling. "I knew Blue was coming with you, so I had one of the staff pick out the bed for him."

Anna thanked Bryan with a gleam in her eyes. She was so surprised that Bryan took the effort to make sure Blue would be comfortable during their stay.

They didn't have to know that Blue always slept in the bed with her. She thought the gesture was considerate. There also was an eating area for her dog with two stainless steel bowls on a mat. Bryan took one bowl into the bathroom to fill it with water, then placed the bowel of water on the mat.

"Thank you, Bryan," Anna said again. "Where can I take Blue to do his business?"

"After I visit with Andre I'll show you the grounds," Bryan offered. "By the way, I'll be staying here in the house with you and Blue, along with the staff. I want to make sure everything will be all right."

Anna knew exactly why he was staying: Lanassa. It didn't bother her in the least. *I'll need all the support I can get*, she thought.

"We'll leave the two of you alone now," Bryan said, "so you can get unpack and make yourself comfortable. Tina the cook will be starting dinner soon. If you have a special request, all you have to do is let her know; I'll introduce you to her a little later."

Both brothers thanked Anna again for taking the job. They found Blue and patted him on the head.

Craig and Bryan then went to Andre's room and found Dr. Baines was checking him over again. "Is something wrong?" Craig asked.

"No, everything is fine. I wanted to give him another examination before I left. Make sure you give me a call if anything changes. I'll see you both tomorrow."

Dr. Andre C. Brass had loss so much weight and the brothers were very worried. "You hold on. Do you hear me, Dre?" Craig said. "You hold on! Don't allow her to take you from us, man." He held his friend's hand and rubbed it with his.

"Dre, you have the best care, and your nurse is such a looker! She is so pretty and will take good care of you," Bryan told him. "She is also very protective of you. I can't wait for you to meet her. She is truly a charm."

Craig gazed at Bryan, thinking, *Does he know this isn't time for a hook-up? What is Bryan thinking?*

Bryan was such an optimist, Craig though. He couldn't get mad at his brother. Craig wished some of that upbeat attitude would rub off on him, because he really needed it. Craig didn't have absolute confidence for Andre recovery that Bryan displayed. And it was taking a toll on him. As always before leaving Andre, they both kissed him on his forehead.

Craig and Bryan went back downstairs and were greeted by Debra Duncan and Bill Gorgon. "How is he doing?" Debra asked, the concern clear in her voice.

"There hasn't been any change in him since he was admitted into the hospital," Craig stated.

"Oh, my," she whispered.

Bill tried to change the topic. "I brought with me the depositions you both should look over concerning Mrs. Brice's case."

While the brothers began to review the depositions, James said he'd go up and visit Andre. The others went into the study and began to work on Mrs. Brice's case.

Later, Bryan went up to check on Anna and take her and Blue on a walk over the grounds. Craig was speaking with the staff that would be taking care of Dr. Brass' home and assisting Anna.

Bryan knocked on Anna's door but didn't get a reply. He just stood there, wondering if he should enter. He decided it was best to leave, in case she was taking a bath or a nap. Bryan went to visit Andre.

He entered the room and found Anna at his bedside, with Blue next to her in his dog bed that Anna moved from her bedroom to Andre's. Anna was seated in one of the armchairs that she pulled from the fireplace and placed it next to Andre's bed. She had her feet on the ottoman. Anna had changed into a comfortable sweat suit. She was reading Andre a biography on different African-American composers from the 1800s. *How interesting that she chose that book. It's one of Andre's favorites*, Bryan thought. She looked up at him as he stood in the doorway. "I apologize," Bryan said, "I didn't mean to disturb you. I came up to take you and Blue for a walk around the grounds of the mansion."

"You didn't disturb me, Bryan. Your presence is always welcome—no telling when I'll need you. I'm also happy you decided to stay. So far so good; I don't feel a chill." Anna saw his face dropped just a little and realized she'd brought up what had been on everyone's mind—would Lanassa's spirit show up at the mansion?

Bryan noticed the concern on her face. "Anna your statement is only a fact. Don't worry about mentioning it. Until Andre is better, we can't be sure about Lanassa's spirit. We all must keep that in mind."

Blue woke up and started wagging his tail. Bryan thought the dog had a look of concern on his face. "You can continue to read to Andre," Bryan said. "I'll take Blue for the walk alone." Blue wobbled over to Bryan as if he was ready to do his business. It seemed as if Blue understood everything that was said. "We'll be right back."

"Thank you, Bryan," Anna said as they both walked out.

Bryan turned and said, "Don't mention it. The little guy is beginning to grow on me."

Once outside, Bryan was surprised he didn't have to call Blue over to him. The dog followed him everywhere. Bryan decided to walk around the grounds with Blue.—They both needed some fresh air and Bryan also needed to think about what would they do if the spirit of Lanassa decided to follow Andre home. That was a big unanswered question.

Dr. Andre C. Brass heard that soft, comforting voice again in his head. She was reading to him. The book was one of his favorites. He could hear her voice and the music of the great composers that he loved to read about. He felt so peaceful and for the first time, he felt alive with vigor. Who was she? What was her name? He tried to turn his head in the direction of that heavenly voice.

Just as Bryan and Blue walked in the room from their stroll, Bryan noticed Andre's head moved slightly in Anna's direction. He stopped dead in his tracks; so did Blue. They both watched Anna reading to Andre, and Andre trying his best to move his head toward her voice.

Bryan wanted to move into the room but didn't want to disturb what was happening. Blue sensed Bryan's hesitation and stayed by his side. Bryan observed how soft Anna's voice sounded. She was changing her voice to make dramatic events come to life from the book. She read so sweetly to his friend. Andre obviously heard her voice. The whole scene brought tears to Bryan's eyes. *Hope*, Bryan thought. *Anna was giving them all hope.* He and Blue walked quietly away from the room.

Bryan carried Blue down the stairs and placed him on the floor. The dog followed Bryan into the study. The room had a bookshelf from the top of the ceiling halfway to the floor. It was built into one of the walls and was made of walnut-wood. The other walls were covered with silk wall fabric in antique white. The sofa and chairs were made of paisley maroon fabric. The floors gleamed and matched a huge desk. There was also a gleaming wooden fireplace. Andre had excellent taste. He designed everything throughout the mansion with a personal touch. Every room in Andre's home was exquisite.

Craig was finishing up his meeting with the staff when Bryan and Blue entered the room. After the staff left, Bryan sat in one of the armchairs opposite his brother and spoke to Craig with excitement in his voice. Blue lay at his feet. "Craig, it's amazing. Anna was reading to Dre, and he moved his head toward her voice. He actually moved again for Anna. Something is going on. She is having an effect on him, and it's a positive one."

Craig viewed Bryan with calmness. Oddly, his calmness came from

Bryan's excitement. It was giving him hope about Andre condition. "We both know she is the one keeping Lanassa from gaining Dre's soul and keeping him alive," Craig said. "I never thought I would believe in such things, but it's obvious the supernatural does exist. I'm so appreciative when it comes to her, Bryan; you have no idea."

Bryan understood. He didn't have all the answers yet. One thing he did know for sure was that he and Craig owed Anna a lot. Bryan reached down and patted Blue on the head. "Craig, I feel about her the same as you. I knew what was going on the very first time we entered Dre's room in the hospital, not to mention your condition and everything moving and falling to the floor. Then later, Dre moved when he heard Anna's voice. I knew she was more than a care provider for him. Anna is Andre's protector, keeping Lanassa's spirit away,"

Although both brothers agreed that Anna was good for Andre, in the back of their minds they wondered how much time it would take for Andre to recover. And would Lanassa come back before he made a complete recovery? Still, they had faith Andre would pull out of whatever Lanassa was doing to him. They would forever be by their friend's side.

Sharon was waiting patiently for the phone call that Craig had promised her. She wanted to get up and drive straight over to Dr. Brass' mansion. But Sharon didn't know what kind of welcome she would receive. As she waited, all kinds of thoughts ran through her mind. The waiting alone was getting to her. Sharon felt like pouring herself a drink.

Instead, she concentrated on the positive and hoped it would all work out for the brothers and Dr. Brass in the end. Everything about the present situation was so unreal to her. She didn't know what to do and the waiting wasn't helping. She wanted to be in Craig's arms; she wanted to see Craig's face and breathe in his scent. She wanted to provide him with as much support as she could. She didn't have the facts, and the lack of knowledge was making her anxious. What she'd read in the newspapers wasn't good. At least, they finally stopped printing the untrue stories. Sharon also wondered how this would affect Dr. Brass' career.

Blue sat up and looked at Bryan as if it was time to go. He wobbled out of the study and stood at the bottom of the stairs. Craig and Bryan followed him and noticed Blue looked at them, as if to say, "*We need to get up to Dr. Brass' room, now.*" The strange thing was that Bryan understood the dog and what he wanted. He picked Blue up in his arms and carried him up the stairs, with Craig not far behind. Then Bryan placed Blue on the floor.

They reached the room and saw Anna bending over Andre. Both brothers stood in the doorway, trying to figure out what Anna was doing. Blue looked up at them, then wobbled into the room. He turned his head back at the brothers with a look that said, "*Are you both just going to stand there?*"

Bryan entered the room and Craig followed not far from his side. Anna's ear was close to Andre's mouth. She saw them entering the room and put up her finger, stopping them in their tracks. Anna said to Dr. Brass, "Speak to me. I know you are trying to tell me something. I'm here; please talk to me, Dr. Brass."

They all heard Andre mumbling something. He was trying to speak. Their hearts beat faster. After waiting for what seemed like hours for Andre to speak, nothing else escaped Andre's lips. The brothers didn't know what to think. Anna shook her head, and Blue barked softly.

Then Andre moved his head toward the sound of the bark. Did they imagine the movement because they wanted to believe Andre moved?

Blue wobbled over to his dog bed and lay down, looking up at Andre's bed. Andre had moved. Bryan, Craig, and Anna knew it wasn't their imagination. He didn't only move, but he also spoke. It was only a whisper, but Andre did make a sound. Then there was silence, without movement. But it left them all with hope.

Bryan approached Anna and asked, "What did he say?"

She turned to Bryan. "I think he was trying to say Lanassa."

Bryan and Craig became instantly rigid. Anna had a look of hope, even though Dr. Brass' first word was Lanassa's name.

Bryan gazed at Craig and asked, "Do you think her spirit is here?"

"I hope like hell that restless evil soul isn't here." Craig replied.

Anna heard their exchange of words, then became nervous. Bryan placed his hand on Anna's back to calm her. He knew it wasn't fear that caused the nervousness. It was her concern, the concern they all shared. Bryan noticed Blue had the same look of concern across his face. Not knowing if Lanassa was present made everyone unease. *Will this uncertainty ever end?* Bryan wondered.

They hoped time would be on their side, but the future was still uncertain. Then Blue barked again. They all looked at him with puzzlement. Had the dog sensed something that they couldn't comprehend? He must have. Earlier, he'd wobbled to the bottom of the stairs, just when Andre was showing signs of activity.

Anna decided it was time to wash Dr. Brass and asked the brothers for some privacy. She wanted to clear her mind of the name Dr. Brass had mentioned: Lanassa. She never would have imagined Dr. Brass trying to speak Lanassa's name. Anna knew she was becoming jealous of the dead woman, now that Dr. Brass had spoken her name. *Why?* Anna wondered. She hadn't known Lanassa during her life. Anna knew she must keep her emotions under control. Her feelings for the doctor were growing strong. No man had ever affected her in such a way. He was sick and being taking over by a dead lover. She didn't doubt the spirit was haunting him, trying to possess his soul.

One thing was certain: Anna was a professional. She wasn't being paid for her emotional attachment to Dr. Brass but for her professional experience as his nurse. Anna had to keep that in mind if she wanted to help him survive this ordeal. And she wanted that more than anything. She looked down at Blue and he smiled. *I thank God for you. You're keeping me strong.* She patted his head and gave him a kiss, then Anna went into the bathroom to prepare herself to give Dr. Brass his bed bath.

The brothers sat in the downstairs study, still in a state of shock. Was Andre calling out to Lanassa? They hoped, for all of their sakes, this wasn't the case. If he was indeed calling her, was he trying to connect with her spirit? That would only create the kind of turmoil no one was ready to accept or deal with, Lanassa's spirit. Her presence in the mansion wouldn't bring comfort to Andre, nor to the people who loved him.

Her spirit was reaching out from the dead, trying to take life from Andre, placing him in danger. No one knew how to stop her. They couldn't blame Andre if he was trying to bring Lanassa to him—he was sick.

"What do you think is happening?" Craig asked.

Bryan had no answers. "I have no idea. We brought him here for protection. But what if he loves her so much that his soul is willing to accept her dead spirit with open arms? How can we protect him from her in death when we failed miserably during her life on earth?"

They hadn't given up on Anna's being able to bring Andre back to life. But was her presence strong enough to do the deed? However, it was something about her dog, Blue, that Bryan couldn't figure out. He only knew he welcomed the dog's presence.

Craig looked across the room as he leaned against the fireplace. He seemed lost in thought as he tried hard to come up with the answers they needed. It was hard to reach any kind of conclusion. Maybe they should call in a priest, someone who could bless the mansion and throw holy water all over the place. He wanted to get Bryan's opinion on the matter, but held it to himself. Why freak out his brother, the same as he was beginning to be freak out. Bryan was handling the situation far better than him. And Craig wanted to keep it that way without bringing up priest and holy water during this time.

Craig had to get out and get some air. Could he leave Bryan and Anna alone, in case something happen?

Bryan observed Craig expressions and said, "Craig there is nothing you can do here. Go and get some rest. We'll be all right. If anything occurs, I'll call you."

"Are you sure?"

Bryan smiled slightly and said, "Yes, I'm very sure. Now go and get some rest, please."

Craig gave his brother a hug, then they said their good-byes. Craig promised he'd give his brother a call later.

Craig reached his Audi and sat in the car for a few minutes. He was thankful that Brenda drove his car to the mansion and took a ride back to Boston with Debra and Bill. He had to regroup. He had to relax his mind and his body. The tension and pain from the stress were gaining control over him. The thought of Lanassa's spirit was invading his mind. Was her spirit in the mansion? Craig flipped opened his cell phone and called Sharon. She again answered on the first ring.

"Hello, Sharon."

"Hello, Craig. You have no idea how relieved I am to hear your voice."

At that precise moment, Craig knew where he was headed—directly over to see the woman he missed, who could provide him with the comfort he needed. "Sharon, I apologize for the late call. I was meaning to give you a call earlier. Things didn't work out the way I've planned. Would it be all right if I dropped by to visit with you?"

Sharon didn't hesitate. "Please do. I can't wait to see you, Craig. Your visit would be good for the both of us."

Chapter 26

When Craig rang the doorbell at Sharon's house, she was there to greet him in a matter of minutes. She was wearing one sexy outfit. Craig couldn't take his eyes off her. Sharon was like a dream to him after enduring such a nightmare. He embraced her gently around her delicate waist. Sharon kissed him and Craig accepted the kiss with desperation. There was much he had to explain about Andre's condition, but for now, all he wanted to do was be with her, if only for a little while. Sharon took him straight up to her bedroom. She saw the stress in his eyes and felt the tension in his body. She knew just what he needed and was more than willing to apply her professional touches to give him relief. In her bedroom, Craig tried to relax in an armchair.

She went to her attached bathroom and started a shower for him, then came back and asked Craig to stand. Sharon removed his clothes, leaving Craig nude in front of her. Then she took him by the hand and led him to the shower. While Craig was in the shower, Sharon prepared her massaging oils. She was on a mission to rid the man she loved from all of his tension. Hopefully, her techniques would reach his mind. Craig was in the shower for some time. He tried his best to relax. It would take far more than a shower to accomplish such a feat. When Craig finished he left the bathroom with a towel wrapped around his waist. He exposed nothing but pure muscles. She loved his body; he was so physically fit. Sharon led him to the massage bed that she'd set up while he was in the shower and asked him to lie on it. Craig lay on his stomach on the comfortable mat. Sharon removed the towel from around his waist with his assistance.

She got up on the massage bed and straddled him. She placed her thighs on each side of his hips, touching his butt with her soft pearly gem. Soft jazz music was playing in the background. The sound added more comfort for Craig. She was enjoying herself just as much as he was. Sharon poured warm oil into her hands that she took from the container by the side of the massage bed. She began to rub it smoothly in her hands and started administering the oil over his shoulders. Then she rubbed the oil over his upper and lower back. Sharon applied just as much pressure as was needed to give him relief from all of the tension she felt in his body. Craig started to moan. Sharon had a way of using her hands, and he knew that before it was over he would feel like a new man. She rubbed over his strong arms, up his shoulders again, and applied pressure down his spine. Sharon moved down and started rubbing his thighs, his calves, and his feet. She got off of the massage bed and rubbed that nice butt of his, over and over again, while she stood by him. Craig went to heaven, he thought.

It took her thirty minutes to complete the magic. Then she asked him to turn over on to his back. She then repeated the process, leaving his erected muscle for last. She felt the liquid from the tip of his penis on her fingertips. Sharon eyes got big as she watched his erected muscle turned hard as steel. Craig wanted her. He didn't know if he could give her what she wanted; he was so tired. But after she placed her warm mouth over his penis, Craig's body came to life. Sharon sucked him with so much passion it took him over the edge. Craig didn't want this to be one-sided. He wanted to return the favor, and he needed to for his own sanity. He gently pulled her head from his penis, then sat up. Craig gave Sharon a kiss that was so heated with so much appreciation and passion, it overwhelmed her. She rocked back from him, but Craig caught her around the waist and continued with the kiss. It was deep and warm and all so tasty. By sucking her tongue it brought him life. Craig left the massage bed and picked Sharon up into his arms and carried her to the bed. He didn't break the kiss along the way. He placed her on the bed and continued with the assault of taking her tongue into his greedy mouth.

Sharon wrapped her legs around Craig's waist and allowed him to feel the warmth of her hand rubbing up and down his shoulders. He couldn't take much more and began to remove the sexy lace garment from her soft brown skin, exposing her completely to him. She assisted him by moving her hips off the bed. She allowed him to pull the garment down her long legs. Craig threw the sexy garment to the floor.

At that time the kiss was broken and she moaned for more. Craig gave her more by moving down her body and placing his mouth over her hot spot. He spread her heavenly lips apart, then placed his warm mouth over her clitoris. He licked and sucked the sweet juices from her body. Sharon grabbed the sheets in her hands as if she couldn't take much more.

He was driving her to the breaking point. But Craig kept at it; the taste of her was so sweet on his tongue he couldn't stop. Sharon started to beg for Craig to enter her with a scream of pleasure. He climbed up her body and placed her legs over his shoulders, and with one smooth push he entered her hot core. Craig took her mouth greedily, at the same time filling her up with his jewel. They made love to each other with abandon, both in need of each other's passion; it seemed as if the world was rocking. Then they climaxed together. Craig rolled off of Sharon and moved her close to his hard body. He placed a kiss on the top of her soft hair. The only thoughts Sharon had were how happy she was to be back in the arms of the man she loved. Craig was thinking how happy he was to have her there with him, wrapped up in each other's body warmth. Sleep was welcome, and it came upon them within minutes.

After Anna finished giving Dr. Brass' his bed bath, she made sure he was comfortable wrapped in the soft blankets. She then picked up Blue and walked down the stairs. Anna tried hard not to think about how beautiful his body was, even though he had lost so much weight. Once she reached the bottom of the stairs, Anna heard voices coming from the kitchen. She placed Blue down on his wobbly legs and he followed her in the direction of the voices. In the kitchen she found Bryan speaking with Tina, the house cook, whom he introduced to Anna. Tina thought Blue was so cute, she went over to the kitchen counter and picked up a piece of boiled chicken breast and gave it to Blue.She turned to Anna and said, "Bryan told me boiled chicken breast is one of his favorites. May I get you something to eat?"

Anna replied, "No, thank you, I'm fine." She didn't have an appetite.

"Anna, you must eat something," Bryan insisted.

Anna decided on cheese and crackers with a glass of milk. Tina placed cheese and crackers on a tray and placed it in front of Anna and Bryan. Bryan pulled out a chair for Anna, then decided to join her with the appetizer. Tina chopped up more chicken breast for Blue and placed the meat in his bowl on a mat, then she excused herself.

"Thank you, Tina," Bryan said.

Blue lay on the floor after he ate his meal, sleeping by Anna's chair. After finishing the cheese and crackers, Bryan asked Anna if she wanted to take a little walk outside. They cleaned up their dishes, then Bryan called to Blue. "Come on, boy. I have a feeling you might want to take care of some business."

Fresh air greeted them as they walked out the kitchen door. Blue wobbled over to the spot his used earlier, and Bryan and Anna walked slowly together, giving Blue time to catch up with them after he finished.

Bryan had to ask; he'd held it in far too long. "What do you think Andre was trying to say? Do you really believe he mentioned her name?"

Anna looked at him; her expression was grave. "I'm afraid to say … but he did say her name." Silence was all that followed. They both patted Blue on the head and headed back inside the mansion.

Once inside, Bryan gathered Blue in his arms, and he and Anna both went straight into Andre's room. They couldn't believe what they saw—Andre was sitting up and moving his head. Anna went to him immediately. She held his hand in hers then asked, "What is it, Dr. Brass? I'm your nurse. What is it that you need?"

"*Lanassa.*"

Bryan was taken back. "What the hell…?"

Dr. Andre C. Brass was searching for her. He hadn't felt her presence in some time. Where was she? Had she given up on him?

Bryan approached Andre's bed. He knew Andre couldn't possibly be inviting Lanassa's spirit into his home—or was he? Bryan couldn't speak. This wasn't good.

"Please, Dr. Brass," Anna said softly, "don't speak her name."

Bryan felt stupid for not having said the same thing to his friend. They didn't want that spirit anywhere near the mansion—or in Cambridge, for that fact.

Then Andre said, "Nurse." He turned his head in her direction.

Anna did something that was so out of character for her. She placed a kiss on Dr. Brass' hand and told him everything would be all right. She helped Andre back on his pillows and covered him with the blankets. Within seconds, he felt asleep.

"What the hell was that all about?" Bryan asked.

Anna thought he was referring to the kiss. "I don't know," Anna said. "I couldn't help myself. I've never done that before with any of my patients."

Bryan smiled at her. "No, I didn't mean your kiss. I thought that was a kind gesture. It's the name I'm referring to. Why would Andre be calling for Lanassa?"

Neither of them had the answer. But the kiss to his hand had calmed Andre down.

They both wondered if Lanassa was in the room, but there wasn't a chill in the air. Bryan told Anna they'd speak more about what had occurred with Andre in the morning. But for now, they needed to get some sleep. Bryan gave Anna a gentle rub on her arm, then bent down and rubbed Blue behind his ears. Were the dog's actions trying to tell them something? Blue did wobbled to Andre's bed once he entered the room and looked up at the doctor with concern in his eyes.

Bryan went to his living quarters to take a long shower. He didn't know if he could take it much longer. He wanted to call Craig, but it was so late. Instead, after his shower, Bryan slipped under the sheets and fell asleep.

Anna took a long bath but wasn't able to sleep, although it was two in the morning. She picked up Blue and went downstairs, gliding around the living quarters of the mansion. Then she saw the beautiful black baby grand piano. Anna couldn't help herself; she placed Blue on the floor and ran her hands over the instrument. A compulsive act made her sit at the bench, placing her fingers over the keys. She began to play a smooth jazz melody from the music sheet on the piano. Bryan was too deep in sleep to hear the smooth tune coming from the piano, but someone did. It was Andre.

It was one of his favorite musical tunes. The one he created. Andre had to find out who was playing the piano like it was meant for his ears alone. Andre sat up and pulled the patches from his eyes. He only saw a blur of objects in front of him. Andre removed the IV needle from his arm but was too weak to pull down the bed rail. He felt trapped in the bed. He slowly began to move to the end of the bed. He stumbled out of the bed on trembling, weak legs. It felt as if he hadn't walked in weeks. Andre walked toward the door slowly, moving his hands over the walls for support. He made it to the door and out to the hall, then reached the banister and grabbed hold of it. Andre began to walk very slowly and unsteadily toward the music. He finally made it to the bottom of the stairs, still moving his hands across the wall for support. He was compelled to follow the sound of the music.

He made it to the living room, where the music was coming from his baby grand piano. Whoever was playing the music was bringing magic from the keys. She created soft smooth jazz, the kind he loved to hear and write. Andre knew it was a woman; he could smell her sweet scent.

Blue got up and barked, and Andre wondered if he'd heard a dog. He didn't own a dog. Then the music stopped. Anna looked over and saw Dr. Brass in his silk pajamas. She stayed there in shock, while Andre followed the funny barking noise. He reached the piano and placed his hand on it for support. The only thing he felt was a tail hitting him gently on the bottom of his pajamas pants. He was about to fall, and Anna rushed to him, gently holding him around his waist.

"Please, keep playing," Andre croaked.

Anna managed to get Andre seated on the bench, then she sat beside him. All he could smell was roses.

Anna didn't know what to do, so she started playing the piano again. Andre closed his eyes, loving the sound coming from the piano and loving the smell of the woman who was playing it with perfection. Anna's hands were steady as she kept playing for him. Blue lay back down against Andre's bare feet. Anna didn't speak a word. She kept playing the piano, feeling the man's body heat as he sat by her side. Andre relaxed his shoulder against hers.

"Tell me your name," Andre said in a raspy voice.

Anna really didn't know what to do; this was out of her line of profession, being so close to Andre and feeling the warmth coming from his body. He didn't feel like her patient. He felt like a pure sexy male to her. She was his care provider, but she felt so much more. Anna wanted Andre to feel relaxed. She moved her head in the direction of his raspy voice and witnessed such a handsome, frail face; it took her breath away. "My name is Anna. I'm your nurse." Anna saw a smile spread across his face and her heart started to do a double take.

Andre said to her, "You play heavenly and smell of roses."

"Thank you." Anna said, with a soft blush that warmed her cheeks.

Andre remembered the sound of her sweet voice, the voice that read to him, the voice that was in his head and kept him strong.

After the music piece was completed, Anna told Dr. Brass politely, "It's time I take you back upstairs. You need to rest; its pretty late, Dr. Brass."

He gazed in the direction of her voice, then replied, "Please, call me Andre. I would love to hear my first name coming from your lips."

Anna's hands began to shake. She didn't expect for him to say those words to her. She didn't know how to respond. His request caught her off guard. Anna kept the woman at bay and tried her best to be the professional nurse. She thought to herself that using his first name would make it personal. She never called a patient by his first name. Then again, Anna never had felt a personal bond with any of her patients, until Andre. She cleared her throat and replied, "Okay, it's time I take you upstairs, Andre."

He smiled.

Anna told Blue to stay, then placed her arms gently around Andre's waist and assisted him back up the stairs. Once they reached his room, she wondered if she should get him settled back into the hospital bed or take him to his king-size bed instead. Andre made it easy for her. "If it isn't a problem I'll like to go to my bed and lie down."

The dilemma was over. She helped him in his bed. Andre helped Anna as much as he could. He could tell she was a delicate woman. Anna almost fell on top of Andre when he was in the bed.

Although he was frail, he was still very tall much taller than she. It was unavoidable not to misstep her position while centering Andre in the middle of the bed. *I must call Dr. Baines at once*, she though.

"Thank you," Andre said in a raspy voice.

"I'll be right back," Anna told him. She went into the bathroom for a glass of water and then returned to him, "I brought you some water to drink."

Andre nodded his head. He was so thirsty. Anna assisted him by climbing into the bed with him and holding his lips to the glass of water. Andre drank the water slowly as Anna watched. He was such a sexy man; watching him drink water brought unprofessional thoughts to her mind.

After Andre had enough of the water, Anna help placed his head back on the big fluffy pillows. Andre closed his eyes and was sleeping before she got off the bed. She placed the glass on the end table, then covered him with the blankets. Anna sat on the edge of the bed and stared at him. Andre was beautiful.

Anna left the bed to go downstairs to retrieve Blue, but before Anna was completely out of Andre's room, she felt a cold chill up her spine. She turned to look back in the room. Had the drapes in his bedroom moved, or did she imagine it? Anna tried to ignore what she felt and what she thought she saw. Anna wanted nothing more than to believe she didn't feel Lanassa's presence in Andre's bedroom. She shook her head and went downstairs. Blue was waiting for her at the bottom of the stairs. Anna gave Blue a big hug. She needed his comfort. They headed up the stairs. When they reached the top of the stairs, she placed Blue on the floor. He wobbled into Andre's bedroom and gave her a look that seemed to indicate that he wanted Anna to move his bed closer to Andre's. Anna moved the fluffy dog bed next to Andre's bed, and Blue lay down in it. *How strange*, Anna thought. She patted him on the head and said good night, then left her dog with the man she was falling in love with. That was one question Anna knew the answer to. She was indeed falling in love with Andre.

Back in her room, Anna took off her clothes and put on a long T-shirt and got into bed. She reached for her cell phone and placed a call to Dr. Baines. She got his answering service and left a message, informing the doctor he must pay a visit to examine Dr. Brass at his earliest convenience. Then she lay down and was asleep in no time.

Andre, what are you allowing that woman to do to you? She is keeping us apart. Please fight for me. Please fight to be with me. I'm here waiting for you. Don't you love me? If you love me, it's time for you to prove it. Come to me and be happy beyond your wildest dreams.

Andre could hear the voice in his ear. She'd returned but something was different. The voice was far away, and all he could hear was the piano playing the heavenly music, along with the sweet voice in his head. For the first time in weeks, he slept uninterrupted. He saw Anna's face. Although it was a blur, he knew she was warm and caring and so beautiful. Andre dreamed about her and the music she played for him. He felt peaceful, the kind of peace that made him wanted to live again.

Chapter 27

It was a lovely morning, and Bryan went upstairs to check on Andre. He was taken back by what he saw. Andre was sleeping peacefully in his bed. And Blue slept next to him in his fluffy dog bed. *What happened last night?* Bryan wondered. Then Blue woke up and wobbled past him into Anna's bedroom. Bryan followed him. Anna was thrashing in her bed, as if she was having some kind of nightmare. She sat up and screamed. Blue rushed over to her and tried his best to jump into the bed. Bryan rushed to Anna, while picking Blue up and placing him in the bed. Blue started licking Anna's face, then Bryan noticed he was licking away her tears.

Anna was shaking from fear.

"Anna, what's wrong?" he asked her.

She couldn't speak. Bryan held her close, trying to soothe her, but she grabbed Blue for comfort and looked up at Bryan. "She is here, in this mansion."

Bryan didn't have to ask Anna who she was referring to. Anna kept crying while in Bryan's arms and holding onto Blue. "I knew I felt a chill last night and saw those drapes move in Andre's room. I didn't want to believe it at the time, but Lanassa is here in the mansion."

It was the first time Bryan had heard Anna speak Andre's first name. Bryan was sure he'd missed something last night but wouldn't pressure her for answers. Bryan tried to help Anna pull herself together, but it was Blue who was having an effect on her. She cried into her dog's body as if he was a pillow. All Bryan could do was rubbed her back and tell her it would be all right. They were only soothing words—he really didn't know what was going to happen next if Lanassa's spirit was in the mansion.

The doorbell rang, and shortly afterward, Dr. Baines entered the room—he'd heard all of the commotion. Blue looked up at Bryan to let him know it was time for him to be placed off the bed. It was time for Dr. Baines to take over. Bryan took Blue out of Anna's arms and placed him on the rug on the floor. Dr. Baines asked Anna what had happened and she told him and Bryan the whole story at least part of it.

They didn't want to believe it but they knew she was telling the truth. Lanassa's spirit had finally come back for Andre.

"Are you all right, Nurse Jordan?" Dr. Baines asked, and she nodded her head, letting him know she would be fine. "I can administer you a sedative to calm you."

"No, doctor that won't be necessary." Anna brought Blue up on the bed with her again. Then she suggested that both men should check on Andre.

When Bryan and Dr. Baines reached Andre's room, he was talking in his sleep. This time, the only name that came from his lips was Anna's. Dr. Baines was surprised to see him sleeping in his own bed. Bryan asked the doctor whether or not they should wake Andre.

"Yes, I have to examine him. Do you know how he got from the hospital bed to his bed?"

"I have no idea." Bryan was trying to answer that question for himself. Something besides the spirit of Lanassa had transpired between Andre and Anna, and he couldn't wait to find out what.

Dr. Baines reached Dr. Brass' bed and placed his medical bag on the bedside table. He viewed Dr. Brass for a short while noticing his breathing seemed to be normal. He placed his hand on Dr. Brass' wrist to check his pulse. Then Andre woke up. His eyes moved rapidly. And his eyelids were blinking fast he was trying to focus his vision.

"Good morning, Dr. Brass."

Andre turned his head in Dr. Baines' direction. He'd know that voice anywhere. "Good morning." He didn't say more, but he was wondering about Anna. He wanted to know more about her. It was as if the past few weeks hadn't happened. He was focused on the present and couldn't remember anything else. Andre started to sit up with Bryan's assistance, then Bryan gave his dear friend a hug. Andre was confused by Bryan's actions, but he hugged his friend back. Andre felt as if he was missing something.

Dr. Baines reached into his medical bag and pulled out his stethoscope, saying he needed to examine him. Andre knew he had been in a hospital but couldn't remember how he got home. He couldn't remember how he ended up in a hospital in the first place. There were pieces missing from his life in such a short period of time. *Do I want to remember?* He wondered.

He did want to remember, but not at the present time. Andre was feeling rather good mentally and physically. Bryan got out of Dr. Baines' way, giving him room to start his examination. The doctor took Andre's temperature, his heart rate, and then he viewed his eyes. Everything was normal. He asked Andre, "How do you feel, Dr. Brass?"

"I feel great, other than I'm starving."

"We'll place you on a very light diet for a week." Then Dr. Baines had to ask, "Do you remember anything that happened to you?"

"No, I can't say that I do."

Dr. Baines and Bryan looked at each other with concern. They weren't about to push him for answers. Besides, if Lanassa's spirit was in the mansion, those answers would surface soon.

Craig woke up in Sharon's arms. He hadn't meant to sleep so late. He had so many things to do. The first thing Craig had to do—even before going home to change clothes and go to his office—was to check on Andre. Craig didn't have time to explain everything to Sharon, but Craig knew he had to give her at least a short explanation before he left. He bent down and gave her a kiss on her smooth brown cheek. Sharon opened her eyes, with a smile spreading wide across her face.

"Good morning," Sharon said to the man she'd spent an incredible night with; the man she was in love with.

Craig gazed into Sharon eyes. "Good morning to you, too." Then he tapped her nose with his finger.

She smiled again. "Care to share a shower?" Craig said with a smile.

He thought he could take the shower with her and update her on Andre's situation at the same time. He got out of the bed. And she held his hand, following him into the bathroom. He moved back the glass shower door and set the temperature of the water just right. Craig allowed Sharon to enter first. As they washed each other, he began to tell her the whole story surrounding Andre. It was the news that hadn't been reported; the news that the reporters knew nothing about—unless that sleazy Ted Pearson decided to break all rules and open his mouth up to the press.

Could it be true? Sharon wondered. *The spirit of Lanassa was haunting Dr. Brass?* Everything she was hearing sounded as if it were written for a horror movie. But it was obvious that Craig was serious and determined to help Dr. Brass with something no one knew how to deal with or how to handle.

As they both were drying off after the shower, Craig noticed tears in Sharon's eyes. He pulled her body into his strong arms, trying to calm her, letting her know it would be all right. Sharon didn't move. She felt protected and that was exactly what she needed to feel—his protection from the unknown. She didn't believe in such things. But the small scar on his head and the serious expression on his face told her that what he'd just shared with her was true.

Craig broke the embrace gently and asked Sharon, "Are you all right?"

She wasn't all right. But she knew it wasn't about her at this time. "I'll be fine; you just take care of yourself and Dr. Brass."

Craig kissed her softly on her lips. They both made their way into Sharon's bedroom and got dressed. She walked him to the front door and told him to give her a call when possible. She wouldn't pressure him and would give him as much space as he needed. Sharon wanted to tell Craig how much she loved him but refrained from doing so. Now wasn't the time. He kissed her again and promised to give her a call later.

As he got in his Audi, Craig thought about how he felt about Sharon. She was good for him, but was he good for her? He didn't have time to think more about it now. He flipped open his cell phone to place a call to Bryan.

Andre walked into Anna's room, but she wasn't there. Then Dr. Brass walked downstairs, with Bryan's assistance because he still was weak. They found Anna in the living room, sitting on the piano bench. Blue was lying at her side. Bryan's phone started to ring from his pants pocket but he ignored the call. Instead, he watched Andre as he approached Anna. She looked up at him, barely smiling. Andre stopped and looked at Blue and began to rub his ears, while Andre was rubbing Blue's ears, Bryan told Anna.

"I want you to get some rest today. Andre is doing well, but there is something I must speak with you about. He doesn't remember what took place in New Orleans. I advised you to allow him to take it slowly. I believe it's best to keep it to ourselves for the time being, concerning Lanassa's spirit."

Anna nodded her head in agreement. If he didn't know what happened to him, she was sure the information would sound crazy to him. That was the last thing Anna wanted for Andre to think of her—that she was out of her mind.

Bryan left the living room, checked his phone, and returned Craig's call. He explained to Craig the new turn of events. Craig advised Bryan that he was on his way. He needed to get to the mansion right away. *What could possibility happen next?* Craig wondered. The news that Andre was alert and doing better was a plus, but Lanassa's spirit in the mansion was a full-blown negative. Was Anna sure about what she felt and what she saw? There wasn't any doubt in his mind that Anna knew Lanassa's presence was there, trying to bring Andre back under her control. What could they do to drive that demon bitch back to wherever she was trying to dig herself out from? They couldn't allow Andre to come this far, only to fall back into her abyss.

Craig made his way to the mansion in record time. Bryan was waiting for him. Craig greeted his brother and asked, "Where is Andre."

"He's upstairs, eating soup and a sandwich. The doctor placed him on a light diet that doesn't have to be all liquids. Tina took him a plate of food up to his room earlier."

"Where is Anna?"

"She's in the living room at the piano. She has been there for over an hour. I think the whole ordeal is starting to get to her."

They both went into the living room to speak with her. Anna had a worried look across her lovely face. Would she be strong enough to handle the ordeal?

"Hello, Anna," Craig said while approaching her.

She turned and faced him with a half-smile. "Hello, Mr. Brown."

"Please, call me Craig; we're all informal here."

"Yes, of course." She gazed straight ahead, the same way that Andre had in the hospital.

Blue barked, and Anna looked down at him; a smile appeared on her face. Blue brought her back into the present time. Whatever she was staring at it didn't last once Blue started to bark. Craig bent over the dog and rubbed him behind his ears.

"Thanks, boy. You are such a good dog."

Blue wobbled to the bottom of the stairs.

Here we go again, Bryan thought. He picked up Blue and went upstairs to Andre's room. Craig reached out his hand for Anna to join them. At first, she hesitated, then she took his hand and they both walked up the stairs behind Bryan and Blue.

They reached Andre's room. He had just finished his meal and was waiting for something. He saw Anna, and the smile on his face was priceless. "There you are. I was beginning to think you had left. Dr. Baines told me you are my live-in nurse. Craig, Bryan, how are you two doing?"

They didn't know how to respond. Andre was acting as if nothing had happened to him.

It's true, Craig thought, *he doesn't remember a thing.*

The brothers knew to take his lead and not ask any questions. "We're doing fine," Craig said.

"Bryan, your dog is attentive, I see."

Bryan looked down at Blue, who was still in his arms, and smiled. Then he placed Blue on the rug.

"Blue is my loyal dog," said Anna. "I hope you don't mine that he'll be staying here with me."

Andre looked at the dog with much appreciation and at his owner with even more. "I don't mine at all. Please forgive me, but is something wrong with him?"

Anna smiled. "Yes, he has cerebellar hypoplasia." Blue wobbled to his bed beside Andre's and sat up looking up at Andre's face.

"I believe he is smiling at me."

Anna was feeling much better. "He likes you."

"Good. I love dogs." Then Andre looked into Anna's eyes. He could see her clearly, there was no blur. "I have a favor to ask of you. Would you mine playing the piano again for me today?"

Anna was surprised to hear the request. She didn't tell anyone that

Lanassa had come to her in a nightmare last night. The spirit told Anna that Andre wouldn't remember her and would be coming with Lanassa very soon. *So pack up and leave. You aren't wanted or needed.* Why Anna kept that part to herself, she had no idea. But Andre remembered last night and it made her gleam. She could fight against the spirit, only if she knew Andre would be there fighting alongside her.

Then Andre asked, "Did Dr. Baines leave a cane? My legs, I must admit, are still a little weak?"

"Yes, he did. I'll go and get it for you," Anna said.

Bryan stopped Anna in her tracks. "I'll go and get it. You stay here with Andre." He didn't want her to leave Andre's side.

Bryan left, and Craig said. "I think you should get dressed Andre and take a walk with Anna and Blue around the grounds."

"I would like that. But first I would like to take a bath. I'm afraid my legs aren't steadied for a shower. I'm sure I'll only fall in the tub."

Craig started to laugh, and Andre joined in, along with Blue, who was barking. Andre was feeling more than better—his humor was surfacing.

Anna became nervous. She would be the one to assist Andre out of his clothes and into the tub. It didn't bother her when he was in a state of unconsciousness while she gave him bed baths. But now that he had all of his faculties together it was a different matter. *You're his nurse; stay professional.* With that thought, Anna said, "I'll go and run you a nice warm bath."

"Thank you, Anna. May I call you Anna?" Anna liked hearing her name coming from his lips, the same way he told her he liked for her to call him Andre.

"Yes, you may." Anna smiled at Andre then went to start his bath.

Craig picked up Blue. "I think it's time for you to eat something, boy, how about some kibbles and boiled chicken breast?"

Andre laughed. "I never thought I'd see the day you'd be watching over a dog."

"I know, but Blue isn't just an ordinary dog—believe me. Aside from his handicap, there is more to him than eyes can see."

Andre knew it was true. He was becoming attached to the dog as well, along with his owner.

Craig told Andre he would visit with him later, once he was finished for the day at the law firm. Then he took Blue and went downstairs.

Anna was in the bathroom and had just placed her hand on the faucet when she felt something grab her wrist. She turned, and no one was there, other than the cold sensation around her wrist. Anna spoke, "You will not intimidate me, nor will you take Andre from me and his friends! Go back, Lanassa, where you belong!" With that, the cold chill left the bathroom. Anna continued to draw Andre's bathwater. Anna wasn't afraid of Lanassa's spirit. She remembered what her mother had said to her before she left. Dr. Brass must allow the spirit to enter his body. If the love isn't felt, Lanassa will leave. But if he still loves this woman, the spirit will possess him. But how could he do that when he didn't remember what had happened to him in New Orleans? Was he still in love with Lanassa? Anna couldn't ask him about his feelings for the woman. If he felt that love in his heart, it would be the end of him—and possibly the end of her soul as well. She was falling for him and falling hard. Anna's heart became saddened. How could she replace that kind of love Andre felt for Lanassa? She knew Andre loved Lanassa unconditionally. He'd accepted the good and the very bad of Lanassa's existence in life; he probably was still in love with her after her death.

Andre felt a chill in the room, then it passed. He hoped he wasn't coming down with a cold. He couldn't wait until he was submerged under the warm bath water that was waiting for him, thanks to Anna. Anna came out of the bathroom. She tried to hide the knowledge of what had just happened. "Are you ready to take your bath, Dr. Brass?"

"I remembered I asked you Anna, to please call me Andre."

"Okay, Andre. Are you ready for your bath?"

They smiled at each other.

"I'm more than ready," he said.

Anna walked with Andre to the bathroom, holding him with less effort than she had the night before.

Anna assisted Andre out of his pajamas and observed his nude body with amazement. He displayed no shyness whatsoever. He was beautiful. Anna's heart started to beat rapidly. She didn't feel like his nurse. She felt more intimately involved with him. She wasn't about to fight against the feelings he brought out of her. Anna always knew he would become more than just her patient. Now her reality of fighting it was gone. Anna wanted him in her life; the feelings were growing deeper and she didn't want them to halt.

Andre got into the warm bath with Anna's help. He submerged his head under the water and came back up, smiling at her. On impulse, Anna dropped to her knees on the bathroom rug and put shampoo into her hands. She began to wash his hair. She rubbed over his hair slowly and massaged his scalp. His soapy curls felt so good in her hands, straight to her fingertips.

Anna asked Andre to lay his head back on the bath pillow. She pulled the shower hose down and began to rinse the shampoo from his hair. Andre felt so good—he hadn't felt like this—or felt cared for like this—by any woman in his entire life. He sat up and took her hand in his, folding their fingers together. Andre just held her hand with their entwined fingers. He didn't want to let go. She didn't want him to let go.

"Do you need me to assist you with your bath?" Anna was hoping the answer would be yes, and it was. Andre released her hand, and she took the washcloth and poured bath wash into it. The smell of spring surrounded the bathroom. With her help, Andre stood up, and Anna began to wash his entire body from head to toe. She loved every part she touched, even his erect penis, which was huge. Anna wasn't shy. She felt as if this man belonged to her, as if she'd done this for him a thousand times.

Once Anna finished bathing Andre, she assisted him out of the tub and dried him off. She wrapped a towel around his waist. They walked back into his bedroom, and Andre took a white polo shirt and black dress pants from his closet, then got underwear from his dresser. All the while, Anna observed how the bath towel hung over his lean waist. Her love for this man was growing deeper. How had her love for him developed with such a force? She'd never been in love before and had never had an intimate relationship with any man. But she wanted to become close—very close—with Andre. He got dressed while she continued to watch his every move.

"I think you are in need of dry clothes," Andre said.

She looked at her clothes and laughed a hearty laugh. "I believe you are right. I'll be back; it will take no more than a minute. Will you be all right?"

"I'll be fine." The smile he gave her was so sweet and sexy.

Andre walked slowly back into the bathroom to brush his teeth. When he returned to his room, Anna was there waiting for him. Andre walked slowly over to her. He pulled Anna gently out of the chair and embraced her. He placed a kiss to her lips and said, "Thank you."

Anna felt the heat from the soft kiss. "You are more than welcome."

He kissed her again, this time with tongue, warm lips, and mouth. Anna never had been kissed this way before. She felt as if she was about to faint.

Andre felt as if he died and gone to heaven. They stood there, gazing into each other's eyes with feelings of trust and passion. It was something very new for Andre. His heart had never beaten so hard and so loudly.

They then heard Blue barking frantically at the bottom of the stairs. And that's when they felt the cold chill enter the room. Anna knew what was taking place, but Andre looked confused.

Downstairs, Bryan grabbed Blue and ran up to Andre's room. It was extremely cold in the room.

Anna yelled, "Go away!" The cold air remained, even though there was so much anger in Anna's voice.

Andre thought she was yelling at Bryan. "What is going on?" Andre asked.

Bryan and Anna just stared at each other. It wasn't good. Without Andre knowing what was happening, it wasn't going to look good anytime soon.

Then Andre started shaking all over. Blue went to Andre's bed, as if to say, "*Someone please get him in the bed before he falls.*" Bryan helped Andre to his bed.

Andre looked at Bryan, then at Anna with a questioning gaze. "Please don't hide anything from me," he begged. "Tell me what is happening. I need to know."

Bryan knew he had to be the one to explain everything to Andre, while Anna sat in the chair beside the bed. Blue was in his doggy bed. The dog was looking at Bryan and Anna. His expression said it was time to tell Andre the truth. Bryan could swear he read the look on Blue's face.

Anna didn't know if Andre could handle the news, but what else could they do? They had to tell him that his home was being haunted by Lanassa's spirit. And that spirit wanted to take his soul. No more dancing around.

Bryan sat down on the edge of the bed and asked Andre, "Do you remember how you landed in the hospital."

Andre was so cold. He knew something was going on, but his memory was blocking it out. Then he heard her voice in his ear. *I'm here for you. Andre, I've never left your side. I know you love me. I know you don't love her. Come to me.* Then the room became even colder. It was Andre who yelled this time. "No!"

Anna almost jumped out of the chair; Bryan held on to Andre. The sound of Andre's voice was so powerful. He remembered it all. Everything came back in such a rush he had to hold his head in his hands. Bryan didn't have to explain a thing to him.

Andre felt pain running through him. His whole body began to quiver, not from cold—because the room temperature had become normal after he yelled for the spirit to go away—but because he remembered everything that had happened in New Orleans: the diamond-smuggling husband, Lanassa on illegal drugs, her lack of love for him. He remembered the deceit, the lies, and most important, the way she died. Lanassa had died in his arms. Shot by her husband, a man Andre had known nothing about. Yes, Lanassa was dead and haunting him, so that he would be with her in the afterlife.

Anna knew Andre had remembered all the sordid details of his visit to New Orleans—and how it had ended. Anna jumped out of the chair and went to Andre, embracing him. Anna didn't know how Andre would receive her, now that his memory had returned, but she had to be there for him. To her surprise, he embraced her tightly while crying in her arms. He was crying hard, and she was crying with him in his frail arms.

Bryan was concerned. He wanted to know if Andre would be able to make it through all of the revelations as they came back to him. Or would Andre allow Lanassa to take control and possess his soul?

Anna and Andre stayed in the same position, holding on to each other. Bryan decided to give them some privacy. He picked up Blue in his arms, and they went downstairs to the study.

Bryan had to think. What could he do? He reached for his cell and called Craig at the office. Craig was relieved that Andre's memory had come back but was furious at the same time. He knew there was a possibility that this could become a setback for Andre. Oh, how he despised Lanassa. She still was affecting them all. And it was a good chance she still could gain control over Andre. Would he want to go to Lanassa in the afterlife?

Bryan mentioned that Anna was consoling Andre, and he was accepting her support. But they'd both seen her in the living room, sitting on the piano bench in a daze. And there wasn't any doubt that Lanassa would start attacking Anna if she hadn't already. *What a mess*, Craig thought. He wanted to drive to the mansion at once, but Bryan convinced Craig to give Andre some time alone with Anna.

"If any change of events should occur, I'll call you," Bryan promised.

"Make sure you do."

After the phone call Bryan took Blue outside for a walk. He needed some air hoping it would clear his mind. Bryan knew the situation was difficult for Andre as he remembered what went down in New Orleans. It could be devastating for him, the man who once loved—and maybe still loved—the person who had always caused him so much pain. They had to find some way to deal with Lanassa's restless spirit.

Blue stopped and looked up at Bryan, his eyes telling him everything would be all right. Or was Bryan just imagining the expression on Blue's face? Whether he was imagining it or not, the dog brought him comfort. He bent down and hugged Blue.

Craig was on the phone with James, explaining everything that happened. The only good news was that Andre's name was out of the papers down in New Orleans and nationally. His job was secure after the summer break was over. Craig and James had to explain to the department board of historical music at Harvard the circumstance that had gotten Dr. Andre C. Brass in such a scandal. Everyone at the university admired Andre and knew he was a great professor and tireless worker and spent his spare time with charitable causes. Yes, Dr. Andre C Brass would be welcomed back. For that outcome, Craig was very pleased. But in the back of his mind, he wondered if Andre would be in any kind of condition to return to work.

It had been over an hour, and Andre and Anna were still in tears. Andre was hurting badly—how could he have allowed himself to be taken again by Lanassa? Yes, he used to be in love with her. Now Andre was facing the fact he was truly blind when it came to her. He overlooked all of the signs. Andre was in denial during the whole relationship. Why had Lanassa decided to bring him back into her world after so much time had passed? It was a world that she knew wasn't meant for him. And how could he have allowed his love for her to lead him back into her arms? Lanassa knew she was living a shady lifestyle.

No, it wasn't her fault but his. Andre had known something wasn't right. He had no one to blame but himself. Now he sat on his bed with a lovely woman that he loved deeply, and she obviously cared for him. But Lanassa's haunting could change the course of his life. Andre wondered why her spirit was coming after him. She didn't love him during her lifetime; why was she there haunting his home and the ones he loved during her death?

Anna saw the confusion in Andre's eyes and wanted to know what he was thinking. Then the room became cold again, this time with a force that slammed Anna down into the bed, not allowing her to move. She wanted to scream but her voice was lost. It felt as if something grabbed her by the throat. Andre panicked. He tried to pull Anna off the bed, but it was as if heavy weights were holding her body in place. He shouted, "No!" but it was impossible to move Anna from the spot where she lay helpless.

Blue started to bark loudly, and Bryan knew something was happening—and it wasn't good. He grabbed Blue up in his arms and ran up the stairs with record-breaking speed. Once he was at the top of the stairs, he placed Blue on all fours. And the dog wobbled fast toward Andre's bedroom. Bryan followed right behind him.

Bryan gasped at what he witnessed. Andre, with his frail body, was trying his best to pull Anna off the bed. The room was so cold. Lanassa was attacking Anna. Blue kept barking while looking up at the ceiling over the edge of the bed. Bryan turned his head and saw a white cloud floating over the bed where Anna lay planted without movement. Blue jumped up, trying to catch the cloud that was holding his beloved Anna in place. It was impossible for a dog with his handicap to be able to do such a thing, but he did.

Then the cold went away. Anna was finally able to move her body. Andre pulled her into his arms with a tight embrace. Then the cold came back, and Andre heard Lanassa's voice in his ear: *She can't have you, for you belong to me!* The voice was so furious. Then the room turned back to its normal temperature.

Andre was determined at that moment to rid himself and Anna from Lanassa's evil spirit. Andre wondered how he could have loved such a woman.

Lanassa had the same evil spirit in life as she possessed after her death. Andre was no longer blinded by her outside beauty. He finally realized that he had loved an unkind soul for too many years. Then the bedside table began to shake and the room became cold again. Anna was in shock, but she showed no fear. She reached down and grabbed Blue in her arms; she didn't want Blue to get hurt. Andre grabbed Anna and held on to her and Blue tightly. Blue began to bark again. Then everything settled back down and the cold air disappeared.

"I must call my mother," Anna whispered.

"I love you, Anna," Andre said. He felt love for the woman in his arms like he felt for no other. He would fight to keep her safe, no matter what happened to him.

Bryan and Anna looked at Andre after his declaration of love for her. She felt warmth inside of her for this man. Andre was still weak but he felt so strong and protective of Anna and Blue.

"I need to speak with my mother, Andre. She'll have some of the answers we need in order to rid this house and you from Lanassa. But only if you want Lanassa's spirit to leave."

Andre lifted Anna's lips to his and kissed her with such passion, it blew her away. Blue looked pleased, and Bryan was caught off guard. Andre released Anna's opened lips from his and said, "You have no idea how much I want to be free from her."

Bryan cleared his throat, trying to get Anna and Andre's attention. He wanted her on the phone, calling her mother, as soon as possible. There would be no Anna and Andre togetherness as long as Lanassa's restless spirit kept invading their lives.

But Andre's focus was on Anna. He remembered those days in the hospital when Anna kept him alive and kept Lanassa from claiming him. He was falling in love with her than. Now he was in love with her. She brought him warmth from the cold. She gave him life from the dreadful draft of death. Andre didn't have to be able to see her. He felt her soul inside of his. Each visit from her made him stronger by the day. When she came into his life during his unconscious state, he felt life. Although Lanassa's spirit was strong and making him weak, Anna gave him a choice to choose life over death. His body may have been weak, but Anna kept his heart strong to the point that he was able to start blocking Lanassa's voice from his ear. Andre knew than he no longer loved Lanassa. Seeing Anna now, her beauty wasn't only inside but outside as well. She was meant for him.

Anna kissed Andre on the cheek and left the bed. She placed Blue on the floor after kissing his head.

Bryan picked Blue up and said, "What a great boy you are." Then they all walked down the stairs, with Blue still in Bryan's arms, wagging his tail. Anna asked Bryan to watch over Blue while she placed the call to her mother. She turned toward Andre and held his hands in both of hers and said, "I'll have to place the call alone."

Andre looked at her with understanding, then placed a kiss on her forehead. Anna left him and went into the study.

Bryan, Andre, and Blue waited patiently in the living room. Both men were on pins and needles. Blue seemed to be far more relaxed than the both of them. He was a major comfort for them all during this time of paranormal activity that was invading their lives. Bryan was in deep thought—so Andre was in love with Anna. She was more than a nurse, more than someone who was getting Andre through the ordeal of Lanassa's haunting. Bryan could also see the gentleness in Andre's eyes when he looked at Anna. No woman had ever displayed so much unconditional care for his friend. And Blue, her dog, kept Anna secure with the warmth of his love. Bryan only hoped that Anna's mother would be able to give them some sound advice on how to handle the woman that refused to give up the man she was trying to claim, Dr. Andre C. Brass.

Chapter 28

Anna waited patiently for her mother to answer the phone. When Florence did, she knew immediately that something was not right. "What is it baby?" She asked. She had no fear for her daughter's life— she knew the restless spirit couldn't harm Anna mentally, which was important. But she also knew Lanassa's spirit could harm her daughter physically. The spirit was capable of playing tricks on everyone's mind. But only a weak mind would succumb to the attacks. Florence already knew what was taking place in the doctor's home—the spirit had followed the doctor.

She knew her daughter could handle the restless spirit, although Anna would have to take some bumps and bruises along the way. She just hoped Dr. Andre C. Brass was strong enough to do what had to be done to get rid of Lanassa.

Anna began to tell her mother everything that had transpired. There wasn't a sound on the other end of the phone. "Mother, did you hear what I just said?"

"Yes, I heard you, baby. The spirit of Lanassa is a strong one and shouldn't be taken lightly, under any circumstances."

"Believe me mother, we're taking this very seriously. But what should we do to send her soul to a place of rest?"

Florence knew the answer. "It's not up to you, Anna, as I mentioned before. It's in the doctor's hands."

Anna chewed on her lip as she considered her mother's words. How could she embrace the advice her mother just shared with her? Anna didn't want Andre to face the spirit of Lanassa alone.

"It will be up to Dr. Brass, Anna. Not you or his friends. You are all just pawns that Lanassa's spirit is playing upon. She is trying to get the doctor's soul by any means necessary, even if she has to attack his friends and you in the process."

"What do you mean, Mother?" Anna asked, her voice trembling. "Are you saying we can't assist Andre with ridding himself of Lanassa?"

"That is exactly what I'm saying to you. When the time comes, Dr. Brass has to be able to send the spirit away with out assistance from you or his friends."

"But how, mother how can he do this?"

"Anna, baby, all I can say is for you to protect yourself by having a strong mind. And tell the others to do the same. If Dr. Brass is the man for you, he'll be able to send Lanassa away. Please believe what I'm telling you."

How can I go back with that kind of information, which isn't helpful at all? Anna wondered.

"Anna, I know you don't understand what I'm trying to explain to you. In time you will. Please remember, keep your mind strong it will protect you. And what is meant to be will be."

They said their good-byes and hung up the phone. Her mother didn't sound worried at all. It gave Anna some encouragement, but she knew the information wouldn't give encouragement to Andre or Bryan. Her mother had talked in riddles. *What is it that Andre must do to send Lanassa away?* Anna wondered with dread.

Anna made her way into the living room and bent down and hugged Blue.

Andre was the first to speak. "So tell us, what must we do to send Lanassa to her final resting place?"

Anna hugged Blue again. Then went to Andre with the confidence she heard in her mother's voice. She placed her hands on both sides of his face, then gazed into his eyes with a smile, and said. "She advised me there is nothing anyone can do, other than you. You will know the answer when it's revealed."

Andre was taken aback. *Is that all the information Anna received from her mother?*

"I have confidence," Anna said, her voice strong, "in what my mother shared with me. I want you all to have that same confidence— and one more thing. Protect your minds. Don't give her the opportunity to get inside of your heads." There wasn't a smiling face in the room with that bit of information. Anna couldn't blame them. She came back the way she left, with the unknown still lingering in all of them.

Andre pulled Anna into his arms and placed a kiss upon her cheek. "Thank you, Anna. I'll be able to fight Lanassa's spirit, and thank your mother for me."

At six o'clock that evening, Andre was getting ready to welcome his dinner guests. The air inside of the mansion was comfortable—no cold draft was felt in the air. Anna was at Andre's side. They welcomed Craig, Sharon, and James, who also were greeted by Blue.

The two women talked with one another while being seated by Craig and Andre. Andre was pleased that Sharon had decided to join them. She was great company for Anna. The menu of the day was rack of lamb with broth-simmered rice, green beans, and buttered dinner rolls, along with red wine. Anna couldn't believe how fancy everything was. It was like going out to a fine diner restaurant. She had never been in the dining room and found it to be warm and inviting. The chandelier over the dining room table was huge and filled with many crystal droplets. Everything was polished and gleaming.

Andre sat by Anna's side and watched her carefully. He hoped there would be no signs of the entity. He refused to say or think the name of the spirit. Craig mentioned to Andre that he and James had gone to the university and spoken with the board. Everything was set for Andre's return after the summer break. Then with a hearty laugh Craig stated, "You need to pick up some pounds. I'm afraid no one is going to recognize you if you don't."

But Andre wasn't yet allowed to eat what the others were eating. Tina kept to Dr. Baines' diet plan of the week. Andre was having chicken rice soup. "I'm afraid you're right. I guess it will have to wait. I'm on this bland diet for a week. Then I'll be able to eat like a man and work out in the gym." Everyone laughed when Andre bent his arm to make a muscle. Anna, on impulse, touched his arm with her hand, giving it a gently squeeze. She did feel his muscle, then blushed. Andre bent down and kissed her cheek. "Thanks for proving me right. I still got it."

"Of course you do," Anna replied. Craig observed the interaction between the two and witnessed the sparks in their eyes. He was happy for his friend. Craig knew for sure Andre had finally found the right woman.

Then, out of nowhere, Blue wobbled over to the dining room table and started to bark. Everyone except for Sharon and James knew what was coming next. Before Andre had the chance to grab Anna, she was tossed out of her chair. She hit the wall behind her with her back. The chandelier above the dining room table started to vibrate, with chiming sounds coming from the crystal droplets. Then the cold air surrounded the room. Sharon had a look of fear on her face. James knew what was taking place, but he was surprised that Lanassa's spirit was trying to cause harm to Anna. He did know the spirit had followed Dr. Brass home. Craig had shared that information with him. Sharon sat frozen in her seat. All of the men went to help Anna, but she was being held against the wall, and no one was able to pull her free. Then there was a white cloud over her, and Anna was gasping for air. Blue continued to bark at the cloud. Then suddenly, Anna was sliding down the wall. She took deep breaths into her lungs. The cold went away as quickly as it had come.

"We must remove her from this house at once!" Craig insisted.

"No!" Anna shouted and pulled Blue and Andre into her arms.

"No what? The bitch is out to kill you."

"I'm afraid Craig is right, Anna," said Andre. "You must leave." Andre pulled up Anna shirt. He found a bruise on her smooth brown skin across her lower back. It broke his heart. Andre was sure there were more bruises under her clothes. He didn't know how to protect her from the force of the dead.

Andre turned his head toward the cold air that had just resurfaced and saw the furious face of Lanassa, the woman he once thought was beautiful. She might as well have presented herself with the gunshot to her head and the blood pouring down her face because all he saw was the ugliness. Everyone else saw a white cloud, but Andre could clearly see Lanassa's face. Blue was trying to escape Anna's hold and get to the cloud. He barked with a fury this time. The cold and the face went away. Andre loved the woman in his arms and her dog, the only one that was able to send the evil back into hiding.

Anna patted and hugged Blue tightly. Then she placed both of her hands on Andre's face and pulled him in to accept her deepest kiss. Andre accepted the sweetness without hesitation. The guests were stunned by Anna's actions. After the kiss was broken, Andre spoke. "I love you, Anna. But I can't protect you from an entity. You have to leave me."

Anna saw the hurt in his eyes. She also saw the anger. He loved Anna and feared for her life. If not for Blue, he could have lost her right there at that very moment. It was too much to bear. And he would not allow that to happen.

Anna looked into Andre's eyes and said, "You don't understand. If I leave, she'll win. As long as she doesn't control my mind, which I guarantee you she doesn't, I'm safe, and it will give you more time to figure out how to send her spirit away. We all must make sure she doesn't get inside of our heads. Andre you must trust what I'm telling you. "

Sharon was shocked by the love and strength Anna had for Dr. Brass, but she knew if it was her, she'd do the same and be there for Craig.

Anna had a determined look on her pretty brown face. "You all have to know there isn't any other way. I'm not leaving. End of discussion."

Craig wanted to shake some sense into Anna's head. Bryan wanted to do the same but in a more diplomatic way, by reasoning with Anna. All Andre wanted was to protect Anna. James walked over and touched Andre's shoulder.

"Andre, you must listen to her. My hunches are telling me Anna is right."

Andre picked Anna up into his arms with the strength he didn't know his frail body could achieve. He carried her out of the dining room to the living room and up the stairs. Andre knew Anna needed to get some rest. And he needed to be alone with her. Bryan picked up Blue and followed them. Bryan knew Blue was the only one at the time able to send the spirit away.

The others stayed down stairs while Anna, Andre, Bryan, and Blue went upstairs. Andre went straight into his bedroom and lay Anna on the fresh sheets on his bed. He was relieved the hospital bed had been removed from his room. He didn't need anything reminding him of his current health. He felt stronger each moment, thanks to Anna's love. Bryan lay Blue in his doggy bed next to Andre's bed. Blue was alert but had a relaxed look on his brindled-colored face. Bryan informed Andre he'd be downstairs in case he was needed. Andre thanked Bryan, then turned all of his attention to the woman lying in his bed. "I'm going to run you a warm bath. You need to relax." Anna smiled at Andre.

"Thanks." Anna knew she needed to relax more than anything. She wasn't afraid of Lanassa's spirit and the attacks geared toward her. But she must keep her strength up. Without a doubt, she had a fight on her hands.

Andre went into the bathroom and poured body wash into the running water. It caused hundreds of bubbles to form in the tub. After the tub was filled he went back into his bedroom to get Anna. He picked her up and carried her into the bathroom. Anna wanted to protest—she was there to take care of him, not the other way around. But she kept that to herself. She knew Andre was feeling guilty for the attacks on her—something that was out of his control and wasn't his fault.

Andre set Anna on a cushioned stool in the bathroom. He began to take off her clothes. Anna saw the look of protection on his face. She knew he was aiming to please her. Anna accepted everything Andre had to offer. Her body felt so sore. That last attack really put a hurting on her. He was finally down to her matching blue panties and bra. Andre's hands felt so strong. He marveled at Anna's body. She was so beautiful and totally in shape.

Her skin was so soft to the touch of his fingers and hands. He placed a kiss on her right shoulder and smiled at her. He removed her bra and next went her panties. He could hardly breathe. Anna shaved the hair from her most private part. She looked so delicious to him. Andre knew he had to get her in the water fast, covering her up with the help of the bubbles. He didn't want the temptation drawing him in. Andre wanted to do nothing more than take care of Anna. He picked her up and placed her beautiful body into the warm water. Anna moved forward, tucking her knees under her chin and relaxed. Andre gasped; she was so bruised. Anna's upper back was covered with red bruises under her smooth brown skin.

"What?" she asked. Then Anna felt the soreness on her back, which Andre was viewing, and Anna realized she had bruises on her back.

Andre began to rub the soft bath sponge over her back, releasing the warm water over her. "That feels good," she told him.

Andre still didn't say a word. He was furious at the spirit that was putting Anna through a bad ordeal because of him. Andre knew all the pain Lanassa had caused him during her life. This was far worse. Andre started kissing each and every bruise on Anna's back while saying he was sorry. Anna could clearly hear the pain in his voice. She didn't want him to feel responsible for what was taking place in his home. And she sure didn't want him to send her away because of his concerns for her safety.

Anna wanted to relieve him from the sorrow she saw in his eyes. "Andre, please know what is taking place is not your fault. You were in love with her. There is nothing greater than to be able to love someone, even if that person turned out to be what you didn't expect."

"No, Anna this is wrong what her spirit is doing to you. She is haunting and hurting me through hurting you. I feel helpless against her attacks on you. I wish I hadn't been so blinded by the love I once felt for her. How could I not see that what she was capable of doing in life, she is trying to finish after death?"

Anna removed her hands from her knees and held his face. "Because you are human, Andre; it's that simply."

They kissed deeply, and she felt his warm tongue tangle with hers. It relaxed her more than the warm bubble bath.

Anna caused Andre's mind to stop thinking clearly, but he had to stay rational. Andre broke the kiss and gazed into Anna's bright eyes of hope, then said, "I love you, Anna, but you must leave me tonight." With that, Andre tried to stand up, but Anna grabbed his arm.

"I love you too, Andre. And there is something you need to know. I'm not going anywhere."

Andre heard the frustration in Anna's voice. He also heard her pain. He bent back down on his knees and held her in his arms. They stayed that way until the water turned cold.

Downstairs, Bryan explained to everyone that Anna was all right.

Craig looked at his brother as if he'd lost his mind. "She is far from all right. She isn't safe here."

Bryan looked back at Craig with just as much determination as Anna had displayed earlier. "Craig, you don't understand. In order for her and Andre to find peace, she has to stay."

"Excuse what I'm about to say," Craig sneered, "but have you lost your fucking mind? We all witnessed what Lanassa's spirit is capable of doing to her."

Sharon placed her hand on Craig's arm, trying to calm him down.

James said, "This is what Lanassa's spirit is trying to do. Get inside of our heads and play everyone against each other. Didn't Anna mentioned Lanassa could never do that to her. Try and take her words of strength and chill out, both of you."

James' words calmed down the brothers' heated argument, but Lanassa's spirit was indeed taking its toll on them all.

The water was cold. Andre reached into the tub and picked Anna up into his arms. He hugged her wet body against his. Then Andre placed her on her feet on the bathroom rug and grabbed a fluffy white towel and covered her body with it. He carried her back into his bedroom and set her on the edge of the bed. The big fluffy towel felt like a comfortable thick housecoat against Anna's body. Anna stayed on the edge of the bed while Andre went into her room and searched for something she could wear. Andre noticed Anna didn't have time to unpack. He searched her suitcase, trying to find her a nightgown. He found a long pink cotton gown with long sleeves. He knew it would be comfortable against her bruised skin. He walked back into his bedroom with the nightgown in his hands. Andre removed the towel from Anna's body. She assisted him by holding her arms up in the air while he managed to pull the gown over her head and arms. Anna stood up, allowing the gown to flow over her hips to her ankles.

Anna wanted Andre to know she felt better. She thanked him by embracing his neck and pulling him down to take in her kiss. Andre responded immediately to her soft lips and warm tongue. He circled her waist with his arms and pulled her close to him. They embraced and kissed each other like there was no tomorrow.

Then it started. Blue's barking. The room became instantly cold. The light from the lamp on the bedside table began to blink on and off rapidly. Andre felt a force trying to pull Anna out of his arms. He held on to her with all the strength he had. The others heard Blue's barking and ran up the stairs, including Sharon. She was no longer afraid but was pissed off.

They all ran into Andre's bedroom. Tina the cook wasn't far behind.

She'd heard the loud noise and advised the staff to stay downstairs. The staff knew there was an entity in the mansion, but only Tina knew the entity was Lanassa.

Blue became furious with his barking while looking up at the ceiling. There it was—the white cloud. When Craig entered the room, he was swung across the floor. Lanassa's spirit couldn't pry apart the hold Andre had on Anna. So the force aimed its powers toward Craig. He was the person that had come between her and Andre when she was among the living. Craig hit the floor hard with his head, knocking him unconscious. Sharon started to scream and went to his side, along with Bryan. James and Tina went to Andre and Anna and were knocked back. The spirit kept them from reaching out to help Andre and Anna.

It was so cold in the room, and everyone was helpless against Lanassa's spirit. The lamp on the bedside table went crashing to the floor. Andre was too busy tucking Anna's body against his. He didn't notice the attacks on the others. A fierce cold wind surrounded them all. Andre finally looked up and saw Lanassa's face, covered with blood and a hole in the middle of her forehead. He also saw Blue attacking the spirit of the dead fiercely, the same way the force of the cold wind was attacking them all. James and Tina couldn't move. Sharon and Bryan protected Craig's body from the force with theirs. Then Blue jumped high, as if he had grabbed hold of the spirit. Immediately everything became calm in the room. Just like that, the spirit was gone. There was a loud yap of pain that came from Blue when he landed on the floor. Anna and Andre went to him immediately. One of his legs was bent as if he couldn't straighten it.

Andre picked Blue up, and the dog had a look of courage on his face. He no longer had the expression of pain. He started to wag his tail. Anna lean her head into Blue's body as Andre held him. She began to cry. Craig regained consciousness but was still in a daze. Sharon and Bryan wanted him to lie still, but Craig refused to stay on the floor. They helped him to his feet. James and Tina didn't know what to do. Who should they go to and offer their assistance? They both viewed the scene as if they were in a bad horror movie. Anna and Andre both asked Craig if he was all right. Craig slowly nodded his head letting everyone know he was fine. Sharon and Bryan walked him over to a chair, where Craig took a seat.

Anna spoke, "I must get my mother up here as soon as possible. You will need her help, Andre. I hope she'll be able to help you discover what you need to do and rid us all from this evil spirit."

Andre heard laugher and words in his ear. *No one can help you, my dear. You belong to me.* He felt cold air by his neck and ear. Blue jumped just a little in his arms. Everyone saw the strange look on Andre's face. Then Andre said, "No, Anna, I'm not a selfish person who would risk another. You all must go and leave me, including the staff."

"Are you serious? Tell me you don't mean what you are saying," Anna said. She couldn't believe Andre would surrender himself to Lanassa.

Andre turned to Anna, still holding Blue tightly in his arms. "I'm very serious." Andre made the statement without a blink. He would not allow his friends to be hurt further. He knew Lanassa would return. He had no other choice but to protect the ones he loved.

Anna knew at that point she must share with them what she knew about her mother. "My mother has the knowledge and experience you need, Andre. She helped my stepfather to rid himself from his wicked dead ex-wife. It's something they both try not to bring up; it's their past. They have been successful at doing just that. But during a time like this, I'm sure my mother will help you any way that she can, even if it means facing her past memories. You'll never find the peace you deserve. My mother and stepfather have been married for over fifteen years, since he fought and won his freedom from the spirit of his dead ex-wife's spirit. We deserve the same peace from Lanassa."

Everyone was surprised by what Anna just shared with them. And Andre began to see Anna's strength. He knew who she inherited it from.

Craig looked at Andre and said, "You'll allow the bitch to knock me out cold and not put up a fight against her?"

There wasn't any doubt in Andre's mind that he was ready to fight Lanassa's spirit. But he knew his friends' safety must come first. Anna placed a kiss on Andre's cheek and said, "As I stated before, I'm not going anywhere."

He wanted to shake her and kiss her at the same time. Andre knew he let Craig down when Lanassa was alive. He wasn't about to make the same mistake. Andre also knew he loved Anna with every part of his soul. He couldn't send her away if she didn't want to go.

Andre kissed Blue on his head and placed him in his king-size bed. His hero should be treated like royalty. Blue had saved their lives in so many ways on so many occasions. It was now up to him to protect Anna, the love of his life, along with his friends. Andre wasn't about to sacrifice his soul and give Lanassa's spirit the chance to claim him. He'd fight back under these paranormal occurrences. Andre walked over to his dresser, picked up his cell phone, and gave it to Anna. "Place the call, my love."

Anna smiled brightly and punched in her mother's number.

Florence answered the phone on the first ring. She knew who was calling and why. The entity was too strong and Andre was too worried for Anna's safety. It was making him mentally weak. "Mother, we need your help."

There wasn't any hesitation in Florence's voice. "I told your father I might be needed. We're ready to make the trip."

Andre walked over to Anna and requested the phone. She placed it in his hand. "Hello, Mrs. Jordan, this is Andre. I'm sorry to impose on you, but I'm afraid I do need your help."

"Please don't apologize, Dr. Brass. My daughter is in love with you. I'll do whatever I can to help. Times will get better Andre, you must have faith. Faith is the most important part of the battle you must face. I'm sure you'll win."

Bryan called Dr. Baines over to check on Craig's head. Andre called a veterinary he knew to come by and check on Blue's leg. He did explain to Dr. Todd Nicholas the events that took placed. Andre didn't want his friend to be caught off guard in case Lanassa's spirit returned during his examination of Blue. Both doctors arrived in record time. Craig had a slight concussion and was advised by Dr. Baines to come into his office the next day for an x ray.

Dr. Nicholas diagnosed Blue with having a mild sprain to his back right leg. His advice was to keep Blue calm and off the leg as much as possible. Dr. Nicholas wrapped Blue's leg with a red-sprain wrap for his joint and said he'd be back in two days.

It was close to midnight and everyone was tired. Sharon and Craig were staying in one of the guest rooms. James had a guest room of his own. He didn't want to walk away until all was resolved. Tina retired to her room and Bryan to his. Everyone left Andre, Anna, and Blue in the living room alone. Anna knew her parents would be arriving within a few hours. She was too excited to rest. Anna decided to play the piano for Andre. He sat on the sofa with Blue's head on his lap while his body spread across the sofa. They listened to Anna's fingers bringing magical music from the keys of the instrument.

Andre heard Anna yawn and told her it was time they try to get some sleep. Anna stopped playing and walked with him up the stairs while he carried Blue in his arms. She hoped for a peaceful night. They all needed it. "Would you mind sleeping in my bed with me?" he asked. "I don't want you or Blue to be out of my sight." Anna understood Andre's concerns and was more than happy to accept. Once upstairs, Andre laid Blue gently in his fluffy doggy bed; Blue closed his eyes immediately and went to sleep. The poor dog was exhausted. While Anna was lying in his bed, Andre told her he'll be right back. He needed to take a quick shower—he wanted to take a shower to stay alert. He hoped there wouldn't be any barking from Blue. There wasn't. Everything was peaceful. As promised, he took a quick shower, dried off, put on his pajamas bottoms, and was back in his bedroom in no time. Anna was still awake when he entered the room. It took some of his worries away. Andre got in bed and wanted nothing more than to have Anna in his arms. He refrained from reaching out to her. He knew Lanassa attacked the most during the times they became intimate with each other. He explained that fact to Anna and she agreed. Andre stayed only inches away from her beautiful body. Finally, they both were asleep without the pleasure of being in each other's arms. The exhaustion of dealing with an evil spirit took them over.

Chapter 29

Sharon lay beside Craig, gazing at him, making sure he was still breathing. She was worried about his safety and very concerned with the injuries Lanassa's spirit had caused to his head. Sharon couldn't rest, so she got out of the bed. She wore a large T shirt that Bryan provided her with to sleep in. He also provided pajamas pants for Craig. Craig refused to put them on and was sleeping in the nude. They didn't bring any night clothes or clothes to change into for the next day. Who would have thought a simply dinner could end up with everyone becoming a hostages in the mansion. All the guests had refused to leave and wanted to stay together. As long as Lanassa's evil spirit was roaming the mansion they had a need to stay and support their friends and family. Sharon saw the strength in Anna and Andre and the courage in Blue and expected nothing less from herself.

She also had seen the will in Andre, Craig, Bryan, and James, trying to figure out how to stop the mess Lanassa's evil spirit was causing. How could any of them be afraid with the circle of support they all had for each other. Sharon started praying again. She prayed that Anna's mother could help Andre release the evil spirit, sending it to the afterlife where it belonged. Craig had told her that Andre was the only one who could rid his life from Lanassa's spirit. By doing so, he wouldn't only be freeing himself but them as well. They all loved him too much and wouldn't walk away during his time of need for their support.

No one blamed Andre for what was taking place. Dr. Andre C Brass had fallen in love with the wrong woman at a young age. Now, he shared a more mature love with Anna. Sharon finally went back to bed and cuddled up close to Craig's warm brown body. He pulled her into his arms. She gazed at his face with the help from the moonlight coming through the windows. She could see his eyes were still closed and his breathing was steady. It gave her comfort. Then sleep overtook her while she lay in Craig's arms.

Bryan lay in bed with his hands behind his head, looking up at the ceiling. He was restless, and everything was taking a toll on him. Bryan wished he had a special lady with him, the same as Andre had Anna and Craig had Sharon. The only women in his life were there as companions during social occasions and occasional sex. He worked long hours and it was beginning to interfere with his finding that special someone. The current events were making him rethink his present situation. Andre and Craig both were thirty and he was twenty-nine—an age when he might have thought about settling down. But for now, it would have to take a backseat to the current dilemma. Lanassa's spirit was affecting them all. Their lives seemed to be on hold until everyone was safe and out of harm's way. Lanassa couldn't break the bond they all shared together. Bryan turned on his side and tried to allow sleep to overtake him. Within an half an hour, he finally went to sleep, with the peace that he only could achieve while his mind was in an unconscious state.

James was having nightmares. As an investigator he had witnessed many things, but an entity wasn't one of them. During the nightmares, he dreamed of all the dead bodies he had to view, connected to his job. He saw wandering souls being released from those bodies, which floated in the air, going to places unknown. Were they going to their final resting place, or were they going to places to haunt the living? Then another dream entered his sleep; it was Lanassa. Her anger was so profound, and she was getting stronger with each moment. James began to move all over the bed. His body couldn't stay still. He woke up abruptly, with a cold sweaty face. James knew he wasn't going back to sleep. He wondered where that evil soul could be roaming—where was she hiding in the mansion until she was ready to strike again?

Chapter 30

Morning came and the sun was brightly shining through all of the windows into the gorgeous mansion. Tina was busy in the kitchen, preparing breakfast. She was so fond of Dr. Brass and only hoped that things would work out in his favor. She wondered if the paranormal events in his life would ever end. Tina hoped they all would be able to come out of the ordeal with no one else getting hurt. She had been the cook of the mansion for five years. No one could have bet her back then that things would turn out the way they had. It was going to be a long day.

Anna and Andre with Blue in his arms were the first to smell the beacon, eggs, and hotcakes coming from the kitchen. They both were surprised that they had a rather peaceful sleep. It confirmed that as long as they didn't become intimate, they might be able to sleep.

Tina approached Anna and Andre and informed them breakfast would be served in the dining room. She had a look of hope on her face, hope that they wouldn't have to experience what took place last night.

Soon all the others entered the dining room. And they all had the same worried look on their faces. No one wanted a repeat from last night. "To set you all at ease," Anna said, "Andre and I have discovered that as long as we stay a distance apart from each other, breakfast shouldn't be disrupted."

"How do you know that to be the case Anna?" asked Craig.

"Because last night," Andre answered, "we stayed inches from each other and there wasn't another attack. It's just a theory."

That theory caught Craig's attention. "Oh, I see. Let's test this theory by having Sharon and Anna sit together. The men can sit on the opposite side of the table." Andre didn't want that kind of arrangement but he also didn't want a repeat from last night so he agreed.

Everyone settled into their seats, with small talk while they ate. The tension throughout the room was palpable. They braced themselves for the unexpected.

"So what time should your mother and stepfather be arriving, Anna?" asked Sharon. She wanted their lives to return to normal as soon as possible.

"I'm hoping they will be here in about two hours," Anna answered nervously. She knew the storm would have to present itself before the calm. Anna could only hope that Andre would be prepared. Blue wobbled away from his meal bowls, and everyone looked at him, waiting for the barking. When he settled by Anna's feet, everyone breathed a sigh of relief.

Sharon advised everyone that she had taken the day off. Craig and Bryan also took the day off from work. The firm knew what was taking place, and they understood. Since James was his own man, he had no one to report to—for now, he was staying put. James knew he could no more walk away from the outcome than the rest of the people in the room. They all were hoping that Lanassa's spirit would be set free some time that night.

Breakfast was over and Bryan told Andre he'd take Blue for a short walk around the grounds. Bryan didn't want Andre along with Anna on Blue's walk—he was too afraid they might touch each other. The way they were looking into each other's eyes during breakfast, it was a surprise that Lanassa's spirit didn't start attacking. Sharon and Craig went into the library to find something to read and try to relax. James stayed in the kitchen with Tina, keeping her company by assisting her with the cleanup, while having a pleasant conversation.

Anna sat on the bench by the piano and played a soothing tune for Andre. He sat on the sofa. Andre hoped their ordeal would be over and soon. Then he would have Anna back in his arms, showing her all the love he had inside of his soul for her. Andre's home was filled with the people he loved, but it wasn't during peaceful times.

Anna glanced over at Andre and saw the pain on his face. She wanted to go to him and almost did, until Bryan walked in the living room holding Blue. He put Blue on the plush rug and sat on the sofa beside Andre. "You play so beautifully, Anna," he said, "I thought Andre was playing the piano."

"Thanks. I had many lessons when I was around the age of nine. I thought my fingers would fall off. Then I started to enjoy playing to the point my fingers became numb. My mother told me I was becoming obsessed. She warned me she'd stop my lessons if I didn't start taking breaks."

Bryan and Andre laughed. They told Anna that the same thing happened to Andre when one of his music teachers in elementary school started giving him lessons. Andre couldn't wait until after school to go over to Craig and Bryan's house to continue playing on their father's piano. Their mother had to bribe him away from the piano with her cooking. It felt so good to be able to laugh again.

And then Blue started to bark—and everyone stood still ... until they heard the doorbell. Anna knew it wasn't Lanassa that brought about the barking but the arrival of her parents. Blue was very excited and so was she.

Blue stood up from the rug with so much excitement on his face. Her dog looked so happy. His tail swung so fast from side to side. It was the most exercise Blue had demonstrated since his leg had been injured. Anna was right behind her wobbly dog and Andre was by her side. Bryan walked behind Andre and Anna with relief. Bryan was hoping for a miracle. He believed only a miracle could send Lanassa's restless spirit to the afterlife. Anna ran to her mother's and stepfather's arms before they had reached the threshold. Anna hugged them both as if she hadn't seen them in years.

Blue was barking with so much excitement, the other guests ran to the foyer as if Lanassa was on the attack again. The relief on their faces was the same that Bryan showed once he knew it was Anna's parents ringing the doorbell. Andre knew their arrival wasn't a frivolous matter. He was showing signs of relief. Anna released her parents from the gentle hugs. Florence and John bent down and gave Blue a big hug. They all knew what was at stake but the meeting was one of pleasure and joy for now. Andre was pleased to finally see the happiness on Anna's face and hoped that one day he would be the one bringing her so much joy.

After the greetings, John bent down to grab their luggage but Bobby, one of Andre's staff, was there to take over. He advised Anna's parents he'd take their luggage up to their room. John thanked the young man and turned to look at Andre. It was as if he could read the man's soul from the other men in the room. He knew which one of them was being haunted. After all, he had been in the same predicament many years ago. Andre reached out his hand and shook John's hand firmly, then hugged him with all the gratitude within him. "Thank you so much for coming, Mr. Jordan. You can't imagine how much relief your presence has brought me."

John smiled at Andre's words. He knew from experience how being haunted could damage the soul. But John witnessed no weakness in Andre. "Please, call me John."

Florence viewed Andre and noted that he would have the strength to be able to get through what would be expected of him. She also observed how handsome and tall he was. After Andre finished greeting John, he turned to Florence and saw Anna's face—the way she'd look as time passed by. Florence was regal and very beautiful with the same curly hair Anna had. The only difference was that Florence's hair was silver, surrounded by a youthful face for her age of seventy.

Andre embraced Florence and experienced a jolt of energy that radiated from her into him. Was she filtering her strength into him?

"Andre, it's my pleasure to finally get the opportunity to meet you. It's going to be all right. I feel your strength. I know you're up for the challenge that is ahead of you."

Andre kissed Florence's cheek and could only pray that her assessment of him would prove to be correct. However, Florence hadn't experience the wrath of Lanassa's spirit. He wondered if Anna's mother knew how powerful the dead spirit was.

"It doesn't matter how powerful the dead soul presents itself. It's your strength and what you choose at the end that would matter the most."

Andre couldn't make out what Florence's words meant. They were like a riddle. He wondered if she read his thoughts. Andre wanted to ask her what her words meant but knew he would know the answer when the time came. It always came back to the unknown, but he clearly knew what he wanted. And that was to free himself from Lanassa and love Anna the way she should be loved.

The other guests introduced themselves to Anna's parents while they all walked into the living room. Andre picked Blue up. He knew

Blue was struggling to keep up. Blue's handicap along with the strained leg was proving to be somewhat difficult for him. The excitement from him jumping up from the rug to greet Anna's parents must have placed more stress on his other three wobbly legs. Blue was obviously slowing down. Anna viewed Blue with concern in her eyes. "He'll be all right, baby. I'll make sure."

Andre knew that was a promise to Anna he must keep. Blue was determined to keep Lanassa away. Andre had to reassure her he'd calm the fearless rascal. "We'll both keep him calm. When the time comes, I'll ask Bobby to take Blue with him to the guesthouse." Anna replied. Andre placed a kiss on Anna's lips in front of her parents and the others. He loved her so much. She was his soul mate.

The guests were in the living room getting acquainted with each other, while being served appetizers and drinks from Tina. Blue lay on the rug near Florence's feet, gnawing on a bone. It would have been so peaceful, except for the fact that Anna was explaining the attacks to her parents. She explained the lack of air in her lungs and the weight that covered her body, preventing her from moving. Craig explained to them the attacks on him as well. Anna also mentioned the effects Blue had on the spirit. Every time he had attacked the spirit, it would disappear, releasing the cold in the air that surrounded them and the fury, along with the force of wind. Florence listened to every single word that was being shared. John also paid close attention, regarding the attacks and the people who so far experienced the spirit's furious energy, which were his Anna and Craig.

John had concerns for what would have to take place in order to send Lanassa's spirit to its finally resting place. John viewed Andre and hoped nothing went wrong, for it could end the doctor's life. Florence and John both knew that part of the equation they unfortunately couldn't share with anyone, including their daughter. They both had to keep faith that the man their daughter had fallen in love with would indeed come out alive. Keeping the secret was driving Florence and John crazy. They should have accompanied their daughter to the mansion earlier. They both underestimated the power of the dead spirit. The only hope that kept them grounded from fear was the man Anna was now deeply in love with. It all rested on his shoulders and in his soul.

Chapter 31

Florence knew that Blue and Craig could be nowhere in the mansion when the next visit from the dead spirit revealed itself. Their presence took the focus away from its aim, which was Dr. Andre C. Brass. Anna was only a pawn to cause hurt, and they knew their daughter had enough faith to fight against Lanassa. Andre must show his ability to fight and fight hard to save Anna and his relationship. Florence felt the love within Andre for their daughter; it was deep and unconditional. The question remained, would he be able to take those feelings of love he had and transfer them into Lanassa's spirit. The answer to that question would be coming soon. Florence felt the presence of the spirit. She said to her daughter, "Lanassa's spirit should have revealed itself by now."

Anna smiled at her mother. "She hasn't because as long as Andre and I stay apart, the spirit doesn't attack. It's during the times we show our love for each other that she reveals herself."

Anna felt weird explaining it the way she did. Anna refused to say the name Lanassa when speaking of the dead woman's spirit. It made her feel more comfortable avoiding her name. But the realization of it all had finally hit her. It was Andre's former lover Lanassa who was causing them so much pain in her afterlife. Anna had to remember just what she was dealing with. She was dealing with a scorned spirit that had no reason whatsoever to be haunting the mansion, along with the owner. Lanassa's obsession after death was making her angry because she was unable so far to take Andre's life. Lanassa was failing at taking over Andre's soul and it was pissing her off. Florence had seen the smile fall from her daughter's face and saw Anna's brown face turn into an under color of red.

Florence also noticed that Andre wanted to go to her daughter and provide comfort to the woman he loved. The fear of doing such a thing was written across his handsome face. Florence went to Anna and hugged her, trying to provide the comfort she knew her daughter needed. "It will be all right. Anna. Keep your faith. We don't have much time. Andre and you must act as if there isn't a Lanassa. You both must embrace each other after we make preparations."

Anna didn't understand her mother, "Preparations? What do you mean, Mother?"

Florence kissed her daughter on the cheek, then began to explain to the guests what would be required to start the proceeding in bringing back the spirit. John went to his wife and daughter while they were sitting on the sofa. He held his wife's hand while she began to explain what must take place. There would be no more avoiding Lanassa.

"Listen to what I'm about to say." Florence still had one arm around her daughter while her right hand was placed in her husband's hand. "Craig must leave the mansion, along with Blue. They both are blockers from Lanassa's full force. The spirit must be totally focused on Andre, which means the spirit will attack you again, baby. Blue can't be a part of this. The spirit must go its full term. The attack must not be interrupted." Craig looked at Anna's mother as if he wasn't getting the full picture. If he was, Craig wasn't encouraged by what he was hearing. Florence witnessed the concerns that her words planted across Craig's face, along with everyone in the room. "I know what I'm saying sounds crazy. It's the only way to rid them from Lanassa's spirit. Yes, it's risky. But it must be done this way."

Sharon was the next to speak. "Are you sure? Is there anything we can do to help? Is there any other way to fight against her?"

Florence looked at the pretty woman, then shook her head. Sharon wanted to cry. "I'm afraid there isn't anything anyone in this room can do to help. Anna and Andre must meet this spirit head on and alone."

Andre started pacing back and forth, wondering how he could deal with such an entity that had proven on more than one occasion just how strong it could be. He wanted to go to Anna right then and take her away from the mansion. He knew it wouldn't solve their problem. Lanassa's spirit would only follow them wherever they would go. Andre was more than sure about that fact. Andre also wondered how he could rid them from the spirit. *When the time comes, you will know what to do.* Those words echoed in his head. Anna, the love of his life, had faith in him. He wouldn't let her or himself down. Anna saw all the worry coming from Andre; it was absorbing him. Anna wanted Andre to believe but knew his doubts came from the fear he had for her safety. For the first time, Anna had to admit to herself that she was beginning to fear the spirit. How in the world could they fight this dead woman without answers? The only thing Anna knew was how much she loved Dr. Andre C. Brass and would do what must be done to bring about peace in their lives.

Bryan stayed stone-faced the entire time. James was amazed by Florence's and John's strength and the calmness they showed, knowing what their daughter was up against. Craig was still not sold on the whole idea; it had to be another way. His head was spinning trying to come up with another alternative. But deep down inside he knew Florence was right.

Andre stopped his pacing and gazed at Anna, while speaking to her mother. "So when should Anna and I begin?"

Florence felt the spirit in the mansion getting stronger and knew they must begin right away. She looked at Andre with a serious expression on her beautiful face. The same face that was similar to her daughter's. "The time has come. Craig and Blue must go to the guesthouse. And for the rest of us, we must stay put downstairs. I suggest Andre and Anna both go upstairs and become the two people who have fallen in love with each other." Florence could clearly see Craig didn't want to leave. He wanted a piece of the action. But his staying wouldn't stop the spirit. It would hinder the outcome and possibly cause Andre great danger. So she stated the fact. "Craig, I know how much this is bothering you. You must have faith; we all must have faith. The dangers of your staying are too great. Your staying would only prolong the haunting from Lanassa's spirit." Florence didn't mention it was a spirit that was drawing in energy at a rapid rate.

If Dr. Andre C. Brass dies, Florence knew, she would blame herself for not coming earlier. Her absence gave the entity time to become stronger by each passing moment. She knew Andre wasn't ready during the days that passed to fight Lanassa. He was so sick and too frail. But it didn't stop her from feeling some form of guilt. Everyone in the room felt like family to her. Their bond with each other was so strong, which allowed Andre to gain some of his strength back, along with the love he felt for Anna. Florence released some of her energy into him during their embrace. She knew Andre had absorbed it into his soul. He was a good man. She hoped it would get him through the ordeal he must face. At the end, she hoped Dr. Andre C. Brass and her daughter would have peace together—and send the spirit to the place of rest on the other side, with the dead.

Chapter 32

Craig felt weird leaving the mansion under these paranormal circumstances that Andre and Anna must face alone. He held Blue in his arms while Bryan and Sharon walked with him to the guesthouse. He knew Sharon would stay by his side. He also knew Bryan would be heading back to the mansion. They all tried to figure out what it was that Andre needed to do in order to win his life back from Lanassa. Craig wondered, would he be able to do it? Andre had always allowed Lanassa to get her way and control him. But he also seen the unconditional love that another woman had brought into Andre's life. Anna was everything Andre deserved. She was beautiful inside and out, with the intelligence and gentleness to make a perfect wife. They both had to be all right. Lanassa mustn't win. *Andre, please, you must have faith within you, my dear friend.* Craig prayed, for he knew only a higher power working through his friend could stop the destruction of Lanassa.

Tina took dinner up to Dr. Brass' room. She informed him everyone was downstairs, trying to relax, and if Anna or he should need anything else to please use the intercom and call her. She'd be in the kitchen. Andre and Ann both thanked Tina as she walked out into the hall and closed the door behind her. Andre turned to the woman he loved with all his heart and was too afraid to touch her. He didn't want to see another attack on Anna. Andre didn't know if he could survive watching helplessly while Lanassa tore into the woman he loved.

Anna finished taking a shower to calm her nerves. She looked so stunning in her long, lacy white garment that hung from her body to the floor. It fitted her very well, and he knew exactly what Anna was doing, thanks to her mother who brought along the sexy get-up for her daughter. Anna was such a brave woman, enticing him without any reservations. She could have worn a brown bag, and he still would have wanted her. She was a part of him like no other woman had ever been. This was the true essence of loving a woman. Andre knew he was blessed beyond measure. But still he was too afraid to touch her beauty.

Andre excused himself and went to take a quick cold shower. He wasn't ready for the attacks to start. He admired and treasured with every cell that ran throughout his entire body the woman in his bed. Andre wanted Anna to be safe and adored. The idea that Lanassa would harm her made him furious. He knew the battle would be upon them and soon.

Andre finished his shower and walked into his bedroom. Anna was sitting up against the pillows on the bed with her sexy eyes meeting his. She was his dream come true, and he had to have her. Andre couldn't allow Lanassa to take this experience from him. He'd fight her every inch of the way. Anna belonged to him, and he belonged to Anna. Lanassa didn't fit into that equation. Tonight would be the biggest battle concerning his love for Anna. He still didn't know how to achieve his goal and send Lanassa away for good. But he refused to waste anymore time. He needed to find out what would be their consequences.

Anna knew Andre was struggling with his emotions. He wanted nothing more than to protect her. But she must free him from those kinds of thoughts. Anna knew what needed to be done. Andre must become intimate with her. And she wanted nothing more than to be in his arms. She wanted to feel his hands gliding over her body and the feel of his tongue wrapped around hers. Anna was getting pretty heated and very wet. Who cared if an evil entity could stop them both during their expressions of mental and physical love that they were about to share together? Anna wanted Andre and could see his desire for her in his heated gaze. Lanassa's jealous, evil spirit was the last thing on her mind. She wanted the man in front of her more than air or food. He was a part of her survival. Anna placed her faith in him. He'd be able to make the right decision when the time came. Her heart was engraved with the faith she had in him.

Anna got out of the bed and walked slowly to him, swinging her hips. Andre held out his hand to her, and Anna placed her hand in his.

He pulled her into a gentle embrace and took her lips. He kissed her lips lightly, then placed a kiss on her neck and cheek, then her slender shoulders. His penis was growing harder, something he had never experienced before with such magnitude. This was true love coming from both sides, and he felt it deep within. Andre placed both of his hands on each side of Anna's gorgeous face and took in her full lips, sucking them as if he was feeding from a baby's bottle. Then he parted her lips with his tongue and took in her sweetness. Their tongues danced together with a rhythm like no other. Andre's heart started to pump hard, moving the blood fast to his penis, which felt as if it might explode.

He was feeling every delicious curve of his woman, while running his hands over the sexy laced garment she wore. Anna was moving with every smooth touch from his masculine hands. She was becoming so wet. Anna never experienced anything like it before. She was afraid but it wasn't fear from a dead woman's spirit. She was fearful of the joy and pain she knew was about to come her way by the man in front of her who would be taking her virginity. He was taking her breath away while making her knees shake with weakness. All of a sudden, without breaking the kiss, Andre picked Anna up into his arms and carried her back to the bed. He lay her down on the thick fluffy comforter. He moved over her lovely body, still kissing her sweet mouth and rubbing his body against hers. Andre couldn't take it much more. He pulled off his silk housecoat that he put on after his shower and threw it to the floor. He rubbed up against Anna's soft brown skin underneath the silky, lacy garment. He was going to explode but not yet. He knew his passion must be restrained.

Anna placed her legs over Andre's hips, still taking in the unbroken kiss. And out of nowhere, Andre broke the kiss and placed his warm mouth over her lacy garment, the part that covered her breast. He smothered that part with his warm breath, and Anna's nipple became instantly hard. Andre wasted no time giving pleasure to her other breast as well.

"Please, Andre, take me."

Andre smiled and started tracing licks and kisses down Anna's stomach to her inner thigh, while pulling up her sexy outfit, moving it out of his way. He needed to feel her smooth skin on his lips and tongue. Andre stopped at her sweet private scent and breathed her in.

He took her with his tongue and mouth. Anna cried out. This had never happened to her before. The experience was blowing her mind. She had no experience in lovemaking and allowed Andre to take the lead. He didn't disappoint her. Andre took every delicious drop of her sweetness into his mouth. He loved everything he tasted, all the lovely scents he smelled from her womanhood.

Andre was relentless. He didn't miss one inch of her clitoris with his mouth or tongue. He also took full advantage of her pink small opening that he knew he'd be entering soon. But for now, he couldn't stop devouring her. Andre couldn't get enough of Anna's juices. She tasted of purity. There wasn't a doubt in his mind she was a virgin. He had to take his time and prepare her for him. Anna looked down and saw the man who took the wind from her lungs making heavenly love to her private parts, and she loved it. She was crying out loud, not caring who heard. When her knees began to shake, Andre knew it was time to give in to both of their needs for each other. Andre lifted his head from between Anna's thighs, then climbed up her body. Anna was shaking all over; it wasn't from any kind of draft or cold air from an entity but from uncontrollable spasms from the loving Andre just shared with her.

Andre pulled the lacy garment over Anna's head, then gazed into her eyes. "I love you, Anna Jordan. I'm so in love with you."

Anna felt the same for Andre. To hear his words of love, Anna wanted to cry. But first she wanted to give back what he just shared. Anna pulled Andre down on his back, then straddled him with her thighs and took in his tongue with so much passion. She went down on him, causing him to groan out in pleasure. Anna sucked Andre as if she wasn't performing the deed for the first time. He just made her feel as if she could do no wrong. Anna sucked Andre all over and licked him to the point of no return. He was too long for her to take him completely into her mouth. So she allowed her hands to do the rest, while she pleasured his testicles with her hand.

Andre couldn't take it. He pulled her up against his body, turned her over, and entered her hot walls slowly. Anna cried out in pain, then pleasure took over. Andre was slow, very slow, moving in and out of her hot tight walls. They made love to each other physically while creating a love of mental bliss. It consumed them both. After they became one, Anna went to sleep in his arms. Andre was in a daze and tried to stay focused. The reality of Lanassa's spirit coming back put him in a very protective mode. He wanted nothing more than to keep Anna as safe as possible. Andre finally experienced an unconditional love shared by two. They shared more than just the physical. He felt her in his mind, body, and soul. This wasn't a one-sided love, and Andre finally experienced the difference.

Anna opened her eyes to see Andre was observing her with all the love a man could have for one woman. He kissed her soft lips and asked, "I think it's time for me to draw you a warm bath." Anna felt a little sore, but she also felt so blissful and sexy. She wanted to go back to sleep but thought a warm bath would do them both some good. Anna said, "Only if you'll join me."

"Of course I'll join you and rub your soreness away." Andre looked into her big brown eyes and knew he'd gone to heaven.

He left her and entered the bathroom and started a warm bubble bath for them. He went back into the room and picked Anna up into his arms.

Andre felt renewed, as if his life had just begun. He carried her into the bathroom and placed her nude body into the warm bubbly water, then followed her. Anna lay her head against Andre's chest and relaxed her body between his thighs. At that point no words were needed; they both became one. Two people who felt each other's needs. It was so overwhelming what they shared. They belonged together. An unconditional love was finally theirs to share forever.

Then it happened. Cold air burst into the bathroom with a wrath like no other. The force grabbed Anna hard out of the water and slammed her nude body on the bathroom floor. Andre jumped out of the tub fast. He tried with all the strength inside of him to pull Anna into his arms. It was impossible to move her. Andre yelled, then the bathroom mirror shattered into many small pieces. Andre covered Anna's body with his. The broken glass from the mirror pierced his skin, and he took in the pain while covering the woman he loved like a blanket.

The guests downstairs heard the noise and knew what was taking place. They all ran up the stairs. All of the doors upstairs slammed closed hard with such force. Bryan and James tried their best to open Andre's bedroom door; it wouldn't give. The force was too powerful. Florence got on her knees and began to speak words of faith and strength, while placing her hand up against Andre's bedroom door. The electricity in the entire mansion went out. The cold air surrounded them all. Bryan started calling out to Andre and Anna. Florence concentrated on her words, while the palm of her hand stayed glued to the door. John took her other hand in his. Tina stood stunned, the same way she had during the other attack she witnessed. They all felt helpless against the force of Lanassa's spirit. Florence and John remained calm.

You don't love this whore. You belong to me, Andre, and me only. I'll take her life if you refuse me! Andre heard Lanassa's voice clearly, as if she was one of the living. Andre gazed down at Anna's nude body that was pinned to the bathroom floor and yelled, "Let her go, Lanassa! Release her and take me!" With that, Anna was thrown across the large bathroom, hitting the wall hard. She was in a daze but was still conscious. Then she noticed Andre's eyes began to roll to the back of his head, revealing only the white part. His beautiful brown eyes disappeared. She screamed but couldn't move to go near him. The force of Lanassa's spirit kept her pinned in place. Anna was motionless and couldn't speak after that one scream. Then she heard the words coming from Lanassa's spirit, the cloud that floated above the ceiling. *He is mine, you bitch. He is coming with me. He doesn't belong to you!* Anna wanted to cry, but the cold air kept pressure on her throat, preventing her from crying, speaking, and most important, preventing her from helping Andre. The pressure was also causing her pain.

Andre began to float from the floor up to the ceiling, where the cloud was lingering. His nude body was very still, and his eyes were still completely white. *Come to me, Lanassa, and I'll follow you.* Andre's body began to shake as if he was having convulsions. Anna noticed his brown nude body turning a shade of gray. *Oh no, she is possessing him. Lanassa is killing Andre.* With that thought, Anna was thrown to the opposite wall. The force kept her motionless once she hit the wall. *Lanassa, enough! Take me; I'm yours! Take me, darling.* Lanassa's spirit entered Andre's body. Anna could only see a blur of the man she loved. But he remained in the same spot. It was the supernatural taking over his body, which wasn't solid but a blurry substance without movement. Anna knew the precise moment Lanassa had entered Andre's body. She wanted to cry out loud, but speech still failed her.

Craig noticed all the lights were out in the mansion and was on his way to investigate, then Bobby grabbed his arm. "Mr. Brown, you can't go anywhere near the mansion. It would only prevent what has to take place."

"The hell with what must take place. The people I love are in that mansion, and I must find out what is happening to them."

"Please be reasonable. You heard what Anna's mother said. You must have faith in Dr. Brass." Bobby said with a pleading voice.

Craig had little faith at the moment. But he had no other choice but to listen to the young man in front of him. He knew what Bobby was telling him was true. Craig must have faith. He didn't want to be the one to interfere and keep the insanity going on. Lanassa must be stopped, and he knew the powers that be didn't include him in the rescue mission. How could he stay away without knowing what was taking place? Blue wobbled over to Craig and looked up at him. Then Craig knew it was time for him to believe in Andre and Anna's love for each other. For that love would be the only thing that could rid them from Lanassa.

Bryan and James kept trying to get the door open. Then Florence held up her hand. "It has come. There is nothing either one of you can do."

Bryan had a panicked look on his face. He didn't understand what Florence was telling them. "What do you mean? There is nothing we can do? We must keep trying."

"No, you must not interfere. What is done is done. Now we must wait for the outcome." Florence said with sadness in her voice.

James wondered if Anna's mother, with the beautiful innocent face, was completely out of her mind. "Your daughter is in there, probably being tortured and thrown across every wall Lanassa could toss her against. Doesn't that bother you? We have to get inside that room and save them both."

"No, my dear, I'm afraid it's too late. The passing has come. The only thing anyone can do now is wait. Time will reveal the outcome and soon." Then Florence began to cry, while being embraced in her husband's arms.

Bryan, James, and Tina just stood there, all hope diminished from their faces.

Andre felt Lanassa's spirit inside of him, taking him to the other side, to the place of the dead. He no longer could see Anna's beauty or feel the hope she had given him. Andre felt nothing but cold inside of his body. All he could feel was Lanassa. Then he felt a cry of love of hope and faith coming from Anna. He loved Anna with every cell inside of his cold body. His love for Anna was making him stronger and pumping blood through him. Then he revealed that love back ten times more powerful to Anna.

Lanassa's spirit felt the power of Andre's love for the woman that was still motionless. The dead woman's spirit who had invaded his body began to jerk violently. He heard a loud scream inside of his head, and he felt the pain that washed over him. Andre was thrown so hard against a wall that his brain started to feel as if it was scrambled. He looked up and saw the face of evil once he hit the floor. It was Lanassa. She viewed him with disbelief in her red eyes—the eyes of evil.

How can you do this to me, Andre? Our love, how could you disregard what you feel for me? Andre viewed the spirit with disdain. Then he said, "I don't love you, Lanassa. I have pity inside of my soul for you. It's time you leave and rest your soul. Give me the one I truly love. And for that, I will forgive you for every hurt you have ever caused me."

Lanassa's spirit felt the emptiness inside of Andre for her. The spirit was overwhelmed by the love Andre felt for the woman who lay nude on the bathroom floor. Lanassa thought in life the way she did in death—that Andre would always love her. That no one could ever take her place. Lanassa wanted Andre because she believed after life the same way she did during life—he belonged to her. Now it was too obvious to deny—he loved this woman more than he had ever loved her. Being inside of him was like being inside of the woman who lay in pain on the bathroom floor. The unexpected had happened, and the spirit became too weak to fight against that kind of love that Andre shared with Anna.

Chapter 33

Lanassa's spirit floated from Andre's body and started fading away. Andre witnessed the beauty of her face returning, the face of the woman he thought was his answer to true love. The red evil eyes were replaced by sadness. Andre was becoming stronger with each passing moment, and the spirit was becoming weaker. Anna saw the white cloud floating out of Andre's body and his brown eyes returned. Then the spirit disappeared. Anna no longer saw the cloud. Andre felt peace invading his body. He stood and ran to Anna. She felt the warmth coming from his body. Andre held Anna in his arms that felt so strong around her body. Then he saw Lanassa standing on the other side, into the afterlife. Just like that, she disappeared; it was finally over. Andre embraced Anna so tightly into his arms, breathing in the scent of her curly hair. They both ignored the pain coming from their bodies. Then every door upstairs opened, and the lights came back on. The warmth of the air surrounded every inch inside of the mansion. They were free from Lanassa's spirit, which took with it the knowledge of his true love for the woman in his arms.

Andre kissed Anna's soft lips and said, "It's over, sweetheart. We're free from the haunting."

"Yes, I can feel it inside of me, how peaceful." Anna felt the defeat of a restless spirit. They both knew it was driven away by their love for each other. Then they heard their friends and family entering the bathroom. Andre grabbed a big fluffy towel and covered up their nude bodies, while he continued to embrace Anna. Florence ran over to them, embracing their sore, battered bodies. But Anna and Andre didn't care; they both embraced her while they were still on the bathroom floor.

"You have done it, Andre. You have defeated Lanassa with the love inside of you for my daughter."

Bryan went to them, helping them to their feet. Andre held on to the towel that secured their nude bodies from their love one's eyes. Florence kept them both in her hug while they all stood. They walked carefully out of the bathroom, avoiding the shattered glass from the broken mirror. It would be a day they all would remember forever.

The guests walked out of the bedroom, giving Anna and Andre some needed privacy and space. Anna was removing particles of glass debris from Andre's upper and lower back. Then they both rubbed each other with menthol cream. They were so sore, but they had won, and it was well worth the battle. They both survived, together, without one broken bone.

Craig received the call that it was safe for Blue and him to return to the mansion. It didn't take long, and he was in the living room with Sharon by his side and Blue in his arms. They all sat on the sofa. Anna and Andre both were dressed and looking rather good, considering what they both went through. They both were walking slowly; it was proof of what they both endured together. Everyone was sitting in the huge living room, waiting for answers from Florence, but it was John who did all of the explaining.

"The love you both have for each other defeated the spirit. It will not bother anyone again. Lanassa is where she was supposed to be after her death, resting on the other side. She attacked you, Craig, for your support of Andre during her life. But she couldn't handle the unconditional love Blue has for Anna. So she withdrew her attacks. The spirit couldn't compete with that kind of love, which was unfamiliar to her soul. Lanassa never had the kind of heart to share love in an unconditional way. She knew the love Anna and Andre shared was too powerful for her to be able to possess Andre. Lanassa's spirit had no other choice but to leave the unfamiliar territory of that kind of love. Lanassa's spirit also felt Andre's love no longer existed for her. It took away her powers over him."

Andre went to John and hugged the man who'd once stood in his shoes. He knew what John was saying was all so true. What he felt for Anna wasn't pity or guilty blame. It was honesty, passion, trust, and a love like no other—a love so deep he didn't have to question it. Andre finally knew what true love between two people really was about. It was peaceful, with faith that the love will always be returned. An unconditional love was so powerful.

"I want to thank you all for staying by my side, especially Anna for sharing so much of your heart and soul with me. I love you so much, baby. Please say you'll be my wife."

Everyone in the room held their breath, waiting for Anna's answer. They didn't have to wait long. Anna embraced Andre gently in her arms, while he bent his head down and took in her deepest, warmest, kiss. After the kiss, she looked him straight into his heavenly bright brown eyes and said. "Yes. I'll marry you, without question. After all, I did almost give up my life for you, Dr. Brass. I love you with all that's in me."

"I wish I could swing you around this room in my arms. You have made me so very happy. But you just wait until we are healed from the bumps and bruises. For now, it gives me pleasure to do this." Andre embraced Anna again, ever so lightly, and gave her the deepest, warmest, most passionate kiss that left her in a daze. Blue started barking with excitement. The beloved dog seemed to know what being human was all about. Everyone started to laugh with tears of joy in their eyes. They all were truly family, Anna and Andre's supportive family.

The next day the sun was shining so brightly, matching the mood inside of the mansion. Tina was busy cooking, as always. James was reading the morning newspaper in the kitchen, while she performed her cooking duties. He felt good wearing fresh clothes, after returning to the mansion that morning from his apartment. Craig and Sharon both arrived back at the mansion that morning as well. Bryan was in the living room, playing with Blue. Florence and John were watching the two at play, while hugging each other on the sofa. Andre and Anna were both upstairs, being examined by Dr. Baines. After the examination, Dr. Baines stated, "I must say the both of you are in good shape, considering what I've heard you experienced last night. No broken bones are always a good thing to be able to share with my patients. The soreness will be gone in a few days. All I can say is keep doing what you are doing for each other. It's more than what medicine could heal during weeks of recovery. Also, let me congratulate you both on the upcoming wedding. I must admit I'm not surprised." The doctor told Andre he was more than pleased that he had put on a few pounds. And Andre knew he owed it all to the woman who was standing by his side. Dr. Baines didn't have to write them any pain prescriptions. It was a good sign, demonstrating their bodies' abilities to heal on their own with tender loving care.

After the doctor finished with his thorough examination, Andre invited him to join them all for breakfast. "It would be my pleasure. I've rushed over here without eating. I heard your cook, Tina, is the best."

"Yes, she is, along with being a great supporter during our time of need." Andre didn't have to explain the meaning of his words. From this day forward, he knew the name Lanassa would never be mentioned from his lips. Leaving the past behind with the help of the woman whom he love like no other, Andre knew it wouldn't be a problem to keep that promise to himself. It's amazing what the power of love can do when it's being returned. He was used to it already, and he was blessed for having Anna to show him the intensity of that kind of love. Dr. Andre C. Brass knew he was one lucky man.

The dining room table was set with a bouquet of sweet-smelling flowers in a crystal vase. Breakfast was ready to be served. Everyone was seated, and it was a pleasure to have Anna by Andre's side. Andre, on impulse, kissed his woman's lips, and Anna took in all the pleasures coming from his warm lips and mouth.

"Okay you two, enough of that. We do have to eat," Craig said, while giving out a hearty laugh. He saw the look on Sharon's face and knew the look very well. But Craig also knew he wasn't ready to go down that road of matrimony.

While eating and enjoying the meal Tina had prepared, Florence, Sharon, and Anna started going over the wedding plans. They felt too much time had been wasted on fighting off a spirit. And they weren't about to waste another second. To them, the wedding plans were a case of pure urgency. After breakfast, Andre asked Craig, Bryan, John, and James to join him in picking out the perfect ring for his wife-to-be. He wanted his friends to share in his joy. After all, they'd stood by him during some very unpleasant times. They all agreed. So after breakfast the men left the mansion on their mission. Andre knew the ring must be special for the woman in his life, for she deserved the best. Dr. Baines headed out with them on his way back to his medical clinic, after he thanked Tina for the delicious breakfast.

Blue was on the sofa, licking his chops after experiencing a good meal of his own. Anna rubbed her beloved dog, while thanking her lucky stars for the outcome from the whole dilemma. Blue had given them time to figure out how to save themselves from the haunting. She would forever be grateful for the love shared by her devoted Blue. He was truly priceless with his handicap and all. What a very special dog she had, and Anna knew it. Sharon experienced the joy that came from Anna. She was so happy for her. How strong could one woman be when it came to loving a man? Sharon knew how much love she had for Craig. But knew it was best not to push the issue of a commitment on him. Only time would tell if Craig felt the same for her. But for now, it was Anna's time to be blissful, and Sharon was happy to be a part of it all.

The haunting of Dr. Andre C. Brass was finally over, and a new life for Anna and Andre, loving each other, was well worth the battle.

During the day, the women went into just about every bridal shop, searching for the right bridal gown. The wedding would be an event well deserved and well overdue. The happiness of two people had proven, time and time again, nothing can keep true love from coming out on top. They only had a couple of weeks to prepare for the wedding because Andre refused to wait another minute longer. He wanted Anna as his wife, living in their mansion, loving each other for the rest of their lives. Anna was just as eager to have Andre become her husband. They both had gone through something that most couples haven't experienced during their whole lifetime together. It was true to say they both had become true soul mates. And to Anna, it was that way the first time she placed her eyes on Andre's frail, handsome face. But now, he had most of his strength back and looked more handsome than ever. No one could have imagined a haunting turning out to be the best thing that could have ever happened to them both. It brought them together.

A week went by, and Andre was throwing Anna the most extravagant engagement party she could ever hope for. His reasoning behind the lavish party was to celebrate their freedom to love each other in peace. He also splurged on the most beautiful engagement ring her eyes have ever gazed upon. It was a huge pear-shaped diamond embedded in five high prongs created on a platinum band. She was more than pleased. She took a large amount of her saving to get him a thick platinum wedding band.

It was well worth every penny spent. Everyone from the Brown's law firm was in attendance, along with the staff from the historical music department at Harvard University and Andre's students. Anna enjoyed meeting Brenda, Debra, and Bill—they had so much humor. She laughed until her stomach tightened up with their joking about their employers, Craig and Bryan. Dr. Baines, Dr. Marvick, Dr. Nicholas, and Nick the investigator, and James were also in attendance, along with a host of other friends who came out to give Andre and Anna their best wishes. Florence had tears in her eyes. Anna hugged her mother who was looking so lovely in her off-white dress. Her stepfather, John, was wearing a tailor-made black suit with a thin blue tie. James and Tina were enjoying conversation together. Tina had the night off to enjoy the festivities with them all.

The catering was superb—all the waiters were in white. The food was the finest in presentation and taste. Blue was wobbling around, greeting everyone with his leg being unwrapped from the sprain bandage wrap. Bryan and Craig entertained Anna's parents. Sharon was holding onto Craig's arms with hope in her eyes, for one day it would be their turn to become as one. Anna hoped one day Craig would be able to see the love in Sharon's eyes for him and feel the same for her. She knew Craig cared deeply for Sharon but wasn't ready for such a commitment.

Bryan had a casual friend by his side, Linda. She had a very sweet, innocent look about her, with a body that had curves for days. She had so much sex appeal.

Finally, it was time for a toast. All of Andre's students were playing music that Andre composed, smooth jazz. It sounded like heaven to Anna's ears. The students stopped playing while Andre raised his champagne glass and dedicated his life to the woman by his side. "With all my heart this is the happiest day of my life. I thank all of my friends and family for being here to witness my love for Anna. Her love for me fills me up with appreciation of joy. And Blue, there isn't enough to be said about my hero." Blue wobbled over to Andre when he heard his name mentioned. Andre bent down and hugged him, then stood back up. "I want to invite you all to New Orleans to witness our exchange of wedding vows to each other. Again, I thank all of you, with much love." Everyone raised their champagne glasses with a cheer, cheer; then took sips, acknowledging the love Andre and Anna shared for each other and the wedding to come.

EPILOGUE

Bryan and Craig weren't surprised that Andre and Anna decided to exchange their wedding vows in New Orleans. It was, after all, a lovely city that was coming back to life, the same way Dr. Andre C, Brass came back from his ordeal. They all loved New Orleans, and the bad memories were in the past for Andre. New Orleans was Anna's hometown. She loved being home to share her joy.

It was a peaceful, beautiful summer day. The sun was bright and the air was comforting. The birds were chirping in the courtyard where the wedding vows would be exchanged. The many flowers were colorful, and the grass was so green. Andre's friends from his college days were playing soft jazz music. It gave his students the time to just enjoy themselves as his guests. Everyone was enjoying the warm breeze, along with the sounds that surrounded them while they waited for the bride to arrive.

Bryan, Craig, and James were Andre's best men. Sharon, Brenda, and Debra were Anna's bridesmaids. The men looked so handsome and tall. They wore black tuxedos with black bow ties with onyx buttons going down their white shirts. The women wore maroon satin gowns, Anna's favorite color.

Dr. Andre C. Brass showed no signs of nervousness. He was too much in love and felt the excitement overtaking him. The past visits to the city never entered his mind and that would always be the case. For Anna had really filled his cup with the love she shared with him. The men stood at the altar, with Blue in front of them sitting on his hind legs, with a black bow tie around his neck. The women were in their positions as well. Florence sat in the front row with Tina, along with Bobby and the other staff members. Craig and Bryan's father and mother were also in attendance, sitting alongside Florence. They couldn't make it for the engagement party but they wouldn't have missed Andre's wedding day for anything in the world. Florence was so happy, tears filled her beautiful face. She would have never guessed in a million years that Anna would have faced what she did and be able to prevail, given the opportunity to love the man who defeated the haunting spirit, just like her John defeated his.

Florence witnessed the look in Sharon's eyes, while Sharon looked at Craig with so much love in her eyes that were filled with tears. Florence knew that look—the look of a woman who wanted nothing more than to experience the togetherness with the man she loved. Florence hoped they would have a happy ending.

The band started playing a jazzy version of "Here Comes the Bride." Then everyone stood up. Anna, along with her stepfather John holding her arm, started walking slowly on the long, thick white runner toward the altar. Anna looked straight ahead at the man she would be spending the rest of her life with. Andre had tears in his eyes, for his wife-to-be was so beautiful. She wore a long Victorian wedding gown. Anna's hair was pulled back in a French twist that had peals intertwined in the French-hairstyle. The hairstyle allowed her lovely brown face to be seen, for the guests to view her loveliness. Her eyes were bright as the sun. She was beaming toward the man she cherished.

Once they were at the altar, John gave Anna a kiss on her cheek and placed her hand in Andre's. John then went and embraced his wife with so much love. Florence embraced him back with the same display of love and happiness. Andre and Anna exchanged their vows with the love that poured from their hearts. Then the minister said. "I now pronounce you husband and wife. You may kiss your bride." Andre took Anna into his arms and swung her around, as promised. Then they kissed each other with so much passion, the guests started to cheered. Blue barked with excitement. The kiss seemed to last forever and the guests continued with their cheers. Then Andre and Anna turned toward their guests and the minister said, "Dear guests, please give more cheers for Dr. Andre C. Brass and his lovely wife, Mrs. Anna Brass."

"Cheer, cheer," the guest shouted and clapped their hands. Then it was on with the partying. The Brasses partied all night long with the ones they loved in the city they loved. In a few days they all would head back to Boston and Cambridge, but for now, it was one big celebration.

Andre and Anna told Anna's parents they could have one of the guesthouses if they chose or could stay in the mansion with them on their visits, which they both hoped would be regular. The two had played a significant role during the whole ordeal. They also knew Craig, Bryan, and James would be regular guests, as always. Anna only hoped it would also include Sharon. Anna knew it wasn't her call, but she couldn't help but hope that Craig would see the light and make a commitment with Sharon.

The wedding party was over and everyone was back at home, entertaining their own lives. Anna and Andre, along with Blue, honeymooned in New Orleans. They were now a family. New Orleans was a part of their survival. Instead of New Orleans being the end for Dr. Andre C. Brass, it was his beginning. He loved his wife dearly, along with their fearless dog Blue. Life couldn't get any better.

Dr. Andre C. Brass' journey for love was finally over. He felt good to finally feel totally complete and thankful to have his better half by his side, making him whole. Andre's beginning was something for which he could only thank the stars above their heads, while Anna and he walked hand in hand during a late-night stroll with Blue, at the park in New Orleans.

Breinigsville, PA USA
30 October 2009
226729BV00001B/10/P